ARMS OF
PROMISE

Crystal Walton

Impact Editions, LLC
Chesapeake, VA

Impact Editions, LLC
www.crystal-walton.com

Book Layout ©2013 BookDesignTemplates.com

Cover Design ©2016 Victorine Lieske

Author Photo by Charity Mack

Name: Walton, Crystal, 1980-
Title: Arms of Promise / Crystal Walton.
Identifiers: LCCN 2016912046 (pbk) | 978-0-9862882-7-2 (pbk)
BISAC: 1. FICTION / Clean & Wholesome Romance 2. FICTION / Romantic Suspense

Library of Congress Control Number: 2016912046

CHAPTER ONE

Home

Annabelle Madison could kill her sister for putting her in this situation. Again.

In a Chicago restaurant's swanky bathroom, she smoothed out the pale yellow dress Reese had managed to talk her into wearing for this blind date. She'd rather be in sweats right now, curled up with her tabby and a *Gilmore Girls* marathon.

The thought expanded into a smile until another cramp tightened her back and stomach. This couldn't be a worse night for a date. Not that any night with "Luke The Lawyer" would've been a good one. His textured tie and Armani cologne had his motives written all over them. Cozy up to her to get in with her dad at the DA's office. Too bad for him, he wasn't the first to try. After twenty-four years, Anna had learned how to dodge the sharks.

Her bracelet clinked against the porcelain sink as she gripped either side. *Just make it through dinner.*

As if laughing at her, an overhead dispenser released a burst of spray directly on her head. Great. Now, she smelled like cinnamon bathroom air freshener. Classy. Then again, if it turned off Mr. Uptown, it might pay off.

Her cell rang from the tiny clutch purse Reese had lent her for the night. She tipped it out and shook her head. Should've known her sister would call to check in. "Just so you're aware, I accept chocolate for penance."

Reese huffed into the line, probably rolling her eyes. "Oh, c'mon. How bad can it be? You're at Blackbird with a total catch."

"I think sellout is the word you're looking for. And he's not even the worst part. I had to get a pad out of the bathroom dispenser." Anna glared at the taunting metal box on the wall. "Have you ever had to use one of these monstrosities? Seriously, if it weren't three inches thick, its crazy long wings would take flight. Now, I'm stuck waddling around like I have a throw pillow stuffed between my legs."

Reese cracked up. "You have a gift for being dramatic. You know that?"

"Comes with being a dancer."

"Okay, drama queen. At least try to enjoy the evening. You could use some fun in your life."

Anna adjusted the lacy belt around her waist. "I have plenty of fun."

"Oh, really? You have no real friends, you avoid your family half the time, and you blow off every guy interested in you. I'm sorry, which part constitutes fun exactly?"

And once again, Reese took first place in the world's least tactful category.

"It's one date, Anna. Stop thinking so much, and live it up a little, will ya?"

Right. Anna hiked up the shoe strap sliding down her ankle and peeked out the bathroom door toward her empty seat across from Luke. "Fine. Let me go before he thinks I fell in the toilet."

"Please promise me you won't make that joke at the dinner table."

Of course not. Because *that* would actually be fun. "I'll call you tomorrow."

"Details later!"

As if there'd be any. Anna shimmied her cell back inside her mini purse and strode for the table, trying not to waddle like a duck. She could handle this. Dinner, small talk, laughter in the appropriate places. She was a performer, for Pete's sake. What was one more routine to push through?

Luke rose halfway out of his chair as Anna took her seat. "Everything all right?"

Hardly. "Yep." She laid a black cloth napkin over her lap. "Just fine."

"Good." He scooted in his chair and motioned to a bottle of wine. "I took the liberty of ordering us a Cabernet while we wait. I hope that's okay. Our waiter said he'll have our plates out in another few minutes."

"Perfect." Okay, one and two word responses probably didn't count as sufficient small talk. Maybe that drink wasn't such a bad idea. She lifted the cool glass to her lips and sipped the full-bodied wine.

A draft from the front door stirred up clouds of cologne on its way across her bare shoulders. If it didn't go against her convictions, she might've asked the lady at the next table for her mink shawl.

Anna almost snorted. Decked out in eveningwear and jewelry, Chicago's finest filled the room with their haughty laughter and ravenous gazes. All caught up in a world of self-absorption and false security—a world she'd almost let consume her once.

What was she doing here? She stayed away from her family's lifestyle for a reason. Until Reese laid a guilt trip on her, anyway. Now here she was, another impractical girl donning a spaghetti strap dress at the end of November. Reese better bring that chocolate over by the pound.

Looking up at the high ceiling, Anna mindlessly swished the liquid in her glass. What were the chances she could talk Luke into cutting the date short enough for her to make a run to the studio before going home? At least there, she could tune everything else out.

Luke cleared his throat. "So, what do you think?"

She dropped her gaze to his. She'd totally missed what he'd just asked. "About?"

"About lunch tomorrow. With your dad."

And there it was. The real reason any of Reese's approved suitors feigned an interest in her. Anna downed two-thirds of her wine to repress the honest response wrestling to the surface.

He leaned against the wingback chair. "You don't really want to be here, do you?"

Way to pick up on the obvious, Sherlock. Maybe you should be a detective instead of a lawyer.

If his glower were any indication, he must've read her thoughts.

She bit her lip, set her glass down, and twisted the napkin in her lap. What was she supposed to say?

A shadow stretched across their table. "Anna?"

The voice she'd given up on ever hearing again eclipsed the droning murmurs of chatter and clinking dinnerware echoing around the room. Her head whipped toward the sound, but every other part of her remained frozen.

Including her vocal cords.

In a dress shirt and dark jeans, Evan O'Riley stood in front of the table with shoulders quite possibly two times broader than they'd been in high school.

Anna blinked, positive she conjured him up. She hadn't allowed herself to admit it, but while in the bathroom, she'd half wished he were still around so they could pull the fake-boyfriend-escape routine they used to do as teens. But he couldn't really be here. There wasn't another logical explanation. She was officially certifiable.

Luke shifted in his seat beneath Evan's towering presence. "I'm sorry. Can I help you?"

"Yeah, you can help by backing away from my girlfriend." Evan held a straight face, intimidating and sultry all at once.

"Girlfriend?" Luke scoured the room of staring faces and lowered his voice. "Annabelle, what's he talking about?"

Evan released Luke from an intense gaze, long enough to signal to Anna her part of the routine was up next.

Except that required breathing.

His brow creased slightly, hazel eyes giving in to a hint of uncertainty.

Dry swallows forced their way down Anna's throat. Water. She needed water.

Without unlocking her gaze from Evan's, she reached in the general direction of her glass until her fingers bumped into it. The goblet clattered over and sent water gushing down the side of the tablecloth and onto the floor.

She jumped up, banged her knees against the table, and backed into their waiter. In case the entire scene couldn't get any more embarrassing, she latched on to Evan's arm to seal the deal. He cradled her close, and her knees almost gave way.

The second Luke rose from his chair, Evan held up a ridiculously muscled arm at him. "I'll take it from here, big guy."

Leaving a speechless Luke behind, Evan escorted Anna toward the door. He grabbed her coat on the way out and draped it over her shoulders. "You okay?"

Only if not being able to breathe counted as okay. She needed to get out of here.

Anna turned and almost collided with a street performer painted in gold. Flinching, she wheeled around and bumped into Evan's solid body. With nowhere to go, she finally backed against the cold brick siding. How could there be no air outside either?

He brushed her hair back from her cheeks and searched her face. "Bells?"

The nickname only he and her mom ever used drew her focus. Her eyes found his. They seemed older, more experienced. Without thinking, Anna lifted her fingers to the strands of hair just above his ear. A hallucination couldn't feel this real, could it?

Evan cupped her hand and brought it down to her side. "I'm sorry. I didn't mean to startle you in there. You were giving our old signals. I thought you wanted me to—"

"I did." Thank God, her voice worked again. "Trust me. You couldn't have intervened soon enough. It's just … How did you …? When did you …?" A lot of good it did for her voice to function if her brain didn't.

When he stepped back, the Christmas lights on the awning illuminated a look she didn't understand. "I'm on leave."

He never came home on leave, did he? If so, why hadn't he ever contacted her? Anna's stomach churned at the possible reasons. She took in the sight of him. Filling out a dress shirt with a stature she didn't recognize. He could've been someone else.

Maybe he was. So much time had passed.

"So, you come home out of the blue and decide to go to Blackbird?" This wasn't his type of scene. Unless that'd changed, too.

Exhaling, Evan rubbed the base of his neck. "It wasn't my choice."

The door beside them opened, and a stunning Latina with lashes almost as long as her heels approached. "Evan, what's going on?" She curled her manicured fingers around his arm and pressed into him.

So much for Anna regaining her breath. A brown paper bag underneath a city bench caught her eye. Hard liquor had never looked more tempting.

"I was helping out an old friend," Evan said in a completely controlled tone.

"Oh, good." The girl bubbled forward and extended a hand. "It's such a relief to have contacts in a new place, isn't it? I'm Marissa ..."

Don't say it. Please don't say it.

"Evan's girlfriend."

The wind coursing over the sidewalk was nothing compared to the way those two words gutted Anna straight down the middle. She begged her face not to wince as she returned Marissa's delicate handshake.

Evan stared at the pavement. The wind had to be cutting through his blue button-down, but he didn't so much as twitch. Why couldn't Anna be made of steel, too?

They hadn't seen each other in five years. Of course his life had carried on. She had no reason to expect anything different. If she could just figure out how to get common sense to infiltrate her heart, she wouldn't be standing here as incoherent as a Macy's mannequin.

Everything about the scene joined the cold, damp air stinging her eyes. Stupid hormones.

"Are you all right?" Marissa transferred her hand from Anna's arm to Evan's. Even a scrunched look of pity didn't come close to diminishing the beauty in her features.

Shake it off, already. Anna slipped her arms through her coat sleeves. "I'm fine. The wine must not be sitting well. I should get going." She buttoned the last notch on her coat, withdrew her gloves from her pockets, and gestured toward the ominous sky. "You guys go back and enjoy your dinner. I'm going to walk home before the rain starts."

Evan looked up and down the dark street. "Not gonna happen."

Anna raised a brow. "Excuse me?"

"You're not walking all the way home."

"I have an apartment off Fiftieth Street now. It'll take me a whole eight minutes to walk to the nearest 'L' station. It's no big deal. Besides, I could use the exercise." After missing her Contemporary Hip-Hop class tonight, her tight muscles were threatening protest.

He sent a yeah-right glance at her heels. Okay, bad cover.

"Why don't you drive her, babe?" Marissa peered inside the restaurant's windows.

"You sure?"

"Yeah, no rush. I think I see Jeff Glibson from the Chicago Tribune." Her striking round eyes glittered with noticeable intrigue. "Never know when a story's brewing." She gave a cute raise of her shoulder. "I'll catch a ride back to my hotel. We'll meet up later."

Anna turned away from them. The strum of a guitar from the opposite corner joined the "L's" constant hum from the nearby train tracks. With the buzz of downtown's street life surrounding them, she should've been able to drown out the smacking sound of the girl's lips meeting Evan's. Anna clutched the bottom of her coat cuffs. Deep breath.

Marissa sashayed inside, and Evan withdrew his keys from his pocket. "She's a journalist."

Anna nodded her understanding. Apparently, her voice decided to go AWOL again. Probably better that way. None of the tangled thoughts unraveling in her head needed to come out in front of him. Or at all.

He led her toward a charcoal Accord with tinted windows and opened her door. Scents of leather and what must've been a trace of Marissa's perfume billowed from inside. Maybe Anna would luck out, and it'd mask the cinnamon bathroom spray still clinging to her hair.

She sank onto the seat, thankful to be out of the wind. Though, seated next to Evan in silence might've been worse. More than his size, his whole aura filled the car. Like an officer who commanded authority without any words. How much had the army changed him?

He turned onto South Jefferson and merged into the bustle of Saturday night traffic. "I'm sorry if I ruined your date with that lawyer."

"How'd you know he was a lawyer?"

Evan peered in his rearview mirror, shifted into third gear, and zipped around a cab into the middle lane. "Something about his hundred-dollar tie gave it away."

She couldn't help grinning. Man, she missed their connection. Missed having one person in her life who really got her.

"Reese is still setting you up on blind dates, huh?"

Anna snorted. "It's gotten worse since she got pregnant. Like it's part of her nesting process or something. I swear the girl's on a mission to marry me off to some three-piece suit."

His fingers tensed then relaxed around the gearshift. "It's only 'cause she cares about you."

Leave it to Evan to be levelheaded. "I know. But she can be really ..."

He cut off a Jetta in the next lane and veered onto a side street.

She gripped the dashboard. "Uh, you know this isn't a training obstacle course, right?"

"Sorry." He eased off the gas while checking his mirrors. "Decided to take a shortcut."

"How do you know where I live?"

He downshifted and kept his face forward. "You said Fiftieth Street. I assumed Stonybrook Apartments."

"I wasn't sure you'd remember your way around."

He cast a sidelong glance across the seats. "I haven't been gone that long."

Maybe it didn't seem that way to him.

Anna slid her hands under her legs while sections of her neighborhood passed by the window. People bundled up on the curb, smoking. Others, collapsed on benches with cardboard signs clutched in gloveless hands.

It wasn't an easy part of town, but she'd fought to build her own life here. For her. For Mom. Even for Evan. She'd chased dreams like they'd promised they'd do together. It wasn't fair for mere minutes beside him to remind her how much was missing from her world.

She pinned her gaze outside, but a faint hint of fresh soap kept luring her eyes to Evan's bulky silhouette and her thoughts to places she couldn't let herself go. She should be mad at him, not ready to climb over the console and throw her arms around him.

Staring at the gray headliner, Anna waited for sense to flow from her head to her heart. Truth was, the amount of time that'd passed didn't matter. Even if the feeling wasn't mutual, she still loved him. Always would.

She set a hand on his forearm. "It's good to see you, Evan." Somewhere lodged inside the web of reactions, that much she knew for sure. Despite how she'd pay for it later.

His gaze strayed from the road to her hand and swept up to her face.

Two seconds. That's all it took to remind her how much those hazel eyes could make her feel. The realization of what that meant burrowed into her chest.

She blinked toward the windshield. "Watch out!"

Evan slammed on the brakes in front of a stop sign, nearly clipping a pickup soaring past them from the adjacent street. Forehead creased, he mumbled something under his breath and snapped on his blinker.

An electric stillness lingered as he pulled up to her apartment building.

A list of all the usual lines she used when ending an awkward date played through her mind. Except this wasn't a date, and it wasn't some random guy. It was Evan. The one person she never imagined ever feeling uncomfortable with.

He turned and held her gaze. "It's good to see you, too, Anna."

Spoken in his sincere voice, his words melted over her. Her heart bypassed her head altogether and sprang right for her mouth. "Do you want to come up for a minute?"

An unreadable expression flitted from her to his side mirror.

What was she doing? Of course he didn't want to come up. He had a girl—

"Got any hot chocolate?" A sideways smile caught the tail end of his question.

She returned it. "Like you have to ask."

Laughing softly, Evan flipped the unlock button. He met her around the bumper, walked her to the building, and opened the door for her.

In the stairwell, Anna headed toward the second floor with Evan right behind. "It's a far cry from my dad's place, but it's home."

"Not unless you've got a rent check for me." Her landlord hovered like a vulture in front of her door at the top of the stairs.

Crap. She ducked, looking for an escape route. What was she going to do? Hop over the banister? Resigning, she climbed the last three steps toward the short, middle-aged Asian man. "Mr. Reyes, you know I'm good for the money."

"I know you're good for saying you're good for the money. I need less of this," he said while making a talking motion with his hand. "And more of this." He rubbed his fingers together to gesture handling cash.

Like she wasn't trying. "I'm giving you as much as I can each week. I have an audition on Saturday. As soon as I make the company, I'll catch up on my back rent. I promise."

"And what if you don't get in?"

The possibility of surrendering her apartment and the vision she'd dedicated her life to only worsened the tug-of-war she was already wrestling.

At twenty-four, she wouldn't get another shot at a dance career. But how could she pursue that dream and forsake the one Mom inspired her to live at the rec center? At the same time, if she didn't make callbacks, she'd be stuck returning home to the life Dad was pushing on her.

Either way, she'd risk losing herself and forfeiting the art Mom believed in. She couldn't let that happen. At least here, she'd have a better chance of remaining tied to the community she and Mom both invested their hearts into.

Keeping her head down, Anna fiddled with her keys and strained to raise her voice above a whisper. "Moving out isn't an option."

"I assure you it is." Mr. Reyes brushed past her. "Your tab is due the last day of the month, or you're out, Miss Madison. Whether you make your audition or not."

"Why don't you cut the girl some slack?" From behind her, Evan's deep voice vibrated throughout the stairwell. "She's obviously doing the best she can."

Heat crawled up Anna's neck. She'd almost forgotten he was there. She shut her eyes, mortified he'd seen her in this predicament. Taking a slow breath, she turned.

Mr. Reyes's gaze slid over Evan's looming profile. "Who are you, her bodyguard?"

Evan's fingers whitened around the railing.

She stepped between them before it got ugly. "Sorry, this is my ..." What? Her childhood best friend? The only man she'd ever given her heart to? The same one who'd walked out with it their senior year and never looked back?

"An old friend," Evan answered for her without releasing Mr. Reyes from a palpable stare.

Right. An old friend. Nothing more. He'd already established that back with his girlfriend. She fumbled over the word, even in her thoughts. He'd never seemed to notice the way girls fell all over themselves to get his attention in high school, but it was bound to catch up with him eventually. She'd just hoped it would be with her.

Evan mounted the last two steps and towered above her landlord. Mr. Reyes backed against the wall and slinked down the stairs with a look on his face like he had the sudden urge to use the restroom. She couldn't blame him. When had Evan become so daunting?

Once he reached a safe distance at the bottom of the foyer, Mr. Reyes called up to her. "I expect a check on the thirtieth. No exceptions." He skirted out of sight.

Evan's silent presence magnified the heat still stinging her ears. Anna shoved her key into the deadbolt, wishing she could shrink inside with it. The night couldn't get any more awkward.

"There's nothing to be embarrassed about." Evan turned her around. "But if you're in financial trouble, why don't you go to your dad?"

"And prove him right?" She scoffed. "No way, Evan. You know I can't do that." Head down, she clutched her elbows. "Listen, things haven't been this bad the whole time. I had an unexpected bill come up six months ago. I've been working on playing catch up, but—"

"You don't have to explain. It's none of my business."

Because they weren't close anymore. He used to know things without her ever having to say them.

Exhaling, Anna tugged her gloves off and faced him with as much dignity as she could muster. "Can we forget this happened? I owe you a hot chocolate for bailing me out earlier. I'd really like to go inside, get out of these heels, and visit with …" She swallowed and pasted on a smile. "An old friend."

One who still held her heart, even if his belonged to someone else now.

CHAPTER TWO

Fringe

Inside Anna's apartment, Evan shut the door behind them. It wasn't much of a security system, but at least the door had a deadbolt. Her landlord sure wasn't going to offer her any protection. Evan never doubted she'd move away from the gated community she'd always felt imprisoned by. He just wished she would've picked a safer location.

Anna turned on the lights and hung a ballet shoe key ring on a decorative hook beside the door. A gray and white cat scurried from down the hallway. Purring up a storm, it weaved between Anna's legs.

"Is that …?"

"Yep. My Bailey's still around." Anna squatted and curled a finger under the cat's furry chin. "Some people just aren't re-placeable."

She had no idea.

"Even kitty people." She pressed a kiss to Bailey's head. "Right, lovey?"

The moment Evan moved from behind her, the old tabby froze at the sight of him.

"Aw, you remember Evan, don't you?"

Bailey tore into the living room before Anna could catch her. Evan had been removed from her life for too long. Of course the cat ran away from him. He was shocked Anna hadn't done the same.

A low growl rumbled from underneath the chair.

"I see she's still got her split personality."

"Very funny." Anna scowled at him. "She'll warm up to you. Just talk to her for a minute."

Talk to her? Sighing, he bent to the floor. "Come here, Bailey girl."

A pair of glow-in-the-dark eyes peered around the chair leg.

"It's okay." He patted his leg. "Here, kitty, kitty." Aw, man, if the guys could see him now—on his knees, calling a cat in baby talk. He'd never live it down.

Bailey wandered over, rubbing her face on each piece of furniture as she went. She sniffed his fingers and pushed her wet nose up under his hand.

"There you go, baby. That's it." He stroked her back until she propped her paws on his knee and raised her head toward his. A giant yawn released a wave of fish breath smack into his face. Eyes closed, he fanned the cloud away.

"See. What'd I tell ya? She remembers you."

And clearly had an opinion about his return.

Anna smiled as Evan rose. "Let me make those hot chocolates. But first things first." She latched on to his arm with one hand and slipped her shoes off with the other. She fluttered her lashes, looking unfairly adorable.

"How can heels be any worse than those pointe shoes you scrunch your feet into?"

The corner of her mouth sloped to the left. "Hey, *everything's* different on the dance floor."

He laughed. "How could I forget?"

Her brow pinched at his words.

That was a stupid thing to say. Not that it'd matter what he said. She didn't understand why he'd left during her audition, and he couldn't possibly tell her.

Fretting with the lacy belt around her waist, Anna stared at the linoleum with enough intensity to drill a hole through it. One he was dying to crawl into right now. Of all the pain his mind and body had undergone throughout his military training, nothing compared to the ache of being near her again.

He cleared his throat and diverted his gaze to the artsy-decorated living room. "The place fits you."

"That's about *all* it fits, but I love it anyway." She breezed toward the kitchen. "Make yourself comfortable. It won't take me more than a sec to make the drinks."

It better be one long second if he was going to get himself in check. Getting too comfortable was exactly what he was worried about.

He strolled into the living room and scoped out the windows. Decent blinds. Hopefully she left them down most of the time. He lifted back the edge and took a bird's-eye view around. Being on the second story helped some with security, but it had its share of disadvantages.

A *thump* from behind drew him around. The top of a purple armchair bounced against the wall as Bailey circled the cushion. She nestled into the corner and went to town giving herself a bath, only stopping once to glare at him as if he were infringing on her privacy.

Chuckling, Evan ran his hand over a tear in the chair's top left corner. Anna had kept the same furniture she'd had in her room since high school. In fact, the whole apartment resembled her old bedroom—globe lights strung around the ceiling, a bookshelf overflowing with Pilates videos and movies they grew up on, scented candles mixing with Anna's distinct fragrance.

How could a place he'd never been in feel so much like home?

An incoming text dinged from his cell. He slid it out of his pocket and grimaced. Another message from Hernandez, looking for a decision Evan wasn't ready to make yet. He crammed the phone back down. He needed more time.

A trickle of lukewarm heat crawled down his neck from the vent above him. He glanced at a pair of open-fingered gloves on a laptop lying on the couch arm. Was she so short on cash she had to freeze inside her apartment?

"Don't you think it's a little cold in here?"

Anna glided in and handed him a bright teal mug that read, *I'm a dance teacher. What's your superpower?* Cupping her own mug, she breathed in the steam. "What do you think the hot chocolate's for?"

He cocked his head at her, and she tipped hers right back.

"Don't tell me you can't hack the winters here anymore."

He didn't budge.

"Okay, you've definitely been away from Chicago for too long. If you tell me you actually put ketchup on your hotdog now, I'm gonna have to stage an intervention."

"Funny." He rolled his eyes but couldn't shake the concern from his face.

Her grin tightened. "You don't have to worry about us, Evan." Anna rubbed a fingertip over the cat's head. "Bailey and I keep each other warm. Don't we, girl?"

The thought of her living like this burned him more than it probably should. She made her own choices. But seeing her strength and resilience had never overridden his yearning to take care of her.

She gestured to his mug, and he obligingly took a sip. Wow. He'd gone way too long without one of these. "Still incredible."

A satisfied grin climbed her cheek. She motioned behind her to a bottle of mint extract on the counter. "My secret in-gredient."

"More like your special touch. It's what makes everything you do amazing."

Pink cheeked, she stood before him, barefoot in a yellow dress that brought out the hints of blond in her long hair. She rolled onto the balls of her feet. "Would you excuse me for a minute?"

"Sure." He stepped back as Anna slipped down the hall and into a room. *Way to be on point, O'Riley.*

Blowing out a hard breath, he moseyed around the living room brimming with picture frames and trinkets. From the bookcase's top shelf, he lifted a photo of Anna and her mom at the last recital she'd made it to before she died. His chest constricted as he brushed a thumb over the image.

Mrs. Madison had been like a second mom to him—a solid foundation during a time in life when he needed it most. But to Anna, she was the whole world. One he watched shatter without any way to pick up the remaining pieces. His failure in letting them both down never left him.

Anna's cell rang from a tiny purse on the kitchen counter. "You want me to get that?" he called down the hall.

"No," she hollered back. "It's probably my dad checking in on me again. The man's driving me crazy."

She strode down the hallway in an off-the-shoulder cotton shirt and a pair of sweats ending at her calves. Only Anna could look even more beautiful in sweats than in a cocktail dress.

At the kitchen counter, she withdrew her phone and glowered. "Like I said." She traded her phone for her mug and joined him in the living room. "I don't know why he's making such a big deal out of this case."

Please tell me she isn't that naïve. "He's prosecuting the biggest black market trafficker in Chicago. I think that constitutes a big deal. It's Michelli we're talking about here. The guy who—"

"I know who he is." Anna dragged her fingers up and down her mug handle. "How do you know about the case?"

Evan darted his gaze to the shelf and the starfish they'd found together on a trip to the Outer Banks. "It's hard to miss the news, Anna."

Thankfully, she didn't press it. She sidled up beside him at the bookcase instead and exchanged her mug for a pair of ceramic frogs painted in funky designs. "A keepsake from one of mine and my mom's prison breaks." Nostalgia colored her voice. "Sophomore year, after I had that stress fracture in my foot. She was so intent on cheering me up."

He feigned offense. "You mean maxing out my lifetime quota of enduring eighties movies didn't help?"

"I didn't force you to sit around with me. And don't act like you didn't love those movies."

"You kidding? Molly Ringwald haunted my dreams for a solid month after that."

She shoved him. "Whatever. You loved it. And this was different. You know how my mom was. The slightest thing turned your world gray, and she went off putting together some crazy project to bring color back into it."

He smiled. That he remembered.

"It's what I loved about her, though. It didn't matter how dark Dad's cases were. Mom never failed to believe the beauty of art could change anything. Like it was proof goodness would always win."

Swallowing, Evan tried to look away, but the pull in her voice wouldn't release him.

"She made it so easy to believe. Especially that night." Her gaze wandered to the frogs and back in time. "We snuck past Dad's security to go to that little art studio on Twenty-Second Street. Spent hours by ourselves. Not as the DA's wife and daughter, just as *us*. Two artists ready to change the world."

Her soft laugh faded into a heartbreaking smile. "No borders. No expectations. No cases ... Man, I miss her."

A series of blinks brought her focus back to him and a look of embarrassment across her face. "Sorry. I don't know where that came from." She escaped to the couch.

With her mug resting over a throw pillow, she bent her foot back and forth with her hand the way she did when lost in thought.

Evan sat in the chair opposite her. Bailey hopped down, shot him a scathing glare, and made her way to Anna's side instead. He couldn't blame her. Despite every shred of logic pounding through his head, he wanted to be beside her, too.

He straightened the chain to his dog tags. "Anna, your dad's—"

"The District Attorney of Chicago. And with that comes legitimate dangers," she said in a proper tone as though reciting an edict she abhorred. The depth in her earnest eyes drilled straight through every piece of armor he had. "I left home for a reason, Evan. Risks or not, I need to live my own life."

He scooted to the edge of the seat. "You can't live that life if it's taken from you."

"Exactly."

His forehead tightened. "That's not what I meant."

She lowered her gaze and sipped her hot chocolate.

Why did she have to be so stubborn? "Bells ..."

She traced her fingertips over the white triangular patch of fur beneath Bailey's neck and lifted those soft green eyes toward him. "Can we talk about something else? If I only have a few minutes with you, I'd rather hear about your life."

Swallowing, he hunched in the chair. "There's not much to tell."

Her wry expression transported him back to the schoolyard when they used to try to one-up each other with the latest secrets. "Why? Is it classified or something?"

Evan shifted, pulled his foot onto his knee, and lowered it a second later.

Her face dropped. "Oh my word, it is. I was just joking. I didn't realize ..."

He lifted to straighten out his jeans and angled toward the window. Why was no position comfortable? He owed her an explanation. Even if it was bare-boned.

"After Basic Training, AIT, and Airborne School, I went through RIP and on to Ranger School."

Anna blinked at him like he'd spoken in another language. To a civilian, he probably had. "You're a Ranger?"

Okay, maybe she knew more about the army than he thought. "Yes, ma'am. Staff Sergeant."

Apparently, the pride in his voice didn't go unnoticed. Her mouth quirked and crinkled the corners of her eyes. "Wow. Should I call you Sarge?"

He strained to keep from showing how cute that sounded coming from her lips.

"I mean, not that I'm at all surprised by how fast you moved up the ranks."

That made one of them. "When you're training to lead a spec ops team, you learn to be laser focused." A lot of good that did him right now. He scratched his brow. "Let's just say I had a reason to be so driven."

Her impressed smile contorted into a glower of concern. "And you talk about *me* facing real danger?"

"The difference is, I'm equipped to combat it."

Anna slid her ankles out from under her thighs and flexed her toned dancer legs. "Hey, I work out every day, thank you very much. I can handle myself."

He didn't doubt she'd try. Which was exactly what worried him.

She tilted her chin. "I'll be fine, Evan."

So much for his skill of withstanding interrogations. If he didn't up his game, she'd figure out why he was here within a matter of hours. He set his mug on the end table and rose. "Mind if I use your bathroom?"

"Of course not." She motioned toward the hall. "First door on your right."

A rainforest shower curtain greeted him once he flipped on the light. Avoiding the wall directly behind him, he tried to ignore the eyes staring at him from the frog-shaped toilet paper holder.

He cracked a laugh. The whole apartment was probably as big as Anna's bedroom at her dad's place. Yet every inch of it bubbled with her personality. After all this time, she hadn't lost herself. Could he say the same thing?

He washed his hands, tapped cool water over his cheeks, and gripped the doorknob. He wasn't here to get attached to her again. For both their sakes, he couldn't afford to. "Discipline on and off duty, O'Riley. Man up." Letting out a breath, he opened the door and trekked back down the hall.

Anna swayed in front of the sink, humming to herself like she always did while doing chores.

His chest squeezed, the need to leave accelerating. "I should probably take off. I have somewhere to swing by before calling it a night."

She spun around with her hands covered in suds and her eyes a dim shadow of their normal brightness. Man, she was killing him.

"Um, yeah, of course." A glance at the clock tugged her smile down even more. She snagged a dish towel from the oven handle on her way toward him. "How long are you in town for?"

He forced his gaze up from his Skechers. "I have three weeks before my leave is up."

Anna twisted the end of the towel around her finger and curled in her bottom lip. "Will I get to see you again before you leave?"

Her soft, vulnerable tone about did him in. He kneaded his shoulder blade.

"You know what? Never mind. I shouldn't have—"

"Twenty-Third Street."

She looked up. "What?"

He strode to the counter to jot the info on a sticky note. "I'm staying at the Extended Suites off Twenty-Third Street." He gave her the slip of paper and crossed his arms before they brought her to him on their own. "I meant what I said earlier." He met her eyes again, despite what it'd cost him. "It's good to see you."

"You, too."

The inflection in her voice prompted reactions he had no business feeling. He unlocked the deadbolt, stepped through the doorway, and inhaled before turning.

She leaned into the door. "Thanks for bringing me home. *And* for rescuing me earlier." Her sweet laugh played around him in the quiet stairwell until the silence beckoned a response he didn't know how to give.

Saying good-bye to her would never be easy, no matter the circumstance. His attention traveled around the hall, down the stairs, and back to Anna. He'd tell her to lock the door as soon as she closed it if she wouldn't get defensive.

He was trained to turn fear into focus. But maybe it was better if he sheltered her from either. He returned her smile instead. "Good night, Anna."

"Night."

Evan stopped on the stairs until the *click* of the deadbolt latching echoed into the foyer. Having to be satisfied with that, he hurried down the last half of the steps and into the night's biting air.

A chilled breeze barreling alongside the brick building collided with his overheated skin. Good thing he'd come home in early winter. Because if he was going to step up to look out for Anna until the Michelli case blew over, he'd need every ounce of help keeping his cool.

He nodded at the black town car across the street and climbed into his Accord. From behind the tinted windows, he scanned for any sign of the Suburban that'd tailed them on the way over. He must've lost them on that side street. But just in case, he did a perimeter sweep around the block before making the ten-minute drive from one difficult situation to another.

The same cutting wind from outside Anna's place whipped him in the face the minute he stepped out of his car in the hospital's parking lot. Yet somehow, the atmosphere felt thicker here. Harder to breathe. Even inside, the antiseptic-cleansed air didn't free his lungs.

Same as the last few nights, Evan slowed on his way up the staircase. His feet knew the way to the third floor. Just like they knew where to stop on the fringe of a threshold he couldn't cross.

He gripped the trim and closed his eyes. The beeping monitors and labored breathing overtaking Mom's hospital room pressed in with the weight of Hernandez's unanswered text. Would the decision to re-up or not even make a difference now? Was it too late? Maybe he should go back to Georgia early. Forget trying to make things right.

A slow exhale leaned Evan into the doorway and into the truth he couldn't run from. Between the remorse at seeing Mom like this and the war of being near Anna again, the consequences of his failures didn't leave him a choice. He had a promise to keep.

CHAPTER THREE

Complicated

The echo of dumbbells clanking into their racks rico-cheted off the gym's ceiling and raced straight for Evan's temples. Working out all morning should've cleared his head by now. Instead, Anna's sweet smile and infectious voice from last night hijacked his thoughts.

His buddy Murphy looked up at him from the bench press. "Bro, I could say I just passed your record on reps, and you'd have no idea if I were lying."

Evan's fingers tightened above the barbell. He was sup-posed to be spotting Murphy, not letting himself get lost in questions that didn't matter, anyway. "Sorry, man. I'm not on my A game today."

"Girls will do that to you." Murphy's triceps shook while pressing the bar away from his chest. He was pushing himself to the limit, a soldier through and through.

Evan spaced out his legs. "Nothing to do with girls. I hard-ly saw Marissa last night."

"Who said we were talking about the J Lo wannabe?"

"Don't call her that, man."

"Hey, I'm just keeping it real."

Evan fixed a glare on him.

"Look, the girl's fly. No question. But it only took me a few hours around her to see she's a walking tabloid waiting to hit the stands." Murphy clanked the bar into the notches and shook out his arms. "I don't get why you're with her."

He wasn't with her. Well, not exactly. She labeled them as a couple, but a few dates didn't count as a relationship to him. And quite frankly, whatever might've been there ended for him before it ever really started. But if he were honest, he'd admit he let her come along on this trip for a reason.

A deep exhale rattled in his lungs. That wasn't fair to Marissa. He needed to make it clear where they stood.

Murphy sat up on the bench, snagged a hand towel from his bag, and wiped his sweaty face. "You need to ditch her, bro. Especially when you could be with Anna right now."

Biting back a comment, Evan rounded the bench and changed out the weights.

"Aw, c'mon, O'Riley. This is *the* Anna, right? Why you acting all Bruce Wayne on me? I've seen your bat cave. Don't try to tell me you're not in love with her."

Evan banged the second weight into the first. "Ever wonder why you always got extra PT in Basic? It's 'cause you don't know when to stop talking."

Murphy laughed. "Just so you know. Brooding isn't helping your case." He stretched an arm behind his head and pressed down on his elbow.

If Murphy weren't his boy, Evan would twist that thing right out of its socket. "There's no *being* with Anna. She thinks of me as a brother. End of story."

Murphy pivoted around on the bench and jutted his chin at him. "You kept the girl's picture in the barracks like a lifeline. Sorry, bro. The we're-just-friends card ain't gonna fly."

Evan craned his head back. Why didn't he bring his headphones today?

Murphy raised his palms. "A'ight. A'ight. If you're not into her, then I guess it's cool for me to take a shot. Dating a dancer would be pretty hot. Especially those private sessions." His notorious Casanova grin expanded beneath his bobbing brows.

Evan's veins bulged on his forearms. "You know I'm a skilled marksman, right?"

"That's what I thought." He pitched a brow at him. "You really think you're gonna pull off moonlighting as her undercover bodyguard?"

The guy never quit. "I don't want to be in this situation any more than she would if she knew. But trust me. It's better if she doesn't." Looking to him as a friend was better than how she'd see him if she knew the truth.

"Better for who? Sure you're not protecting your heart instead of hers?"

The answer stung. He'd messed up the last five years being that selfish, staying on the periphery when he should've been by her side full-time. But with the Michelli case putting Anna in real danger, watching out for her from the sidelines wasn't good enough anymore.

"Better for both of us."

Evan grabbed his water bottle from the floor and chugged half of it down. The gym wasn't helping. He needed a stress shoot out on the range.

Murphy planted a solid grasp on Evan's shoulder. "Just trying to watch my boy's back."

"I know. You would've made a good Ranger."

"Our RI didn't seem to think so." Murphy scratched his jaw.

"Yeah, well, he was a real ..." The front door opened. A guy, five foot six, strode in carrying a duffel bag with two carabiners hanging from the handle. Probably a rock climber. Not a threat.

"Earth to O'Riley." Murphy waved a hand in front of him. "You good?"

Evan shook it off and picked up his bag. "Yeah. I'm gonna hit the showers." If he couldn't sweat out his tension, maybe a hot shower would drain it instead.

In a bathroom full of steam, he braced a hand against the shower wall as jets of water beat into his tight muscles. He rotated his neck and rubbed off the water cascading down his face, but thoughts kept pouring in.

Murphy didn't get it. Evan killed whatever remote chance there'd been of sharing a life with Anna the week her mom died. He wouldn't risk jeopardizing what was left of her future. He'd keep his feelings off the table and get the job done without causing her any more pain.

It wasn't that complicated. Anna needed surveillance whether she liked it or not, and he owed her that much.

Working the shampoo from his hair, Evan released a hard exhale. Images of her in those sweats with her bottom lip curled beneath her teeth washed over him without mercy. He turned the water all the way to cold but couldn't shake the reality staring him in the face. After nineteen-hour days mastering the ability to operate under extreme physical and mental stress, it'd only taken one look at Anna to confirm he'd never mastered his heart.

Who was he kidding? Complicated didn't begin to cover it.

Anna slid her leg warmers off and chucked them by her bag in the corner of the studio. Winding her braid into a bun, she crossed the floor to her iPod speaker dock to reset the song for the fifth time. If she didn't start connecting with the choreography, she was going to scream.

She wiped the sweat rolling into her camisole bra top. Why did Evan have to show up now, of all weeks? With the bind she was in, a shot at making the Chicago Dance Crash company was her only hope at continuing what she and Mom had started together.

She couldn't afford to repeat history. Couldn't afford any distractions. Especially a gorgeous one who melted her insides just by calling her "Bells."

Focus. She tapped her fist to her forehead. Yet all it did was unleash images of Evan's assuring eyes latching on to hers, as if the need to take care of her trumped any military op.

If Anna didn't know him as well as she did, she'd be tempted to wish that look was for her alone instead of for Marissa or anyone at all who needed help. The sting of rejection she'd worked so hard to bury threatened to burn right through her walls.

Shaking it off, she spotted her focus in the mirror and restarted her audition piece from the top.

She dropped to the studio floor, rolled a quarter turn, and faced stage left. An upper body roll brought a silhouette from the doorway into view.

Heat spread through her until the sunlight streaming from the windows lit a face she recognized. Recovering, she gathered herself up and traipsed toward her iPod as her dance instructor, Mr. Jamison, strode in.

"You're off today, Annabelle."

If it was that obvious from only a short combination, it was worse than she thought. Anna dug her fingertips through the top of her hair. "I know."

"You want to talk about it?"

Definitely not. Talking would only stir up more convoluted emotions she didn't want or need to explore. "It's just one of those days. Nothing to talk about." She swept her things up from the corner, turned, and almost bumped into him.

Mr. Jamison gave her the stern teacher look he pulled off as if he were fifty instead of thirty-five. "Whatever it is, it's not more important than your dance career."

Tell that to her heart. Anna stared at her bag's handle clutched under her fingers.

"I got a call from Vicky last night."

Her head flashed up. "What'd she say?"

"They're moving the auditions to the twenty-fifth."

"Black Friday?" Not good. Reese would kill her if she bailed early on their Thanksgiving weekend plans.

"A snowstorm's scheduled to hit on Saturday." He shrugged. "They didn't want to risk having to cancel."

So, she'd have to audition after a full day off the floor. Great. She pinched the bridge of her nose.

Mr. Jamison cupped her arms and angled his face in front of hers until she had to meet his eyes. "Don't stress. There's not a single company that'd reject your technique. I wouldn't have booked the audition if I didn't think you were ready. The choreo's there. The only thing holding you back is this." He motioned to her head. "There's no room for doubts on the dance floor."

Anna nodded. After failing her audition for Hubbard Street Dance Chicago at the end of her senior year, she knew that better than anyone.

"Do you want to do some partner work before you leave?"

"Not today." She slung her bag around her back.

He offered an understanding smile. "I'll see you tomorrow, then."

"Bright and early," she called on her way to the bathroom.

The studio had been a refuge for her these last several years. It was enough. Why did life have to mess with that? And why did Evan have to be here to complicate it even more?

After patting down with a damp towel, Anna traded her tights for a pair of jeans, changed into a bulky sweater, and tugged on her tan boots. It might not have snowed yet, but the wind coming off the harbor didn't know the difference. Just like her emotions didn't heed the warning trying to knock some sense into her every time last night replayed in her head.

She could kick herself for asking to see Evan again like a doe-eyed girl on a first date. He had a model lookalike girl-friend, for crying out loud. Not to mention, he'd obviously left town for a reason. What made her think running into him yesterday changed any of that?

At the sink, Anna unraveled her braid, wishing her con-nection to him were as easy to undo. She had to throw away that paper with his number on it when she got home tonight. Plain and simple. He wasn't the only one who could be laser focused. Mr. Jamison was right. On or off the floor, she had no room for second-guessing.

No room for daylight without coffee, either. A mocha was calling. Big time. If there were ever a day—scratch that—*a month* to splurge on comfort drinks, it was now.

Anna looped her infinity scarf around her neck while backing out the door into the blustery morning. The urge for a caffeine fix led her toward Forty-Second Street on her way to the rec center.

A guy in a long wool coat on the opposite sidewalk caught her eye. Something about the way he looked in her direction gave her goose bumps. He flicked a cigarette to the ground, and she would've sworn he nodded to someone behind her.

She shot a cautious glance over her shoulder to a burly guy a block away. Were they tailing her? Anger flared. If Dad had assigned her protection detail without telling her, the two of them were going to have words. A few choice ones, for sure. She'd made herself clear this time.

Mr. Trench Coat Wearer mirrored her strides. Still gripping her bag, Anna picked up her pace. A step ahead of her, the man reached the crosswalk first and hustled across the street.

A pang of apprehension coursed through her body. What if they weren't her dad's men?

Her pulse jumped into double time. Blood swooshed in her ears, amplifying each heartbeat. A rolling gate clattered open beside her at the same time a jackhammer drilled through pavement up the road. Noises crowded in from all angles, but none louder than the heavy footfalls gaining ground on her.

Adrenaline spiked. She cut around the corner. Ahead, two more bulky guys came out of a building. She stopped, heart pounding.

"Anna?" Evan lowered his sweatshirt hood.

Thank God. She ran the last several feet separating them.

"You okay? What's going on?" His gaze rebounded off her to the street corner.

"Yeah." She cast a backward glance. "Someone was ..." Aside from a few pieces of loose trash, the sidewalk couldn't have been emptier. A mix of relief and embarrassment settled over her shoulders. Wow, now she had to add paranoid to her list of crazy responses since running into Evan last night.

He turned her around. "Was what?"

"Nothing." Anna inched her bag up her arm and evaded the intuitive stare she knew was tearing her lie apart right now.

"It's 0700. What are you doing out this early?"

"I needed to go to the studio." *To dance out frustrations about you.* She let her hair fall in her face to shield her warm cheeks.

Like it mattered. When he dipped his head low enough for his intense eyes to roam hers, the knot in her stomach took a whole different spin. So much for being laser focused. Why did he have to be so …? Her gaze sloped from his defined arms to his gear. "Wait a sec. Look who's talking. What are you doing here?"

Evan lowered a duffel bag to the concrete. "Just leaving the gym."

She glanced up at the building. Of course he had to work out at a gym along her everyday commute. Perfect.

The guy beside him whacked his bicep, and Evan almost shoved him off the curb. Laughing, he butted his way forward. "Darius Murphy." He swept her hand in his and kissed it. "Pleasure to meet you."

"Easy, Casanova," Evan said in a guarded whisper behind him.

Their banter relaxed her tense muscles. Despite his playful charm, something in the guy's stature gave her the impression he'd be the kind of friend you'd want to watch your back.

She returned his warm smile. "Anna Madison. Pleasure's mine. Not too often you meet chivalry on the streets. You must be one of Evan's Ranger comrades."

He puffed out his shirt. "Hear that? I don't need no gold and black tab on my uniform. I got pure bona fide Ranger swag going on, right here, dawg."

Evan looked like he was restraining an eye roll, but he winked at her instead. "Thanks for encouraging him."

One wink shouldn't launch an entire fleet of wings flapping in her stomach. "I should, um ..." Learn how to form a coherent sentence around him. "Probably ..." Stop talking. Jeez, what was her problem?

He stared at the pavement with the slightest grin hitching up his cheek. "Where you headed?"

Anywhere but here. "I'm gonna swing by Sip and Savor Chicago."

"Mind if I join you?" His crippling gaze met hers, and that was it. Brain-mouth coordination, over.

She shook her head, unable to look away from him.

Darius clasped Evan's hand before climbing into a Jeep at the curb. "Tomorrow, bro."

"Later." Evan gave him a chin flick. Smiling at her, he motioned toward his car.

Anna peeked behind her. No way she was returning the way she'd come. Then again, facing a stalker—real or imagined—might be easier than standing three inches away from the man she wished was the one pursuing her.

CHAPTER FOUR

Infiltrate

Evan pressed the seat warmer button as soon as he started the car.

Anna cocked a brow. "The café's only, like, two minutes away."

"That's all it takes." One of his favorite features about his Accord.

"You didn't turn into one of those testosterone-driven guys who have car separation anxiety, did you?"

Laughing, he shifted into second gear. "Something like that."

"Wow, Sarge. If you start pec bouncing next, I might have to leave."

He cracked up. She was going to crush his willpower before this was over with. He checked his side mirror, wondering how she snuck into his blind spot every time. "I'll try to hold back for you."

"I appreciate that." The afterglow of her impish smile rivaled the seat warmer.

Evan knocked the heat down and willed his mind to stay on track.

Parked beside the curb in front of the three-store strip, he cast a glance around the neighboring brick apartments and abandoned basketball court before unlocking the doors. The city had a Dunkin Donuts and Starbucks on every corner, yet Anna insisted on traipsing off the beaten path by herself.

Evan refrained from commenting. He should be thankful she acted like she hadn't noticed anyone tailing her. It made his task of pretending this was just a random encounter with a friend a lot easier. He'd play along to curb any suspicions but not at the expense of lowering his guard.

"You still drink coffee?" She opened her door.

"Are you kidding?"

"What? That's not a valid question?" Her innocent expression made it even funnier.

"Not even in the near vicinity of valid."

"Then you, my friend, are in the right place." Flaunting a grin, she ambled outside and up to the windowed door.

With Anna, any place felt like the right one.

"Don't be stupid, boy. You'll never belong in that girl's life." His dad's words hovered right beneath the surface. Always ready to remind Evan of his place the second he edged past it.

But the truth kept him focused. He scanned the street on his way to the door.

"Ready to be in heaven?" She peered back at him with green eyes capable of causing any guy within a hundred yards to turn his head. Her unassuming beauty made her more of a target than she knew.

Burying the thought before it showed on his face, he held the door for her. Inside, the purple walls, abstract paintings, and black and yellow chairs sang Anna's artsy love language. No wonder she preferred to come here instead of a chain.

A plastic green tag sticking out on her jeans' waistband caught Evan's eye as she unzipped her coat.

She followed his line of sight, yanked down her sweater, and laughed. "You didn't see that." Lips tight, she scampered toward the counter.

"You don't seriously think I'm gonna let that slide, do you?" Not with such an incriminating expression.

She dished out a *whatever* face at him. "I got these jeans at the Goodwill the other day ... and *might've* forgotten to cut the tag off after I washed them."

"The Goodwill." He blinked at her. "You're shopping at a thrift store when your dad can buy you anything you want."

"Not independence."

Evan crossed his arms.

She matched his scowl and raised a finger. "Don't start." Banishing the conversation, she skipped the rest of the way to the counter. "Can I have a Bull Frog Mocha? With extra whip, please?" After tucking her hair behind her ear, she fished through her purse for a fabric wallet.

Like that was happening. Evan withdrew his billfold and set it on the counter. The overhead menu stared back at him with dozens of choices. She was right. His mouth watered just from reading the descriptions.

"I'll take a Caramel Royale Latte." He paid for their orders, despite her resistance, and looked over to an impossibly wide grin. "What?"

"Nothing." She gave a wry shrug. "I just figured now that you're a big bad Ranger, you would've graduated from frou-frou drinks to black coffee." Her infectious laugh trailed the dig.

Evan pocketed his wallet, a grin harder to hide. "Old habits die hard."

The slightest crease crinkled her forehead.

He moved to the end of the counter and out of danger territory before she could press the subject. She didn't need to know he'd kept drinking hot chocolates and lattes all these years because they reminded him of time they'd spent together.

Anna either missed it or let it go. Instead, she leaned her shoulder against his. "So, Casanova, huh?"

"Don't let him fool you. Murphy talks a good game, but when it comes down to it, he's a one-woman kind of guy."

"I wouldn't expect any less from a friend of yours. Is he in your platoon or battalion or whatever it is you guys call it?" She slurped a mouthful of whipped cream off the top of her drink, looking way too attractive.

Heaven help him.

Releasing a gruff breath, Evan strode to the bar chairs along the windows. Anna sat next to him with an earnest expression, as though genuinely clueless of the effect she had on him.

He swirled a stirrer in his cup. This wasn't what he wanted to talk about, either, but he'd take the subject change. "Murphy and I met in Basic. We went through training together all the way through RIP."

She slid him a questioning stare.

"Ranger Indoctrination Program," he clarified. "Murphy's a good soldier. Even recycled when he failed the first time. But Ranger School will break the best of them."

An older man walking an even older looking mutt passed by the window. Beyond him, on the opposite corner, a guy smoking a cigarette leaned against the bumper of an SUV with a stare trained on the café.

Evan's senses jumped to alert. A single Suburban. No other tails. Two men—muscle for hire. The one behind the wheel held status but not final authority.

"What's the school like?"

Anna's innocent voice cut through his focus. He inhaled and risked looking back at her but couldn't find the right words.

"Oh." A torn expression streaked her face. "It's classified, isn't it?"

She had no idea how much it killed him to keep things from her. "There's a reason the sign at the camp says *Not for the Weak or Fainthearted.*" He set a hand over hers without thinking and rubbed her fingers with the back of his thumb. "Even if it didn't violate code to tell you, you wouldn't want to know."

The concern welling up in her tender eyes confirmed his need to shield her from his life and the risks around her every day.

A car door closed. Evan looked up in time to see the Suburban backing up the street and out of view. Had he been made?

Anna slipped her hand out from under his and dropped it to her lap, her voice even lower. "This can't be your first leave in five years. Why haven't you come home before now?"

The painful questions obviously weren't about to end. Leaving the SUV in the background for now, Evan lined up the logo on the cardboard sleeve with the one on his cup and wrestled over what he could tell her. "My mom's in the hospital."

"What happened?"

"She had her right lung removed."

Anna covered her chest. "I just saw her maybe six months ago at her pottery shop. She didn't say anything."

"We only found out about a month ago. She went to the doctor's thinking she had bronchitis." She didn't deserve to face anything worse. Evan shoved the cup away from him. He should've gotten Mom out of that smoke-infested apartment and away from his dad's verbal abuse years ago. If Evan had been stronger, he could've spared her the consequences of all those years of pain.

Gentle fingers slid over his. "I'm so sorry." Anna lowered her head to meet his eyes. "Your mom's one of the bravest women I know. She'll beat this."

Her assurance tightened the knot in his chest. Anna had always been quick to credit other people's strength yet never recognized her own. He couldn't pull away.

Returning her hands to her cup, she faced forward. He cleared his throat and chugged half his coffee. They needed something else to talk about. Fast.

"How was the studio this morning?"

Her grunt said enough. "I have less than a week to polish my audition piece."

"I'm sure it's already perfect."

She sat back and huffed.

O-kay. Wrong word choice?

"Perfect's not good enough. Every dancer who hits that floor will have perfect technique. I have to find a way to stand out. I'm not competing against skill. I'm competing against passion."

"Anna, your entire life exudes passion for art. You have nothing to worry about."

Staring at the ceiling, she tugged her scarf away from her neck. "You don't understand. If I can't clear my head and immerse myself in this routine, I'm not gonna make it. And the possibility of what that means ..." She closed her eyes, as if shutting out the thought.

"What's holding you back? You thinking about your dad's case?"

She hurled a blank stare at him, let out a strange laugh, and pushed up from the table. "Guys are so blind."

Evan scurried up from his seat, but she beat him to the door. Outside, he scoured the sidewalks, cars, and buildings while jogging to catch up. "Where are you going?"

"To the rec center."

The girl's stubbornness never ended. "Let me drive you."

Anna stopped beside a black gate leading to a park that could've passed for a cemetery. The tension radiating off her kept him a foot away.

"You, Evan." She spun around, wavy hair a beautiful mess in the wind. "You're the reason I can't think straight."

Her words clawed into his gut. She had every reason not to want him around. He'd fully expected it. But no amount of prepping could neutralize the pain of seeing it on her face.

Watery eyes approached him. "Five years. You left and haven't been back in five years. No phone calls. No visits." Her gaze plummeted to the ground, his heart right behind it. "Can you at least tell me why?"

The hurt in her voice wound around his own so tightly, no sound came out.

She looked up long enough to intersect his gaze. "Something else you have to keep from me. I get it." She turned, but he caught her hand.

"Bells, please. I'm sorry. For more than you know." More than he could ever tell her. "I left because I had to." His heart took over as he brushed back the strands of hair billowing across her cheeks. "That doesn't mean I went a day without thinking of you."

Her lashes swept up, and an ache to hold her seized every part of him. He urged his eyes to stay even, his pulse to slow.

An unreadable expression propelled her into his arms. "I'm sorry, I just ... I've missed you so much. Without you here, without knowing what was going on ..." Anna squeezed him tighter. "You're my best friend."

He didn't understand her response. Didn't deserve it. But he couldn't bring himself to step away. He curled his arms around her back and nestled his cheek to her hair. Her softness decimated his discipline of holding memories and desires at bay. The closer she pressed in, the harder the waves hit and intensified the yearning to tell her everything.

Swallowing, Evan slid his hand down her hair and loosened his hold. He'd led ambushes in Iraq, assisted Special Forces in Afghanistan, and conducted dozens of raids against Islamic terrorists. Yet, the most dangerous place he'd ever been in was right here in Anna's arms.

Later, Anna would regret allowing herself to sink into the warmth and safety of Evan's embrace. She knew better. Had been coaching herself to act like running into him again hadn't even happened. But right now, she didn't care.

The honest feelings Evan ignited in her when they were kids hadn't waned, but this soldier-version of him did things she'd never felt before. Visceral things she shouldn't be letting him see.

Ignoring the warning, she drew tighter and breathed in lingering hints left from his soap and shampoo. Evan had never been one to wear cologne. At least that much hadn't changed.

Her body tensed at the thought of what she must smell like after dancing up a sweat this morning. Anna eased away from him until her heels leveled with the pavement.

A self-conscious laugh slipped out in response to his confused expression. "Sorry. I just realized I probably stink." *And must look like a blubbering idiot draping myself all over you.* Did she have no control whatsoever?

He rubbed a knuckle across his brow. "You smell distinctly you."

Like a sweaty dancer? Fabulous. She curled a strand of hair around her finger and brought it to her nose. "My own smell, huh? That can't be good."

As if his smile couldn't get any more attractive, it deepened until the slightest dimple emerged beside a tiny scar she didn't recognize. He moved her hand and let her hair slide through his fingers. "Trust me. It's a good thing."

If her diaphragm would listen to her brain for a change, maybe she could conjure enough breath to form a reply.

A pink hue dusted the tops of Evan's cheeks as he stepped back. Poor guy. She seriously had to stop putting him in awkward situations. She pointed behind her. "I should get to work." *And pick up some self-control along the way.*

He gestured to the Accord with his eyes.

"It's practically around the block, Evan. I'll be fine."

"We're not really gonna have this argument again, are we?"

Anna tapped her foot, prepared to have a stare down. With Mr. Hazel Eyes? Bad idea. She should know better than to go toe-to-toe with a soldier. Her bag was in his trunk, anyway.

"Okay, fine. You win." He'd drop her off, and she'd go on her way with yet one more thing to pretend never happened. What was new?

Beside a metal garbage can, Evan intercepted her empty cup when she went to toss it. "We can recycle that."

She stared at him.

"What?" He flattened the cardboard. "You don't care about the environment?"

"No, I do. I just didn't peg you for a tree hugger."

Evan hit the unlock button on his key fob and opened the door for her. "I defend the country. Might as well save the planet while I'm at it."

"An everyday hero, right there." A laugh followed her into the car.

Behind the wheel, he cranked the engine. "I do what I can."

Probably more than he was admitting. No doubt, he'd finished at the top of every training he'd gone through. Evan was an all-or-nothing kind of guy. Always had been.

The possibility of what danger that put him in on the field terrified her. She didn't need to add any more strain to his life. Burying her feelings, she buckled her seat belt and faced forward.

He hadn't fully answered her question about not coming home before now. Chances were, he never would. His classified missions were one more reminder she didn't fit in his world anymore. If she weren't such a glutton for punishment, she'd leave it at that and let the rest go.

Anna directed her thoughts to the work she and Mom started at the rec center instead. Just thinking of the lovies there, and the way art impacted them, brought life back into perspective. Mom wouldn't want her to give up on that.

"Sometime before you leave, you should stop in and tell the kids about the army. They'll eat it up. But I gotta warn you. They'll have you wrapped around their little fingers in seconds." Anna laughed. "The girls in my Ballet One and Two classes are utterly adorable. And don't get me started on the tykes who come play basketball through the week. I'm telling ya. There's no way you're going to resist their charm."

Evan rubbed his smooth jaw. "I don't know. We go through hardcore discipline training in the military. You think these kids can break me?"

"Hands down, Sarge. You've met your match."

"If you only knew," he mumbled softly.

Sunlight broke through the clouds and cast a glare over the windshield. He flipped down his visor, something in his demeanor drooping with it. "It's great what you're doing here, but teaching a couple of classes at a rec center doesn't sound like much of a salary."

She scoffed. "They taught you some mean deduction skills at Ranger School, didn't they?"

"You're lucky I'm driving right now." Grinning, Evan circled the wheel.

Her laughter petered into a sigh. "It's hard to pay the bills, but I don't care about making money. I care about making an impact. We're supposed to be the paintbrush—"

"That cheers this dark world. I know. Your mom's words left their mark. Believe me. I haven't forgotten."

Except he had. Just like Anna had for a time. Even now, some moments made it all feel pointless. Realigning her life with the original vision they'd shared would never be enough to make up for losing time with Mom the year she died, but it was all Anna could do.

"I wasn't given the chance to stop someone from stealing my mom's paintbrush, but I refuse to let someone rob me of mine."

Evan idled the car in a parking spot and held her with those unsearchable eyes of his. He shifted into park, severed their connection, and cut the engine. "I never thought you would."

And she never thought she'd be doing this alone. What happened to their plans? She stamped down the disappointment, climbed out, and welcomed the cool air hitting her flushed face. There was no point harboring resentment. She just had to say good-bye and move on.

He hustled around the bumper. "I would've gotten the door for you."

She pushed down her emotions and smiled away things he didn't need to see. "Can't have you cramping Casanova's style."

His sobered expression wasn't letting her off the hook. "Anna ..."

Up the street, a woman resembling Marissa sauntered out of a building and cozied up to a clean-cut guy in a suit, who wrapped his hand around her hip. Anna did a double take.

Evan pinned a questioning look on her.

Shoot. She grabbed his sleeve to keep him from turning. "Why don't you run inside with me to meet the kids real quick while you're here?" She'd blurted it out so fast, he probably thought she was desperate to keep him near. Latching on to his arm like a groupie definitely didn't help. But the possibility of his seeing his girlfriend cheat on him was worse.

Anna backed off once a peek behind him showed Marissa had rounded the corner.

Evan sent a scrutinizing glance around the street and zeroed in on something over Anna's shoulder. Probably his car.

Couldn't blame him. They were supposed to be saying good-bye. "Listen, you really don't have to come in. I shouldn't have put you on the spot like that. Thank you for the ride and the coffee. But we should both get on with the day." *And our lives.*

A flicker of something unreadable passed his eyes before he secured a grin back in place. "You kidding? I'm dying to meet the kids able to crack the United States Army's toughest men."

Great. Resigning, she plodded inside.

Of all the schools available to train a soldier to defend his country, why wasn't there a single one able to train a girl to defend her heart?

CHAPTER FIVE

Shrapnel

E van kept a smile painted on until Anna passed under his arm and through the doorway. He cast a subtle glance toward the Suburban parked on the opposite corner. As hard as it was on him to be close to Anna again, he wasn't leaving until he got some leads on who'd been tailing her.

Inside the rec center, he took advantage of the stroll down the long hallway to iron out his composure. The squeak of sneakers gliding across a floor led them around the corner and into the musty smell of an old gym. Pockets of kids occupied the basketball court—an older bunch playing a pickup game at one end, younger ones messing around at the other.

Evan glanced at his cell. "Are they always here this early?"

"On the weekends, they basically live here." Anna's smile competed with the overhead industrial lights. "What did I tell ya? Cute, right?"

A kid, probably about nine years old, with one pant leg hiked up and a backward ball cap on, turned when they approached. He jogged to the sidelines and flung a once-over up and down Evan's profile. "Dang, Miss Madison, you didn't tell us you was bringing the Hulk with you today."

Evan barely squelched a laugh. Anna's pinched lips weren't helping. One look from her amused eyes to the kid's expectant ones, and he couldn't resist. He squared his shoulders and busted out a series of exaggerated pec bounces.

Anna shook her head. "You did not just do that."

"Couldn't help it." His mouth quirked.

The kid jumped up to touch his bicep. "Yo, you think you can arm curl me?"

"Let's see."

The kid locked his fingers around Evan's hand, and Evan curled him in the air.

Anna rolled her eyes. "Show-off." She reached to tickle the kid's sides. "Better be careful, Shaun. You're leaving yourself wide open."

Shaun's laughter joined the echoes of conversation bouncing around the high ceiling.

Evan lowered him back to the ground and picked up a basketball. "So, what do you think, big guy? You ready to ball?"

Shaun adjusted his tattered sweatshirt, stole the ball, and dribbled it between his short legs. "All those muscles gotta slow you up." He pivoted around Evan. Twice. "And since I'm, like, a hundred times faster than you, I'd say you got no game, old man."

Evan blinked. Who was this boy, Kid President?

"I tried to warn you." Anna visibly fought a satisfied grin.

Pec bounces weren't the only thing he couldn't resist. Eyes on her lips, he sidled closer. "Oh, yeah?"

A middle-aged woman with a headband holding back her puffy hair strolled up to them. "It's about time you brought a good-looking guy up in here."

Anna darted her a look of warning. "Evan, this is my outspoken coworker, Robyn Thomas. Robyn, this is Evan O'Riley, a childhood *friend*."

Evan tipped his head. "Pleasure, ma'am."

"Oooh, and he's got manners, too." Robyn swatted Anna's arm. "Girl, you better keep this one."

Anna's cheeks flamed. "You're seriously trying to embarrass me right now, aren't you?"

"Aw, don't you worry about that, Miss Thang." Robyn bobbed her brows toward Evan. "The color on your face is only attracting that boy even more."

Anna's jaw dropped.

Shaun folded in half, laughing. "Ms. Robyn just called you out, yo."

"Miss Madison!" A spindly-legged redhead, who looked slightly younger than Shaun, skipped across the floor wearing a worn tutu over her jeans. She sprang into Anna's arms. "I've been practicing my pirouettes."

Anna diverted her attention from Robyn to the little girl, clearly thankful for the interruption. "You have? I can't wait to see them. You think they'll be as pretty as you are?"

The girl blushed, nestled her face into Anna's shoulder, and shook her head.

As if seeing Anna's heart come to life earlier hadn't already threatened to undo Evan, watching her with the kids did him in.

"Megan, I'd like you to meet my friend." Anna's lips curled to the side. "Mr. Hulk."

Another bashful look colored Megan's expression as she said hello. Keeping her chin down, she tugged on Anna's hand. "Can we start class early?"

"Of course. Let me just…" Anna looked around. "Shoot. I left my bag in the car. I—"

"I've got it." Evan lifted a hand and backed up. "I need to make a quick phone call, anyway. Give me five minutes. Is there a bathroom I can use first?"

"Sure." She motioned behind him. "Just down that hall on the left."

"Perfect." He strode in the direction she pointed. Once out of view, he passed the bathroom and traversed a series of hallways and corners until he reached a side exit.

Evan scanned the alley without opening the door all the way. With his hood swept up, he slinked between two brick buildings across the street and approached his Accord from the back.

Inside the car, he grabbed his Nikon D3300 from a bag in the back, swapped the regular lens for the telephoto zoom, and focused on the Suburban. "You're not the only ones with tinted windows, boys." He zoomed in on their license plate and shot a handful of photos, including a few of a crater-faced guy pacing the sidewalk beside the SUV.

If Evan had to guess, he was the one who'd scared Anna this morning. Even in broad daylight, the guy could startle any woman with pure ugliness.

He lowered the camera and called his buddy at the police department.

"Corporal Harris."

"What's up, man, it's O'Riley." Evan scrolled through the pics. "I need a favor."

"Nothing like cutting to the chase." Harris laughed. "You gonna stop by the station while you're in town, or what?"

"Maybe next week. I need you to run a plate for me."

The pause on the end of the line stretched.

"On what basis?"

"Friendship."

Harris breathed into the phone and lowered his voice. "All right. Give it to me."

Evan held up the camera. "Bravo Two Five Foxtrot Romeo Six Three. Call me when you have something."

"Roger that. But stay out of trouble while you're here, huh?"

Evan's job led him into the heart of trouble every day. That was one promise he couldn't make. "Later, bro."

He hung up and rifled through his bag for the tracker he'd picked up last week. From the backseat floorboard, he snatched a ball cap and exchanged his sweatshirt for a coat. The jokers might be packing guns, but he'd gamble brains didn't come with the gear. He didn't worry a second over blowing his cover.

Quietly easing out of the car, Evan tugged the bill of his hat tight over his eyes. He circled back the way he came and approached the SUV from behind. With Maps pulled up on his cell, he glanced up and down until he bumped into the guy.

Evan gripped the dude's shoulder, pretended to catch his balance, and tucked the tracker under his coat collar. He turned on the Texas drawl he'd learned from his boy Hernandez. "Sorry. I'm supposed to meet a friend. You by chance know how to get to..." He looked at his phone. "Grant Park?"

Crater Face shoved him back and readjusted his coat. "Screw off, man."

"A'ight. Easy. Just looking for some directions." Evan kept walking with his cell out.

Behind him, a car door closed, followed by tires screeching around the corner.

Evan pulled up the GPS app and watched the dot on the screen pulse down South Calumet Avenue. "Yeah, keep driving, buddy."

He slid the phone into his pocket, grabbed Anna's bag from his car, and hustled back to the rec center. He'd deal with Tweedledee and Tweedledum after nightfall. Right now, he had someone even more intimidating to tackle.

Inside, he spun his ball cap backward and shed his coat while jogging onto the court toward Shaun. "Let's ball, big guy."

Amazing how quickly the hours passed while interacting with the kids. Evan hadn't meant to spend the entire day at the rec center. But after the way Anna had completely mesmerized him while teaching her ballet class, he doubted he'd be much use doing anything else, anyway.

Standing beside him, Anna rearranged some things in her bag without looking his way. Whatever was on her mind confiscated her smile. Did he want to ask?

She rolled up a pair of tights. "Thanks for staying today. It meant a lot to Shaun. He desperately needs a male role model in his life."

"Looks like the kid's got a good head on his shoulders."

"He really does. If life would give him half a chance, he'd go places." Another frown emerged.

Evan cupped her hand to stop her busywork and lifted her chin. "You give him that chance every day by caring about him." What would it take for her to see the difference she made just by being who she was?

She inhaled softly, and he let go before he lost the last thread of restraint preventing him from crossing a line.

Anna kept her head down while zipping up her bag. "How long have you known Marissa?"

The question sank dead into his gut. He could kick himself for being in the predicament of ever needing to have this conversation. "Four months."

Her hand stalled over the bag. "You love her?"

One sucker punch after the other. He raked a hand through his hair. Anna deserved his honesty as much as Marissa deserved him to be honest with himself.

"No. Truthfully, we hardly know each other. Between my trainings and her travels, we've gone out only a handful of times. I'm not even sure how it got to the point of her calling herself my girlfriend." He faced the industrial ceiling. "I need to set her straight. I was going to before I came. But when she asked to join me on this trip, I guess I thought it'd make things easier."

"Make what easier?"

She really had no idea, did she? He leveled his gaze with hers and dug inside for the bravery he staked his life on. "Seeing you again."

Her lashes gave a flutter as she looked away.

He searched the room, dying for a topic changer.

Anna clutched her bag. "How'd you meet?"

A topic change wouldn't be that easy. "On deployment. She was in Afghanistan, covering a story."

"And she ended up in danger." It wasn't a question.

"Yeah."

Comprehension touched Anna's face. She inched forward, lowered his hand from his hair, and met his eyes with piercing compassion. If she moved any closer, he'd have absolutely zero chance of hiding how fast his pulse was thrumming.

"You're a protector, Evan. You can't help it."

She was wrong. Both of their moms were proof of that. But with those green eyes showering confidence over him, he almost let himself believe it.

A twinge of discomfort furrowed her brows. "It's why you looked out for me like a big brother all those years. I'm not surprised you were drawn to her. It's easy to confuse protection with something more."

Even though he knew Anna would eventually realize that was the same thing she did the night she almost kissed him, his heart sank at hearing her say it. He couldn't blame her for reacting in the moment. Caught up in leaning on his comfort and protection during such a tumultuous time, it was easy to confuse her feelings. But she would've regretted kissing him later when the emotions of losing her mom settled. Even more so when she found out why she died.

He wouldn't have risked ruining their friendship. Still wouldn't. Even if he didn't deserve it any more now than he had then.

Evan backed up, and Anna's forehead creased deeper.

Megan bulldozed between them and bounced on the balls of her feet. "Ready?"

Anna wiped any trace of their conversation from her face and ruffled Megan's hair. "Yep. Just give me a minute to say good-bye to …" Her lips pulled to the left. "*Mr. Hulk*, and then we'll go."

Megan scurried off toward the door, and Anna stalled in front of him. "Miss Allison's a single mom. Basically a kid herself. She's never around when I come by. So, I walk Megan home each night."

Of course she did. In the dark. To a sketchy neighborhood, no doubt. And she wondered why she needed security. With how easily his feelings for her undermined his steadfastness, maybe he wasn't the best one to offer it.

No. He could do this. Straightening, Evan crammed the mixed emotions under his armor where they belonged. He was built for close combat, trained for direct-fire battles. What were a few more pieces of shrapnel added to the ones already spearing his heart?

He withdrew his keys and faced her head-on. "I'll drive."

CHAPTER SIX

Barrier

Megan tapped her shoes against the back of Evan's seat in rhythm with the music coming from the stereo. Thankfully, he'd slipped out ahead of them and transferred his gear from the backseat to the trunk. Otherwise, she'd be annihilating it right now instead of his spine.

A glance in the rearview mirror caught her smiling up at him with that cute freckly nose. Anna was right. Everything about Megan's appearance screamed neglect, yet her face held nothing but joy.

His stomach soured at the thought of what conditions they were bringing her home to. No one deserved a childhood like his. Especially not an innocent girl.

In the passenger seat, Anna stared out the side window. Away from him. Hard to blame her. A charged awkwardness hadn't stopped surging between them since their conversation about Marissa.

No telling what Anna thought of him now. He'd essentially admitted to hiding behind having a fake girlfriend in order to handle facing her. His knuckles whitened over the steering wheel.

"Up here on the right," Anna said, still without turning her head.

He pulled beside the curb and noted six cars lining the street in front of a shabby apartment complex with everything he'd expected written all over it.

Clenching his jaw, Evan unlocked the doors. Thanks to his gut, he'd already secured his Sig in his concealed holster before the girls had made it to the car earlier.

Megan skipped up a set of metal stairs on the side of the building while Evan and Anna trailed cautiously behind. The stench billowing from a nearby dumpster churned Evan's already-uneasy stomach a little more with each step.

After knocking, Anna twisted Megan's hair into a braid from behind.

The door creaked open, and a guy in an oversized black T-shirt and jeans hanging halfway off his butt let his gaze roam Anna up and down. A smug grin expanded beneath bits of greasy blond hair. "You didn't tell me you called a friend," he hollered behind him.

Evan stepped into view, and the punk flinched backward.

"Heather, what the—?"

"I didn't call anyone." A young woman with sallow cheeks and red hair to match the rims of her eyes tottered up from the couch. A spoon and lighter clattered onto the coffee table. While scratching her arm with one hand, Heather wiped her nose with the other. She stumbled forward, glared at them, and tugged her daughter inside by the shirt. "It's just her dance teacher."

Megan reached for Anna.

Don't say it. Don't say her name.

"Miss Madison," she whimpered.

Evan swore to himself. Now the loser had something to go on.

The grimy creep traced a hand down Megan's hair. "Aw, you won't mind hanging out with Mommy and her friends tonight, will you?"

Anna slapped the jerk dead across the face. "Don't you touch her."

Vehemence darkened his bloodshot eyes.

Evan swept her behind him. "Back down, man."

Grease Boy shoved him and went for the Glock in his waistband. "You the one who better back down." He waved the gun in Evan's face like he was posing for some hip-hop video. "What's up now, punk? Not so tough with heat up in your grill."

Evan should've gotten a badge for restraining an eye roll. With a twist of the guy's wrist, Evan disarmed him, released the magazine, and pulled the slide back to empty the chamber. He backed up to chuck the magazine off the railing outside and thrust the empty gun against the guy's bony chest without wasting his breath on a response.

Grease Boy shifted his glare to Anna and yelled over his shoulder. "Have my money by Friday, Heather, or you ain't the only one who's gonna pay."

Just what Anna needed on top of everything else. Some lowlife thug putting a hit on her. Evan barricaded her behind him so the punk couldn't memorize what she looked like.

An all too familiar fear lit Heather's glassy eyes as she watched her dealer jog down the steps. She closed the door, blocking the shaken look on her face from Evan's view but not from his heart. He'd endured that kind of helplessness too many times.

Anna clawed around Evan's shoulder. He understood, but now wasn't the time. He caught her at the waist. "We gotta roll." Grease Boy would be back with his crew.

"No." She fought against his pull. "We can't leave Megan here."

"We have no choice."

Anna shoved away from him, hair a hot mess, eyes sharp. She whipped out her phone. "We at least need to call someone. The police, Child Services—someone!"

It wouldn't make a difference in the end. He knew that better than anyone. Even if they charged Heather for neglect, or put Megan in foster care, it'd probably make the situation worse.

"We'll call Harris on the road, and I'll swing by later to check on her, but we gotta go."

Anna burrowed her feet. He stole her phone and tucked it into his pocket. A glare he'd pay for later pummeled him. Sighing, he heaved her over his shoulder. She always had to do things the hard way.

"You did *not* just do that." Anna wrestled to free herself from his hold.

He pinned her legs tight across his chest to avoid taking a knee to the gut. She could probably out leg press Casanova.

At the car, he opened the door and slid her inside. She reached for his neck and held his face an inch away, heated breaths meeting his. The tension already teeming through his body rocketed into an entirely different sphere. He needed to move. Now.

He shut the door and craned his head to the dark sky. *Breathe, O'Riley.*

Behind the wheel, he cranked the engine and exhaled. Frustration radiated off her seat. Anna could be mad as long as she was safe.

"I'm gonna come back, Evan."

God, give him patience. "No, you're not."

She turned. "Yeah, I am."

"Do you have *any* concept of danger?"

"Yes! Why do think we have to get her out of there? It doesn't matter if I get hurt."

"It does to me." His fingers tensed around the gearshift.

Anna clenched her jaw, curtailing the beginning of tears.

She might've been angry, but it was obvious she was scared, too. More for Megan than for herself. Heaving an exhale, Evan climbed back out of the car. On the other side, he opened the door, pulled her up, and closed her in his arms.

Her initial resistance waned as her body melded to his. She clung to his shoulders. "Promise me she'll be okay, Evan."

Keeping her close, he cupped her head. "I promise." He leaned back and searched her face. "But I need you to let me take care of you right now. Please."

She nodded, and he helped her back into the car.

Once on the road, he scrolled to Harris's number.

"I'm working on it," Harris said, skipping the hellos.

Evan flipped on his blinker and refrained from telling him to work faster. "I got another plate for you to run. Echo Kilo Oscar Six Zero Delta One."

Anna gawked at him as he merged into traffic, but he veered his gaze back to the road. "Put out a BOLO for a midnight blue Chevy Impala. Driver's a local dealer, about five foot seven, blond, medium build. Last seen at intersection of Stewart and 58th."

"Charges?"

"Drug possession, dealing, brandishing a firearm. Take your pick."

It sounded like Harris dropped his pen on his desk. "O'Riley—"

"At least run the plates."

A drawn-out breath filtered through the line. "Give me an hour."

"Later." Evan hung up, slipped his cell into the cup holder, and caught another gaping stare from the passenger seat. "What?"

"How do you know what car that guy drives?"

Evan bumped his wipers on. The blades dragged across the windshield, smearing several raindrops in their path. "The Impala was the only car missing when we came out."

"Wait. What?" Anna pulled one foot up into the seat and twisted toward him. "You're telling me you memorized the cars outside the apartment and each of their license plates? We were out front for, like, two minutes, tops."

He shrugged. Studying an area was part of any op—so ingrained, it was as natural as eating and sleeping.

"You know, the whole Jason Bourne thing you've got going on is starting to freak me out a little."

Before Evan could respond, a *ding* from his cell announced the tracker he'd placed on Crater Face was on the move again. He swiped the screen to check the GPS. The guys tailing Anna weren't nearby yet, but he didn't doubt they would be soon. And now he had to add that loser from Megan's place to the list of people they had to dodge. Evan swerved to the right.

Anna gripped the door panel. "Where are you going?"

"Scenic route." He didn't see a tail, but they'd stayed longer at the apartment than he'd intended.

Rain beat onto the window and sent rivulets streaking down the glass. He rotated the wipers up another notch and glanced in Anna's direction. Streetlights cast soft shadows across her face as she traced an erratic pattern up and down the seat belt, clearly lost in thought.

Surely, things like tonight showed her she needed protection. He struggled for the right words. "Anna, I know you value your independence, but would it really be so bad for your dad to want to offer you surveillance?"

"From one of his Secret Service wannabes?" Scrunching her face in feigned seriousness, she raised an imaginary wrist mic to her mouth the way her dad's guards did any time they found her. "Radiance secured," she mimicked. "Come on. I'm not the president's daughter. I don't need a code name or bodyguards following my every move. You, of all people, know what growing up like that did to me."

Without facing her, Evan shifted into third gear. "Some people might call protection love."

"And some might call it a cage." Anna clutched her elbows, her words like a vise around him. Would she ever see it differently?

He coasted into a parking spot alongside her apartment complex. "Regardless of how it seems, the streets are a dark place."

"Relax, Batman. This isn't Gotham. It's Chicago."

Close enough. And what was with people making superhero references today?

He unbuckled his seat belt and met her gaze, thankful her eyes had never seen the things his had. "Anna, listen to me. Soldiers don't train to pacify civilians' fears. We train because evil's real. The moment you think it isn't is the moment it wins."

"But admitting it's real doesn't mean it loses, either." Chin lowered, she toyed with the hem of her sweater.

After losing her mom, Anna had every right to think that. But if she'd just trust him, he'd never let that darkness near her.

"You're right, you know," she said after another moment. "About Social Services. I've tried calling before. I knew Megan didn't have a good home life, but I didn't realize..." Eyes closed, she cut herself off.

"You can't change her situation, Anna."

She stared at her lap and released a hard exhale. "I know. I just hoped teaching her dance might help make life more bearable ... the way it did for me." Anna raised her head. "I'm not giving up on her, Evan."

Like she hadn't on him. "I wouldn't expect anything else."

"I wish things were different for her."

It'd only taken one day with the sweet girl to feel the same exact way. "I know." He traced his thumb over the back of Anna's hand and nodded outside. "C'mon. I'll get your bag."

Cold beads of rain landed on his neck as they jogged up to the building.

She led the way to the second-floor apartment, where high-pitched meows carried on from behind her door.

"Who are we gonna get today?" he mumbled.

Anna pulled out her keys. "What?"

He pointed to her apartment and the incessant meowing still coming from inside. "Split personality. Sméagol or Gollum?"

Rolling her eyes, Anna unlocked the deadbolt, inched the door open, and nudged the gray tabby back with her foot. "Hang on, Bailey girl. I know you're hungry." Anna flipped on the lights, and the cat weaved through her legs, purring with enough gusto to rival a train on the "L."

Sméagol. That was a good sign. But just in case, he'd check the place out. Evan motioned toward the hallway. "I'm gonna drop your bag in your room and use the bathroom, if that's all right."

"Sure." Anna set her purse on the kitchen counter and went for the cans of cat food in the pantry.

Down the hall, he withdrew his Sig and inched the bedroom door open. After sweeping the room, he slipped into the bathroom and checked behind the curtain. Nothing but a few paw prints. He secured his gun, washed up, and headed back to the kitchen to find Anna humming while preparing hot chocolate.

Nothing hampered her spirits for long. She popped a few mini marshmallows in a mug with *One Kitty Away From Becoming A Crazy Cat Lady* written on it and turned. "Want one?"

And stay longer with her? More than he should. "I need to get going."

"Right. Yeah." Anna left her mug and shuffled across the peeling linoleum, hands in her pockets. "I, um … Thanks for today. All of it." She peered up with an adorable frazzled expression on her face, as if she found saying good-bye as awkward as he did. An almost bashful grin touched her lips. "I really enjoyed hanging out with you."

His throat turned to cotton while he stood in front of this amazing woman looking at him with such honest vulnerability. "Me too."

He opened the door, stopped across the threshold, and swallowed before turning. Leaning her hip and temple against the edge of the door, Anna sent another unassuming smile his way. Man, why'd he turn around?

A damp breeze blew in from the front door. His gaze shot from an older guy walking in back to Anna. "Don't unlock this door for anyone. You understand me?"

She gave a quick nod.

"If so much as a single hair rises on your arm tonight, you call me. I don't care what time it is. Okay?"

"Okay."

He blew out a breath. *Now, back away.* For the first time since being around her again, his legs actually obeyed and stepped backward. "Good night, Anna."

"Good night." She closed the door.

He didn't move again until the deadbolt clicked into place. Gripping both sides of the trim, he pressed his forehead against the door, thankful for the steel barrier keeping him from a battle he would've lost if he'd stayed.

She'd be livid if she knew her dad had one of his town cars staked across the street, but at least Evan could leave with some peace of mind knowing she had surveillance for the evening. As much as he wanted to stay and make her feel safe, Anna needed him on the field, which was exactly where he was headed.

CHAPTER SEVEN

Present

Staked out in his Accord across from a park near Anna's place, Evan drank the Americano he'd picked up on the way to follow the GPS tracker. The men had ditched the Suburban for an Escalade. Nothing like trying to keep a low profile.

Evan adjusted his camera lens and zoomed in on the SUV right as Crater Face got out and lit a cigarette. What were they standing around waiting for?

His cell buzzed in the cup holder. Harris. He swiped the screen. "Tell me you've got something."

"Yeah, I've got something. It's called a warning. What are you getting yourself into?"

Whatever he had to.

"Is this why you asked me where to find a tracker? Jeez, O'Riley. Michelli's not a guy to mess with. Neither are his hired guns. Let the DA's Office handle it."

So, they *were* Michelli's thugs. Evan swore away from the phone.

"I'm telling ya, man. Walk away from this one."

"You know I can't do that."

"You won't do Anna any good if you're dead."

Evan massaged his forehead. He didn't want to argue with his high school buddy about what he could handle. Even though all service men held a given respect for each other, jealousy over his elite training somehow always found a way into these types of conversations.

He took another swig of the bitter coffee that was supposed to keep his focus off wishing he were with Anna right now.

"I know the risks, Harris." Some more than others. "You got a name and address with the plate I gave you, or what?"

His pause grated on Evan's already-tense nerves. "Registered to M. J. Industries."

Michelli's front company. Why was Evan not surprised? "And let me guess. The address matches Adele's Little Italy's." He'd already scoped out the restaurant once. It served as a rendezvous point, but they must headquarter somewhere else. He just had to find out where.

"Like I said, man. Leave it alone."

"What about the other plate I gave you?"

"Stolen."

There was a shocker.

"But I think the guy you're talking about is Jamie Painter. The kid's got a list of priors longer than his age."

"So, you picked him up?"

"Not yet."

Evan clenched his coffee cup. Were they waiting for a personalized invitation?

"Two units patrolled the neighborhood you gave us. No sign of him. The guy's a drifter. Never stays at one address longer than a few weeks."

Maybe the punk was smarter than Evan gave him credit for. "Set a squad car at Brookfield Apartments. He'll be back."

"You know we don't have the resources to run a stakeout on every low-level drug dealer."

"The guy's walking around, waving a gun up in people's faces." Evan ran a hand back and forth over the top of his head. "If nothing else, pick him up for illegal possession. I guarantee he lifted that Glock on the streets."

"Him and two-thirds of the guys in that area. Look, my department's swamped on a case right now. When things die down, I'll see if we can get an informant to wire up for us, all right?"

"That's not good en—" Coffee dripped onto his shirt as he scrambled up in his seat. "Let me go, Harris." He dropped his phone on the center console and stared out the window.

Across the street, a bundled-up Anna hurried down the sidewalk with a drink carrier in her hand. What the heck did she think she was doing?

She ambled over to a woman and two children huddled together on the corner and handed them each a hot drink. The rain had let up, but the damp cold wasn't as merciful.

Evan shook his head at her unfailing empathy.

The door to the Escalade opened when Anna started down the sidewalk. Tweedledum lumbered out and jutted his chin at his partner. One flanked left while the other gained ground on Anna from behind. *Bells.*

Evan shot a glance toward her dad's town car creeping down the street. If Anna saw them, she'd flip. He grabbed his Sig and drew back the slide to check the chamber. Why'd he think she'd actually listen to him and stay inside? The girl was going to be the death of him.

He glanced up right as another man from the opposite direction strode for her.

Halfway out the door, Evan halted at the sight of the dude wrapping his arms around her. She obviously knew him. Even the dark couldn't hide the look of comfort on her face. Evan's whole body froze as she returned the affection.

The Trench Coat Duo stopped short, exchanged a measured glance, and backed into the shadows. A left-hand turn steered the town car out of view just in time. Her dad's men would be circling back around to their post, just as Evan should be tailing the Escalade.

But when the guy with Anna draped an arm over her shoulders and prodded her forward, Evan slumped back into his seat. Her dad's men had Anna covered. Still, if it didn't feel like a Humvee was sitting on his chest, he would've followed them.

Someone banged against the passenger window. Marissa pressed her face against her cupped hands while trying to peer into the tinted glass. Anna was tripping him up more than she should. He never let someone sneak up on him.

A quick glance back caught Anna and the guy disappearing around the corner. Evan's stomach twisted at the thought of him walking her to her door. Or worse, going inside with her.

Boxing out the image, Evan rolled the window partway down. "This isn't the best time, Marissa."

Headlights circled past them as the black Escalade turned the bend and careened in the opposite direction. Evan's hand sloped down the face of the steering wheel. At least he still had GPS on them.

"No time like the present." Marissa hiccupped. "Isn't that what you always say? Or is it some Ranger motto. I can't remember." An airy giggle flitted into the car.

Was she drunk? Releasing a hard breath, he stashed his gun in the glove box, unlocked the door, and pushed it open for her.

Marissa sank onto the seat as if relieved to be off her feet. "You soldiers think you have it tough, but woo, I'm telling you. Girls..." She slid off her heels. "*We're* the real warriors."

Warrior? Wasted and in an outfit that left little to the imagination, she could convince most any guy on this block to call her whatever she wanted. But all he felt was pity.

He'd tried with her. Tried to talk himself into being in a relationship. But she wasn't Anna. No one ever would be. He had his training, his missions. There was no point looking for anything else. He knew better than to complicate his path.

"You know what? You're right. No time like the present. We need to talk."

An alcohol-infused laugh trickled from Marissa's glossed lips. "So serious," she said in a baby voice while cupping his cheek. "Lighten up. The night's still young."

Keeping his calm, Evan transferred her hand to her lap. "What are you doing out this late?"

She lifted a finger to her mouth. "Shh …" The slurred noise intensified the stench of alcohol already overtaking the car. "I'm undercover."

If he hadn't grown up with a drunkard as a poor excuse for a father, he might've been tempted to throw back a few brews himself right about now. "Undercover for what?"

"Uh-uh-uh." She wagged a finger at him. "We said we'd never kiss and tell, remember?" Grinning, Marissa pressed the same finger into his bicep and leaned against it for balance. "*You* have your classified missions." She waved the finger back in her general direction. "And *I* have mine."

Evan gritted his teeth.

She must've noticed his lack of amusement. Wiggling up in the seat, she smoothed out her silky shirt and her expression. "C'mon, Evan. You didn't really think I was going to sit in my hotel all week, pining for you while you're out romping around, did you? I'm a journalist. I'm going to be wherever I can find a story. And let me tell ya. I'm working on a big one."

She flipped down the visor, popped open the mirror cover, and tweaked her makeup with her fingertips. "You understand the need to be in action better than anyone. That's why this thing we have between us works."

A devilish grin flashed his way. "Ooh. Speaking of action. We're going to a gala on Wednesday. Make sure you rent a tux. People here might not know my name yet, but they'll sure remember the power couple who walks in and steals the show."

Evan cupped her shoulders and moved her back into the seat before she got close enough to kiss him. Visuals of that guy sliding his hand over Anna's back snaked through his mind again.

Marissa fumbled around the door panel for the handle.

Evan clicked the lock button. He might not want to be around her, but he wasn't going to let her stumble down the street in a drunken stupor, either.

Marissa's laugh merged into a sigh against the window. She dragged her fingertips along the breath mark left on the glass.

He reached over to buckle her in. "I think it's time to call it a night." They'd have their conversation later—when she was coherent and he wasn't already on edge.

Not to mention he had work to get back to. At least the tracker app had recorded the thugs' movement. He'd log their routes and figure out where their base was as soon as he returned Marissa to her hotel.

The streetlight outside Anna's apartment buzzed on and off, each flicker mirroring the static in his head. She had her own life now. He shouldn't have thought he could slip back into it. He'd serve her better where he belonged. In the shadows.

CHAPTER EIGHT

Chains

The tension of not seeing Evan the last two days stung right along with the lactic acid left from Anna's jazz class early this morning. What was her problem? She'd gone without seeing the guy for five years. She should be a pro at this.

Sprawled in a sunbeam on Anna's bed, Bailey stretched her legs in opposite directions and yawned. Cats had the life. No drama. No traitorous emotions screwing up their sanity.

Anna crammed three pairs of socks into her top drawer and eyed her sister folding a sweater on her bed. "I can fold my own laundry, you know."

"That's debatable." Reese winked.

Anna gave her a stiff smile, turned, and propped her elbows on the dresser behind her. "You sure you're not here just 'cause Dad sent you?"

Hurling a sharp glance her way, Reese clutched a pair of dance shorts above her protruding baby bump. "I'm gonna pretend you didn't ask that."

"I'm just saying. It's not like we've hung out a lot lately."

85

"Whose fault is that?"

"Aren't we feisty this morning? Is the baby sitting on a nerve, or something?"

"No worse than you."

Anna chucked a pair of socks at her.

Reese dodged the incoming missile and flexed both hands on her back. "Seriously, I miss having you nearby."

"And you call me dramatic? I live a whopping thirty minutes away." Anna snagged the last pair of leggings from the basket and added them to the pile of clean clothes on her bed.

"Might as well be a world away."

Hard to argue with that. "You know the Gold Coast isn't my scene."

"And you know that's exactly why Dad worries about you."

"Because I want to live my own life?"

She set a hand over Anna's forearm with an expression equaling the soft gesture. "Because you think you have to abandon roots for freedom."

If Dad hadn't turned those roots into chains, maybe things would be different. "Be honest with me, Reese. Did he put a security detail on me again?"

"Truthfully? I don't know." She shuffled into Anna's closet and unhooked a hanger. "But I wouldn't be surprised. With the Michelli trial going to court on Monday, you know he's thinking about Mom. Can you blame him?"

Yeah, she could. "Don't start. Mom died in a car wreck."

"A wreck that happened right before Dad tried to prosecute Michelli the first time. Why can't you accept it might've been rigged?"

Anna wheeled around. "Because that'd mean they're in control." Over her. Over life. It was easier to believe in a world where she still had a say in who hurt her and who didn't.

"Anna—"

"The investigation ruled it as an accident. End of story."

"It doesn't matter. Dad'll never stop blaming himself for her death."

Maybe he *should* blame himself. Mom wouldn't have had to sneak out that night if she wasn't trying to flee Dad's overbearing security.

Shoulders down, Anna twisted the bracelet Mom had given her around her wrist. "If he's so worried about the case, why doesn't he sick his Robocop men on you, too?"

Reese flaunted a no-brainer look and hooked one pointer finger over the other. "Let's see. One, I live within walking distance of him." She extended a second finger. "Two, I have a husband who looks out for me every day." Another finger. "Three—"

"I get it." Anna held up a hand. "I'm the single daughter living in the slums."

"Again, whose fault is that?" Reese disappeared into the closet. "How many dates have I set you up on?"

"Fifty too many," Anna mumbled.

She stuck her head around the doorframe. "I heard that."

Anna turned to keep Reese from seeing her eye roll. Sunlight filtered through the blinds and onto her dresser with a reminder of how long it'd been since she'd last dusted. Life kept her plenty busy. Why did it have to feel like something was missing?

She set her brush down and swiped her favorite knit beanie from the top of her jewelry box. "I don't need a line of suitors, Reese. I just need the right one," she said more to herself.

"Oh my word. What is this?"

Anna's mind sprinted through a rapid inventory of what she kept in her closet. She jogged over. "What?"

Reese waddled out with a scrapbook open in her arms.

Crap. Anna reached for it. "Give me that."

Reese pulled away and crawled over the mattress to the other side of the room.

"Reese!" Anna scurried across the bed after her, but she'd already sailed around the corner to the door.

She flipped the pages while backing down the hallway. "Tell me this isn't a shrine to Evan."

"It's a scrapbook from high school. He's a photographer, remember?" Or used to be one, anyway. Anna snatched the album from her and cradled it to her chest.

"Wow. This explains so much."

"What's that supposed to mean?"

"The *right* guy, Anna? All this time, you haven't moved on. No wonder you won't give any of your dates a chance."

Really? "Give me a break. Those pompous lawyers are nowhere near Evan's league."

Reese's stark expression all but screamed the comment she didn't have to say. "Please don't get started on an Evan-roll, or I might have to stuff a leg warmer in your mouth."

Anna cocked her head. "He used to be like a kid brother to you, in case you've forgotten twenty-plus years of your life. What's your problem with him?"

"Oh, gee, I don't know. Might have something to do with watching my little sister bawl her eyes out after he ran out of the first audition she'd been to without her mom. Seriously, how long did you wait in that hallway, thinking he'd come back?"

She wasn't about to admit the answer to that.

"Has he even bothered to offer you an explanation since he's been home?"

Anna's lips thinned. Any other gut-wrenching questions she wanted to sling at her?

"That's what I thought." Reese pried the book from Anna's hands and set it on the end table beside them. "You guys were glued at the hip over half your lives. Don't you think if something were gonna happen between you two, it would've by now?"

"We were best friends. Neither of us wanted to ruin that." And yet they had. Because of her.

Reese sobered. "He left you, Anna. What does that say about how he feels?"

The sting of regret and rejection slithered inside and coiled around her heart. She'd tried to mask it with so many things. Dance. The rec center. Serving the community. Doing anything to prove pain in life didn't have the final say. But the truth resurfaced like phantom pains from a limb she lost when he left.

She couldn't pinpoint the moment she'd fallen in love with him. Maybe it'd been from the very beginning. But she'd never forget the night she pushed him away. One slipup of almost kissing him, and he was gone a week later.

She glared at her sister. "Thanks for the encouragement."

"I'm sorry." Tipping her head to the side, Reese squeezed Anna's fingers. "But it's time you moved on. He obviously has."

Part of Anna prayed she was wrong. A deeper part knew she wasn't.

Still holding her hands, Reese wiggled Anna's arms. "Shake it off, girl. You're a gorgeous, talented, available woman. Bring a date to Dad's Thanksgiving party." She pitched a manicured brow. "A *girlfriendless* date. And finish the last month of the year as if it were the beginning." She nodded, voice softening. "It's time, Anna."

Except time was no different from love. Moving forward wouldn't sever the connections to her past. Whether roots or chains, they'd never let go.

"About Thanksgiving …"

"Uh-uh." Reese wriggled up her little five-foot-two frame as tall as it would go. "You're not getting out of this."

And Evan called *her* stubborn. Anna started for the door. "My audition is Friday. I need to be rehearsing nonstop."

"A day off isn't gonna kill you. Mom would want you there."

Anna turned. "She'd want me to make the callback."

"She'd want you to put family first." Reese's crisscrossed arms sealed her resolve.

Two sides of Anna's heart pulled at the fissure running down the middle. Mom made her family her life and encouraged them to do the same. But she'd also made Anna promise not to lose herself. How did she expect Anna to do both when she knew what life with Dad was like?

Memories from her senior year zinged with regret. Anna had let the pursuit of a professional dance career crowd out everything that had real meaning. She'd stopped going to the rec center with Mom, insisting she couldn't afford to spend any time away from training. Then she was gone, and it was too late for Anna to make up for her selfishness.

Reese rubbed her belly. "If you won't come for Mom, at least come for little man, here."

The wry smile on Reese's face drew Anna out of the past. She shook her head. "Way to make it so I can't say no."

"Well, I *am* married to a lawyer. Persuasion kind of runs in the family."

On Dad's side, anyway. Good thing Anna had more of Mom's genes.

Guilt conquered any last chance she could decline. Mom would want her with the family. For that reason alone, Anna would go.

She looped her scarf around her neck and offered Reese the most genuine smile she could assemble. "I gotta run. Will you be all right getting home?"

"Mark's sending a car." Reese grabbed her hand. "Promise me you'll find a date."

"I'll try." She might as well spend the evening before her audition practicing her performance skills. Anna tossed her bag over her shoulder, tipped her head at Reese, and kissed her on the cheek. "See you tomorrow."

She needed to get back to the studio to clear her head. ASAP.

Once outside, Anna slipped in her earbuds to hold thoughts from their conversation at bay. But as soon as she neared Sip and Savor Chicago, the floodgates reopened. Great. Evan had only been home a few days, and he'd already colored over her routine with new memories she'd be stuck missing once he left again.

"Annabelle?" A guy she didn't recognize retraced his steps on the sidewalk and looked her over. "Annabelle Madison, right?"

She tugged her earbuds out. "I'm sorry, do I know you?"

The red marks left on his cheeks from the cold deepened. "Not exactly." He pulled on his ear. "I'm a JD student at the University of Chicago. I've been hoping to get an internship at the DA's office."

Of course that's what this was about. Her father. Anna re-situated her bag. "Well, good luck with that. I need to get going." Without waiting for a reply, she opened the door to the café.

A woman in a business suit and fluorescent orange sneakers bumped Anna's shoulder on her way out. Why couldn't Anna have been that invisible a minute ago?

After the eager soon-to-be lawyer left, she crept back outside. He'd reminded her of a phone call she needed to make. One the entire coffee shop didn't need to hear.

Dad answered on the third ring. "Annabelle, everything all right?"

"That depends. Did you put a security detail on me again?"

His hesitation answered for him. "Anna, the trial—"

"Is going to come and go just like any trial." She paced the sidewalk. "I can't believe you. We talked about this. How could you put someone on me and not even tell me?"

"I never said I did."

"You didn't have to. You know what? Forget it. I gotta go." She jammed her cell into her coat pocket and strode back into the café's warm aromas.

A middle-aged man behind the counter offered a sympathetic smile. "Rough morning?"

She begged her face not to show her inward cringe. "Nothing a little caffeine can't fix." *Please let it be that easy.*

"I hear that." He chuckled. "What remedy can I get for you today?"

Anna scanned the overhead menu until her gaze stopped on the drink she knew better than to order. "The Caramel Royale Latte, please," she said anyway.

"You got it."

Minutes later, she plopped onto a chair in front of the windows and stared at the empty seat beside her while drinking the same latte Evan ordered last time. She pulled off her hat and wacked herself in the face with it. It didn't get much more pathetic than this.

So, he'd spent one day with an old friend while in town. And he probably wouldn't have hung out Sunday at all if she hadn't run into him in front of the gym. Good grief, he brought another girl home just to avoid seeing her.

Anna sank her forehead into her hand. Reese was right. She needed to let him go. She'd made it on her own all this time, pressed through the aches. She couldn't go back to emptiness again.

But the harder she pushed out the memories, the more they shoved back—cold air searing her numb body at Mom's burial, the warmth of Evan's embrace holding her while she came undone, the turmoil on his face when she leaned in to kiss him.

Gray images from that day clashed into ones from her audition a month later. The glare of spotlights couldn't block her view to the empty seat where Mom had sat through every routine, cheering with raised arms ready to hug her. Anna latched on to Evan's face in the crowd instead. But when the music ended and the lights dimmed, he was gone, too. And the only arms left to hold her were her own.

A breeze swept in as the bell above the door chimed, jarring Anna back to the present. Hints of vanilla whirled past her. *Mom?* She spun around in the seat. A woman in a floor-length coat shook off the cold and grasped a young girl's hand beside her.

Anna hung her head, missing Mom more than ever. Missing their talks, their escapes. She always knew how to make it better. Art was supposed to do that. But without her, the colors had turned gray.

Anna tugged her hat back on and rose from the chair. With her bag and cup in hand, she turned and bumped into her dance instructor. "Mr. Jamison. What are you doing here?"

"Sorry. Didn't mean to startle you." He swiped a napkin from the nearest table and dabbed at the coffee dripping down her fingers. "I saw you through the window as I passed. You looked … lonely."

She glanced behind her to the windowed wall she'd been sitting in front of like a hopeless artist waiting to be picked for a callback. Okay, that was it. She had to get a grip.

Grasping for some shred of dignity, she straightened her features. "Nope. Not lonely at all." She tapped the side of her bag and passed off a smile. "I've got my dance gear and music to keep me company. That's all I need."

The look in his eyes said he didn't buy it. "When I walked you home last night, I didn't want to pry, but you seemed down." He cupped her shoulder. "You sure everything's okay? I've been worried about you."

"I know. And I appreciate all you do to look out for me, Mr. Jamison, but—"

"I'm never going to get you to call me Andreas, am I?" With an almost coy smile, he backed up and scratched his brow. "You headed to the studio?"

"Um, yeah, actually. I had Advanced Jazz at Visceral this morning, but this ballet piece I've been working on is calling to me." She smiled again. Sincerely, this time.

Despite everything else, the dance floor had a way of making everything right. Just picturing the routine lifted her spirits. The feel of her pointe shoes while doing relevés, the soft breaths in step with the music. Everything about the passionate, fluid movement sang to her heart until it reminded her who she was.

Evan may no longer be tied to her life, but dance always would be. Anna blinked away the sheen building over her eyes. "I need to get going. I have somewhere I need to stop first." *And something to say good-bye to.*

Evan's arms held him in a suspended pushup above photos and notes strewn across the hotel carpet. He'd ended the call with Mom's doc five minutes ago, but the conversation hadn't released him yet. Given his medic training, the jargon wasn't the issue. The uncertainty was.

Mom would be in the hospital another ten days before release and then another four to eight weeks off work as she recovered. Waiting. Hoping. Easing back into a normal routine without any guarantee of indefinite remission.

Childhood memories, shadowed by his dad's volatile nature, pried to the surface. Evan couldn't go there. Not now. He finished one last pushup, sat on the floor, and hunched over the notes he'd been studying all morning.

No surprise, the tracker's path had led him to Adele's Little Italy Restaurant and a bunch of low profile activity. He'd staked it out most of last night, anyway, hoping for a lead. And what did he have to show for it? A raging headache.

Keeping an eye on Anna from a distance instead of up close was supposed to get him back on target. He was used to operating on the margins. Yet now that he'd spent time with her again, being with her was all he could think about.

Evan pinched his forehead between two fingers and tried to rub some sense into his brain. For the twentieth time, he sifted through a handful of photos he'd taken of Michelli's men. There had to be something. Some clue. Some trail he could hunt down to cut them at the base. What was he missing?

His throbbing temples steered his gaze toward the kitchen. Coffee. He needed a cup. Pronto.

His cell rang before he'd made it up from the floor. He swiped the screen. "O'Riley."

"Man, I was hoping you were too ill to answer your phone," Murphy joked. "Unless you got a better reason for standing me up at the gym this morning."

Evan ran a palm down his face. "Sorry, bro. Long night."

"Out on a bat chase?"

Evan swept the mess on the carpet into a disheveled pile, stood, and dumped it on the desk. "You could say that."

"Yo, man, I get wanting to fly solo. Girls dig the dark knight mystique. But since you don't have an Alfred there to nurse you back to life, you might want to ask a friend to watch your back. Just sayin'."

"You offering?"

"As long as I get my own bat mobile. And a few battle scars. Gotta keep my game up with the ladies."

Evan shook his head. "And who you gonna be? Captain Casanova?"

"Like you can talk. You get rid of the Devil Wears Prada yet?"

"Dude, she has a name." Even if Murphy's nicknames fit better. "And ..." He let out an exhale. "I'm working on it."

"Are you seriously trying to pull that—?"

"Today, all right. I'm taking care of it. Speaking of which, you want to help a boy out? She's gonna need a date to a gala tonight."

Murphy wheezed through the line. "Even I have limits, bro."

"C'mon. Dinner, drinks, women in fine dresses. This has your name all over it."

"I do look pretty fly in a tux." Murphy's swaggering lilt clung to every word. "Considering there'll be plenty of other ladies there, I'd probably make an exception, but my baby sister would kill me if I missed her party. I'll be up in Milwaukee with the fam all night."

"Don't worry about it." Evan closed his laptop. "It's my responsibility, anyway."

"Get off it, man. You don't always have to be responsible. Just tell her how it is."

"Thanks for the advice."

"Hey, if you'd listen to me, you wouldn't still be mucking stuff up with Anna."

"And what would you do?" Evan strode away from the desk. "You know what? Never mind. I gotta run."

"A'ight. But I expect you to give me Anna's number next time I see you if you haven't—"

Click. That conversation was definitely over. And that blasted coffee was three hours past due.

A knock on the door stopped him at the edge of the linoleum. Drawing his Sig, Evan crept toward the peephole. At the sight of Marissa, he released his gun and a heavy sigh.

She strode inside the second he unlocked the deadbolt. "What are we, like, twelve?"

"What are you talking about?" On second thought, he turned toward the kitchen, not ready to deal with female riddles before a caffeine recharge.

Marissa followed. "I know you have an issue with drinking, but I was just a little tipsy."

"Tipsy? You passed out in my car. I had to haul you over my shoulder to get you up to your room."

Her heels clanked behind him across the floor. "Fine, but do you really have to give me the silent treatment over it? You could've called me the last two days."

"I thought you were undercover. Didn't want to interrupt." He rummaged through a cabinet for the coffee grounds, tempted to shovel a giant spoonful straight into his mouth.

"We already went over this."

Not about the one thing that mattered. He dumped two heaping scoops into the filter and swung the basket shut on the coffee maker. "Marissa, we should talk."

She flung her hand up. Shaking her head, she retreated to the suite's living area. "You're back in your hometown, Evan. Seeing old friends, old places. It makes sense to have old feelings come up, too. Now's not the time to make hasty decisions."

"I'm not." He followed her. "And this has nothing to do with being here. This place isn't home anymore."

Head angled, Marissa slid a glance toward his camera lying on the desk. "Thought you said photography was an old hobby."

"It was—is." He made a beeline to the desk and shoved everything into a folder before her journalistic instincts jumped into full investigation mode.

"Like I said. The past has a way of stirring things up." She sauntered toward him. "Look, I'm not blind, okay? But just hold off until we leave. I'm close to breaking a story. This gala tonight…I need to be there." Her eyes softened. "I can't show up alone, Evan. Please. It's important."

The urgency in her gaze lowered his shoulders. "Okay. I'll escort you tonight…but as a friend."

"Understood." Marissa lifted on her toes to kiss his cheek. "Thank you." She grabbed his hand. "Come on. We need to go pick up your tux."

"Coffee first."

"We'll grab some on the way." Marissa dragged him out the door and down the stairs.

With each step, a battalion of thoughts from the morning overpowered the speed talking reverberating in the stairwell. The world of image-building and name-dropping meant squat to him. Especially when his phone call with the doc kept pulsing with the blood drumming against his temples.

Mom needed someone nearby to take care of her. How was he going to do that from Georgia? Was it finally time to come home for good? But how could he let down his team? Not to mention having to watch Anna be with someone else.

That thought alone capsized him. He'd always known that'd eventually be the end result. He was supposed to be ready for it this time.

One step outside, and a brisk wind slammed into him. Just like reality. Cutting and unrelenting.

"Do I need to write any of this down for you, or are you good?" Marissa stood in front of him, waiting for a response to whatever she'd been rambling on about nonstop.

Evan scratched the back of his hair. "Uh ..." A red coat up ahead caught his eye. *Bells.*

Anna halted just around the corner with a string of emotions chasing each other down her face. Her gaze swung from him to Marissa. She backed up, turned.

He jogged toward her. "Anna, wait."

Anna hustled the way she came. *Don't be a coward.* A backward glance caught Marissa glaring from beside the door. *Okay, fine. Be a coward.* She picked up her pace.

"Where are you going?" Evan called.

To go search for the resolution she had five minutes ago.

"Anna, will you wait a sec?" He caught up to her. "What's going on?"

"Nothing." With her fingers clasped around the slip of paper with his address on it, Anna inhaled and faced him. "I was just ... walking." On a path that happened to lead directly to his hotel. Right. She made herself meet his gaze. "Actually, I came to tell you ..."

An unreadable expression moved through his eyes. But in classic Evan-stoicism, he nodded for her to go on.

"That ..." She fiddled with the strings on her hat. "Shaun's been asking about you. Megan, too. She's itching to show you the routine we've been working on. She had a tough bout with pneumonia six months ago, so it's taken her a while to get back into dance. But she's been loving every minute." *Stop talking.* "You should come by the rec center tonight ... if you want."

Wow. In case she wasn't pathetic enough before, now she was resorting to using the kids as an excuse to see him. Steam rose from a grate beside the curb and added to the flush claiming her cheeks.

Evan squeezed the back of his neck. "I can't. I have this gala I have to go to tonight."

Anna's focus wandered to Marissa, messing with her phone while waiting for him.

An internal scolding snaked up Anna's insides. Even if he wasn't really dating Marissa, things were the way they were. "Um, yeah. I'm just gonna ..." Anna pointed behind her.

"That doesn't mean I don't want to." His brow furrowed. "Trust me. I'd rather be with you guys."

His intense eyes exuded the protective strength and concern that made him Evan. *Her* Evan. The one she grew up with, whose friendship she didn't want to lose again. Why did this have to be so hard? Just looking at him pillaged her resolve.

Deep breath. Finding her own strength, Anna gripped her bag and rehearsed the conversation she'd had with Reese in her head.

"Actually, it's probably better if the kids don't get attached to you." Same as it was for her. "I shouldn't have asked." She almost reached for him but stopped herself and offered him a genuine smile she hoped he'd understand. "Bye, Evan."

"Wait." He caught her wrist as she turned. "What are you doing the rest of the day?"

Anna peered over her shoulder toward whatever held his stare. Other than a beat-up canary yellow Bug and a dark SUV, the street looked empty. A slow turn brought him into view again, but whatever held his attention didn't release him.

"I'm heading to the studio right now. Then I'm taking Megan to Millennium Park for the afternoon before work. Why?"

"I have a few free hours before the gala." The indefinable look on Evan's face grabbed hold of her stomach. "Would you mind if I came along?"

Say no. Walk away.

His earnest gaze sent her heart beating against her chest, longing against reason. Darn gorgeous eyes. As if the question alone weren't hard enough to turn down.

Anna toyed with her bag's zipper, words still not coming. Dance revolved around discipline. She'd mastered most every muscle in her body. You'd think she'd have control over her tongue, too.

Evan broadened his shoulders but hung his head. "Unless there's someone else you'd rather go with?"

"Like who?" She raised a questioning brow.

"I don't know." He splayed a hand to the side. "There's no other guy … friend … no one at all?"

Lips together, Anna shook her head slowly. "No."

"You sure?"

"Yeaaah."

"Okay, then." Whatever had his forehead wrinkled a second ago disappeared with a definitive nod. "I have an errand to run first, but I'll swing by your place to pick you up at one."

"O-kay." What just happened?

Evan took her hand and started back down the street.

"I thought you said you'd meet me later."

"Yeah." He stopped beside his Accord and opened the door. "*After* I drop you off at the studio." He motioned her inside with his eyes, his chauffeuring obviously not up for debate.

Anna dodged the cutting stare Marissa lanced between them. As if Anna needed one more reason to think this was a bad idea. Sighing, she climbed into the backseat and sank against the leather at the same time the other two closed their doors.

Marissa wrenched her seat belt out with enough grit to be a tug-of-war champion. In case she hadn't noticed, Anna wasn't in the running.

An electric silence chafed against the engine's purr. She should say something to put Marissa at ease. But the air held enough thickness to consume a single word before she even thought it, let alone said it out loud.

The tension soared past heated and into the ridiculous. A laugh built inside her. She couldn't help it. With her hand covering her mouth, Anna faced the window before the inward cackle became audible.

This emotional stress had to go. Look what it was doing to them. To her. They used to be so comfortable with each other. Used to live in the moment. Maybe if she started acting halfway normal around Evan, he'd remember that and might even want to stay in touch this time.

Because honestly, all the logic, heartache, and pep talks in the world wouldn't change the fact she wanted to keep him in her life. One minute with him was all it took to prove that.

She needed to stop worrying about what might or might not happen when he left again and focus on reminding him of their friendship. An afternoon at the park would be a good start.

Her shoulders relaxed against the cozy seat. With any luck, she could make up for her mistake and restore things to the way they once were.

As long as Reese didn't kill her first.

CHAPTER NINE

War

Sunlight streaked across the stairwell as Evan knocked on Anna's apartment door. A few hours of running errands and dealing with Marissa's silent treatment hadn't kept his mind off this afternoon.

If he hadn't seen the Michelli Escalade earlier, he wouldn't have impulsively asked to go with Anna to the park today. He released his grip around his coat cuffs. Who was he kidding? Seeing her stammer on the sidewalk had nixed any chance of thinking he could keep his distance. Not to mention he had a job to do. One he was royally messing up.

From the first time he ever came home on leave, he knew he couldn't handle this role. But falling short on his promise wouldn't stop gnawing at him. He had to find a way ...

A *thump* rumbled from inside, followed by the deadbolt clicking open. He straightened.

Anna peeked through the door with her brows knit together. "Sorry."

"For what?" He almost tripped over Bailey at his feet.

"For losing track of time." Anna rolled a yoga-ball-turned-chair under a desk in the corner, closed her laptop, and kicked a fuzzy pair of owl-patterned slippers out of the middle of the floor. "I stopped to check the mail on my way home from the studio and got sidetracked. I meant to be ready by the time you got here."

A cluster of envelopes beside the computer grabbed his attention. Probably unpaid bills stacking up. No wonder she seemed frazzled. Collection notices were the last thing she needed on top of her fast-approaching rent deadline. If she weren't so stubborn, he'd take care of them for her.

Bailey sprang to the desk and nestled beside the laptop. Trying to keep warm, no doubt. Evan glanced at the thermostat—sixty-four. Couldn't blame her.

Anna spun around with her fingers threaded through her hair as though trying to pinpoint what to do next. "Drinks." She whisked past him into the kitchen and rummaged through a cabinet. "I wanted to make us something to take along. Is hot chocolate okay? Or I can brew coffee."

She stretched on her toes to reach a top shelf. The bottom of a loose-fitting green sweater crept above a pair of tight gray pants.

Why did his training have to give him such heightened senses? Even from here, he could smell hints of her herbal shampoo and hear the soft fabric moving against the sliver of bare skin along the small of her back.

"What do you think?"

That this was a very bad idea.

"Hot chocolate?"

As if he needed anything else to increase his body temperature right now.

Anna turned when he didn't answer. Her gaze ping-ponged from his fixed stare down to her outfit. If her cheeks felt anywhere near as warm as his did, she did better at hiding it.

She left two travel mugs on the counter and tugged on the hem of her sweater. "I haven't had a chance to change yet. It'll take me two seconds. Can you grab a few clementines from the fridge to take with us?"

"Sure." And climb in the freezer while he was at it.

Anna glided by him and disappeared down the hallway.

Before he turned, a logo from the papers on her desk jumped off the page. Rush University Medical Center. He scanned the bill. Looked like something for Megan. An ER visit. *The pneumonia.*

His chest sank as Anna's words from the other day blazed to mind. "*I had an unexpected bill come up six months ago.*" A bill that wasn't even hers. For all the concern Anna carried in her heart for others, how could there be none left for herself?

Evan dropped the page and plowed to the refrigerator. Aside from the basics, a box of clementines, and a container of leftovers, bare shelves looked back at him.

"How old is this Chinese food?" he called down the hall.

"What Chinese food?" she yelled back.

Evan lifted the lid and smelled the Asian mixture. Surprisingly decent. "Whatever this noodle concoction is." Leaving the door open, he twisted when she shuffled around the corner in dark jeans and a fitted button-up flannel shirt. As usual, she made casual look gorgeous.

"Oh, that's pancit. Mrs. Santos from across the hall made it for me. I watch her adorable shih-poo when she's out of town."

"Is she out of town now?"

"No, why?"

"I didn't hear any barking when I came up."

Anna angled her head at him. "Some owners actually train their dogs, you know."

Like that ever stopped a yapper. "So, you watch her dog, and she pays you in food."

She shrugged. "She's my neighbor. It's the right thing to do. And it's a really good dish. You should try it."

"Not the point." Evan returned the container to the shelf. "You have bills piling up. Your kitchen's empty."

"I'm waiting for my next paycheck. And it's not empty."

He cocked his chin. "Clementines don't count."

"Sure they do." Anna leaned around him, tossed three into a handbag, and nudged him in the shoulder with it. "You shouldn't neglect your immune system. Especially this time of year. They're actually great for strengthening your bones and muscles, believe it or not. And vitamin C is amazing for your skin. You …" Meeting his gaze, she curled her lip in but couldn't stop an embarrassed smile from pushing through. "… probably don't need to know all that. I'm gonna stop talking now."

Too late. It'd floor him if she could get any cuter.

He set a hand on her arm when she turned toward the empty mugs on the counter. "We'll pick something up on the way."

"Okay." A soft smile played on her lips. "Did you remember your camera?"

"Yeah." Evan rubbed his neck. "Though, I have to warn you. I'm out of practice. Doubt the shots will be any good."

"It doesn't matter how long an artist sets his paintbrush down. The minute he picks it up, the world becomes a canvas again." A matter-of-fact look met him dead in the eyes.

Before he could find his voice, Anna bent to a bottom cabinet and swiped a can of cat food.

He grinned. "I'll buy you lunch, too. Don't worry."

"Very funny." She returned his smirk while heading toward her coat on a hook beside the door.

Anna pulled on a knit hat with puffy balls hanging from the strings and opened the door. He followed her outside. But instead of going to his car, she circled the corner toward a parking lot behind the building.

"Where are you going?"

"To take care of a friend." She approached an eighteen-gallon Rubbermaid tote beside the dumpster and popped open the can of cat food.

A dingy-looking orange tabby with uneven whiskers scurried through a square hole carved into the side of the container.

"Come here, you." Anna picked him up, nuzzled her nose against his, and set him and the food down.

"What is that?"

"An impossible-to-turn-down kitty."

Evan's lips tightened. "I meant the tote."

She lifted the lid. "A makeshift shelter. It has a Styrofoam cooler and a layer of hay inside for insulation." She knelt beside a series of oil stains while the stray wolfed down the food. "It's the best I could do for him. I found the little guy a few weeks back, scrounging around the dumpster. Thinking of him being out here in the winter about killed me, but I can only have one cat in the apartment."

Evan took in the sight of her, kneeling on the cold ground beside a destitute animal everyone else overlooked. The woman never failed to give without hesitation. But if she wasn't careful, life's unforgiving realities would squelch that gift of compassion right out of her. And having to watch that happen would pulverize him.

"There'll always be strays, Anna. As sad as that is, you can't change the way things are."

Tender yet headstrong eyes met his. "I can try." She shifted her weight but not her gaze. "I know what you're thinking. And I get it. The world's a dark place. But that doesn't mean I can't add color to it." Anna ran a loving stroke down the cat's back and up his tail. "Otherwise, I mean, what's the point of all this?"

A knot in his throat blocked his voice from coming out. She sounded so much like her mom.

The mangy cat licked his lips and walked his front paws up her knee. Anna leaned her nose down to his. "And who can turn down this face? Isn't he a cutie?"

Was that what she called it? "He's missing a chunk of his ear."

"Battle wounds. They build character." She rubbed a finger over a streak of white fur on the top of the cat's head. "Isn't that right, Strider?"

"Strider?" Evan hiked a brow at her.

She pushed up on her thighs to stand. "Well, he *is* kind of a ranger. Though, I'm not sure if he's from the North."

Evan cracked a laugh. "I think you've watched *Lord of the Rings* one too many times."

"No such thing." A playful grin led her toward him. "Speaking of rangers. I might just start calling *you* Strider, too." Studying him, Anna lifted her cool fingers to the hairline above his ear. "I thought army guys were supposed to be clean-cut."

"Spec ops guys tend to get a little slack in regulations."

She feigned a look of being impressed. "Well, aren't you special?"

He rubbed his jawline.

Her sweet laugh succumbed to a pensive expression. "You are. You know that, right? Special, I mean."

Not like her. Standing this close, Evan couldn't help being enveloped by it. Her strength, compassion. There was no way he could move home and stand by her side without letting her know he wanted to experience every part of life with her.

Evan blinked away, afraid she'd see the tension escalating behind his eyes. "Anna—"

"Miss Madison?"

They both turned toward Megan strolling around the corner.

Anna's face paled. "You were supposed to wait for us at the rec center."

"I got bored." Megan jogged the rest of the distance separating them.

Anna zipped up Megan's soiled coat and pulled the hood over her head. "I know you're on your own a lot, kiddo, but you can't roam the streets by yourself, okay?"

Megan's chin drooped to her chest. "Yes, ma'am."

"Okay." A motherly smile overrode the look of reprimand on Anna's face. "Now, are you ready for some fun, or what?"

Megan nodded with enough enthusiasm to knock her hood back down. With eyes almost as eager as the stray's, it wasn't hard to tell why Anna had fallen so hard for her.

"Sweet." Anna roped an arm around Megan. "I've been looking forwar—" Her wide-eyed stare streamed across the lot. "What's that?"

Evan followed her line of sight to the row of cars parked along the fence.

"Don't tell me." She hurried over to an old, white Kia.

The dread coating her voice set Evan on alert. He grabbed Megan's hand and hustled after her.

Anna swiped some kind of ticket off her windshield. Confusion wrinkled her forehead. "Wait, what are they talking about? I just paid for my renewal."

Evan took the ticket from her and scanned it. A sixty-buck fine for a past due registration. "Did you put the stickers on?"

"Yeah, last week." She motioned to the license plate. "I ... No, no, no." She bent for a closer look, then rose and slumped against the quarter panel. "Perfect. Now I have to pay a fine *and* the fee for new stickers."

Evan squatted and rubbed a thumb over the ridges on the plate where someone must've used a razor to scrape off the decal.

She massaged her temples. "Don't cops have better things to do? And, really. Who steals someone's registration stickers?"

"Someone who's desperate." People short on money did all kinds of things. She was lucky they hadn't done worse. "Not everyone's as kind as you."

Megan leaned into Anna's side as if to add her agreement.

This close to the ground, mechanical odors reached Evan's nose. He pressed a palm to the grainy pavement, angled his head under the car, and spotted a few drops of murky liquid glistening near the wheel. A tendon on his neck pulled taut as memories of her mom's accident hit him in the chest. If someone tampered with Anna's brakes, so help him.

He dabbed his fingers in the liquid and brought it to his nose. Just oil. Relief swept in until he noticed a tracker under the wheel well. Michelli's guys were here. His muscles constricted.

Anna crinkled the ticket and shoved it into her pocket. "It's always something."

The dejection in her voice pulled Evan up from the asphalt. No way he was about to add to it. He dusted off his hands and glanced over the car. "When was the last time you had this thing in the shop?"

"I don't know." Anna lifted off the panel. "A few months ago, maybe. Why?"

"I'll schedule an appointment for tomorrow. Don't drive it until then." He made it only two steps before she caught his elbow to stop him.

"Why? What's wrong?"

Smoothing out his face, he turned. "Nothing."

She crossed her arms, and he upped his acting skills. "I'm not in town for very long. While I'm here, let me help where I can."

A trace of disappointment touched her eyes. Blinking it away, she curled her wavy hair over her shoulder. "Thanks, but tomorrow's Thanksgiving. I have to drive to my dad's for his dinner party."

"I'll take you."

"That's sweet, but there's no need—"

"It's not up for discussion."

Brows raised, she drew back her shoulders. "Excuse me?"

That obstinate expression got him every time. "Relax, Bells. I'm just looking out for you. It's what friends do." He leaned down to pet the stray. The second he extended a hand, the cat released a low growl and skittered away.

Anna smirked. "Your bossiness must've turned him off."

Eyeing her impish grin, Evan stood up and fought one of his own. "Apparently, he must overlook your stubbornness."

"Oh, really?" She inched forward in an adorable attempt at intimidation. But instead of backing him away, her penetrating gaze rooted him in place.

Megan let go of Anna's hand and tugged his instead. "Can we go now?"

He broke eye contact with Anna and diverted his focus to Megan. "You got it."

Good thing she was there. With how easily a single look from Anna could undo him, he definitely needed the distraction. He scooped Megan up, swung her onto his back, and headed toward his Accord.

After stopping for coffee, they parked on Randolph Street and strolled toward Michigan Avenue beside bright shop windows decked out in Christmas decorations.

It was hard to beat Millennium Park in the summer, but the winter months held their own perks. Fewer people being one of them. The lack of activity made it a heck of a lot easier to scan the area. So far, the place looked clean.

He'd lost the signal on the tracker the night after they'd almost cornered Anna in the park. Either Crater Face had gotten rid of his coat, or someone had gotten rid of him. Something gave Evan the feeling it was the latter. Chances were, Michelli would be sending in someone new for the job.

Anna sipped her latte and gave a contented sigh. "You know you're spoiling me with these drinks, right? I don't need the calories. But, man." She lifted the cup. "Total guilty pleasure, right here. Why do the things we want most have to be the ones we shouldn't have?"

If she only knew. Evan took a swig of his coffee, swallowed the painful truth, and toyed with his cup.

A soft laugh escaped beside him.

"What?"

Anna raised her drink to shield her smile. "Sorry. Your OCD-ness is really cute sometimes."

"What are you talking about?"

Following a slow blink, she took his cup and waved a hand up and down it as if issuing evidence into a court case.

His gaze trailed over the lid and sleeve aligned perfectly with the cup's logo. He snagged it back. "Hey, nothing wrong with a little symmetry."

Another snort-laugh wrinkled her nose.

"Ooh." Megan pointed at a playground. "Can we stop here?"

"You betcha." Anna squatted to her level and set her coffee down. "You have gloves?"

When Megan shook her head, Anna pulled out a pair of knit ones from her own pockets. "Here." She tugged the fingerless glove part on and flipped the monkey-patterned mitten part over them. "Now you'll be the coolest kid out there." With a wink, she sent Megan off to the miniature rock wall and Evan's heart up his throat again.

He cradled his warm fingers around Anna's cold ones. "Sure you don't need those?"

She put on her game face. "I'm tough."

More than she probably gave herself credit for. If he learned how to love half as selflessly as she did, maybe he'd find a way to make up for the pain he'd caused Mom.

He released Anna's hands and started toward a bench on the border of the playground.

Anna's arm grazed his as they ambled together. "Something on your mind?"

"You could say that."

"Worried about your mom?"

Evan gaped at her. It was like she operated with night vision goggles on, nothing hindering her from seeing straight to the heart of things.

The bench's cold slats met the back of his jeans. "I spoke to the doctor this morning. She's doing okay, but it's hard to know what her recovery will look like."

"I'm sure having you home is a big encouragement to her." Anna sat beside him.

He twisted the lid on his cup back and forth. "She doesn't know I'm here."

"What?" Her coat scratched against the bench. "What do you mean?"

"I haven't spoken to her yet." He'd stayed outside Mom's hospital room. Went in only when she was asleep. He couldn't face her any more than he could face the confusion in Anna's expression right now. Layers of regret overlapped each other and propelled him back up from the bench and into a pace.

"Before I left, I opened a bank account for her. I've been wiring money ever since I got my first check from the army." He rolled a twig on the ground with his Skecher. "I thought a few years of help would be enough to get her away from my dad."

Comprehension tinted Anna's eyes, questions welling up right behind it.

Please don't ask.

She stared at the turf and bit her lip. "Is that why you left?"

A long exhale expanded a puff of warm breath into the air. "Yes." One part. He couldn't look at her, or she'd see the rest. "I had promises to keep."

"I thought it was because ... I mean, it happened right after I ..." The slight tremor in Anna's voice drew his gaze back to her. "You could've told me, Evan. I would've understood."

"It's complicated."

She looked at him like he'd dished out the lamest excuse in the book. Better lame than heartbreaking. Sometimes the truth hurt worse. His dad had taught him that much.

Reaching his side, Anna touched his sleeve with her signature tenderness. "Regardless, I don't know why you'd be worried about seeing your mom. You've done nothing but provide for her. She got her own place—"

"*After* my dad died." He withdrew his arm. "I should've gotten her out of there sooner. Now, she's dying." Because he couldn't protect her. Didn't she get that?

Anna drew closer. "She started a new life with your support, opened up her own pottery shop."

Too little, too late.

Now where did things leave them? Would she depend on his monthly payments even more? Would she need him home to care for her? What was he supposed to do?

"My contract with the army is up in three months. I have until the end of next week to decide whether to reenlist."

Turning, he forked his fingers through his hair. "I honestly don't know which is better for her." Taking leave was supposed to give him time to think this through, not make it more muddled.

Anna's warm green eyes embraced his with unmerited grace. "Serving your county may have made you a soldier, Evan. But serving your mom is what makes you a man of valor. You're doing everything you can." Her fingertips curled under his. "And it's enough. It always has been. Don't underestimate your strength or hers."

Except she didn't know the extent of his weaknesses. "Just because someone's strong doesn't mean he isn't broken."

"And just because he's broken doesn't mean he has nothing to offer."

It didn't matter how long he knew her. He didn't have a single doubt she'd leave him undone every day of his life.

In the background, barking dogs joined kids squealing while chasing each other up the slide, but nothing could pull Evan's focus away from Anna. Holding her gaze, he edged closer. The smallest breath parted her lips and reignited the war he'd fought before he left.

Same as that night at the burial—having her this close, seeing her vulnerability—his pulse thundered over shouts of warning until he almost surrendered to the question that'd consumed him most of his life. How would it feel to kiss the one girl he'd always loved?

CHAPTER TEN

Candid

Megan barreled into Evan's legs from behind. One day, he might run out of interruptions keeping him from wrecking things between him and Anna. But for now, he thanked God for each one.

"Can we show Mr. Hulk our routine?"

Anna pressed her lips together and looked from Megan back to Evan.

"I'd love to see it." He swung Megan around by her hands.

Anna's smile swelled with affection. "Mind if Mr. Hulk takes a few pictures?"

Megan shook her head and beamed, as if the slightest interest in her made her whole world.

Anna set her coffee down again and stretched her arms, one at a time. "We might have to find somewhere out of this wind, though. The cold is hard on your muscles." She bent at ninety degrees and hugged her nose to each knee.

Evan groaned. "What are you doing?"

Anna peeked up at him through the curtain of hair falling into her eyes. "Never seen someone stretch before?"

121

Sighing, he scanned the periphery. "You're not just some-one. Trust me. Every guy in this twenty-five-acre park is looking at you right now."

"Not *every* guy." The somber pull in her quiet voice drew his gaze back to her. She stood tall, but something palpable weighed on her shoulders.

Megan pointed to the Jay Pritzker Pavilion. "Can we dance over there?"

Anna mussed the top of her hair. "I'm pretty sure that's off limits." A glance around brightened her eyes. "But I think I know the perfect place."

Evan followed Anna's line of sight to a distant structure on the outskirts of the park. Away from the beaten path.

Bad idea.

"You don't want to eat first?" Evan tipped his cell out of his pocket. "We could stop at a food truck. How about The Fat Shallot?"

Anna's blank stare ruled that out of the question. "If you want a sandwich, you should try the flatbread ones from Naansense. They have amazing salads, too."

She had to be kidding. "I don't do Indian food. And I definitely don't do salads."

"You're missing out. I'm telling ya." Anna started forward.

He reached for her hand. "Why don't you let me take you to Hugos?" They needed to stay somewhere public.

She snorted. "Blackbird. Hugos. When did you start high-rolling?"

"Must've been around the same time you started sticking your nose up at people wanting to treat you well."

Her feisty glare gained a chuckle out of him. Any attempt at looking riled-up made her even cuter than normal.

"I'm not hungry." Megan wedged between them. "Can we dance first?"

Anna shifted her attention to Megan. "Sure, love." Another spunky gaze flitted back to Evan. "Mr. Hulk could use a little lesson in culture."

Before he could dish out a response, Anna raised her drink to her mouth, craned her head back, and tapped the bottom of the cup.

Relenting, Evan did the same and held out a hand.

A lopsided grin followed Anna's glance from him to a city trash can. She surrendered the cup. "One more piece of cardboard saved from the fate of landing in a garbage dump."

"Laugh it up." He flattened their cups together and shoved them into his back pocket.

Anna grabbed a clementine from her bag, tore into it with her nails, and tossed a piece of the peel at him. "In case you want to start a compost pile while you're at it."

A trail of laughter circled around her as she spun out of reach.

Megan tugged on Anna's coat, her brows pulled together in consternation. "Is he afraid of garbage?"

Anna stopped herself before fully doubling over.

"Real funny," he muttered, catching up to them.

"No, sweetie." Anna kept her eyes on his. "Some people just have weirder quirks than others."

He cocked his chin. "Says the girl who has a frog toilet paper holder."

"He's cute." Anna swatted Evan's bicep.

"He stares at you when you pee. That's not cute. It's creepy." He turned to Megan for a little support.

Nose scrunched, she gave a hesitant nod. "Sorry. Mr. Hulk's kinda right."

"Ohhh!" Evan raised his hands for a double high five. "Now who's the smack talker?"

"You're such a dork." Still smiling, Anna shoved him off the path, curved an arm around Megan, and leaned down to her ear. "Boys."

He didn't have to see her face to know she'd just dramatized an eye roll as if she were Megan's BFF, joking about the boys in homeroom. She'd always be a kid at heart. She made childhood innocence and joy seem so easy to keep, so within reach.

He adjusted his dog tags under his shirt. Only a few days with her, and Anna already had him remembering the way life could feel with her in it. If she understood what that did to him, she'd understand why he'd stayed away.

Evan brought up the rear as Anna led them to a long, courtyard-like area with huge brick arches bordering one side and a solid brick wall on the other. Its artsy flare fit Anna's style to a T.

He stopped them at the entrance. "Stay put." He had come to the park ahead of time to reorient himself with the layout and get a feel for any liabilities. This wasn't part of the plan. Secluded from everything else, it made them vulnerable.

After a quick sweep through, he jogged back down the hall to find Anna and Megan unloading their coats beside the wall. "I told you to stay."

Anna lowered her lip balm from her mouth and deadpanned him. "First of all, I'm not a dog. And you try standing out there with the wind flying up your shirt." She tossed her bag on the floor. "Relax. No one comes around here."

That was what worried him.

"Wow." Megan spun in a circle. "This is so cool." Her visible excitement gave way to a puzzled expression. "But what do we do for a barre? We can't start without warm-ups."

Anna chuckled. "Spoken like a true ballerina, if I've ever heard one." She tucked her Blistex into her pocket and surveyed the wide corridor. "Guess we'll just have to brace against the wall." She prodded Megan toward the bricks, moved a few paces ahead, and faced opposite her. "Ready?"

Megan's vibrant nod almost outshined her smile.

"Okay, first position. Tighter turn-out. There you go." Both girls angled their feet at a hundred and eighty degrees, heels together. "Demi-plié, slow tendus, and stretch. Very nice. Now, fast."

Seated on the ledge beneath one of the arches, Evan took out his camera and gauged the level of natural light casting a warm color over their skin.

"Slow dégagés." They both lifted pointed toes several inches from the floor, slid them back into place, and repeated from different angles.

Ten feet away, Evan shot a handful of takes. A quick scroll through the underexposed images was enough to remind him how long he'd been away from this. He adjusted the ISO to four hundred and tried again. Much better.

Nailing the exposure sent his creative instincts into high gear. The backdrop, the lighting, their movement. Everything came to life, just as Anna had said it would.

"Now, balance in fifth position. Perfect." She gave Megan an enthusiastic clap. "Awesome job."

Megan twisted the tip of her sneaker on the ground, head tilted to her shoulder. "I think we should get Mr. Hulk to try it."

He fumbled the camera. "Not happening."

Anna sauntered up to him. "Oh, I think that's an excellent idea. Big Ranger like you, doing an arabesque." She winked. "C'mon, Strider. It'll be fun."

More like humiliating.

He turned, full-on ready to sprint if he had to, but she caught his belt and tugged him over to the wall.

Anna stole the camera, pulled the strap over her head, and squatted to adjust his feet. "You gotta turn out from the hips," she said through a ridiculously sassy grin.

Heaven help him. He forced his attention straight ahead.

She moved beside him and set one hand on his lower back, the other on his stomach. He tensed, praying she didn't detect his inside-the-waistband holster.

"Relax."

Easy for her to say. His skin burned through his clothes against her cold hands.

"Draw those abs back, ribs in, and support from underneath."

He slouched. "You can't seriously expect me to do this."

"Mm. More than expect. I'm thoroughly enjoying it." She straightened his frame. "Chest up, release the neck. Now, extend your arm." While holding his hand from behind him, she swayed his arm forward and out to the side in a grand sweeping motion.

He twisted toward her. "That's good en—"

"Shh." She rotated his neck forward and pressed closer. Soft breaths touched his neck and sparked every nerve ending. "Now, port de bra to fifth."

"Port de what?" His gravelly voice barely got the question out.

Megan giggled. "I think we need to show him, Miss Madison."

Evan stepped away from the dangerous currents surging in Anna's graceful movement against him. "Never heard a better idea." He extended a hand for his camera.

After reluctantly handing it over, she joined Megan in the middle of the hall and stared him down. "No falling asleep."

"Me?" He aimed a finger at his chest.

"Says the guy who falls asleep in a dentist chair."

He laughed. She had him there. Wild conditions on his deployments had only increased his natural ability to fall asleep anywhere. But she couldn't really think her dancing bored him.

Anna angled her feet outward as she'd done before, rounded her arms in front of her, and nodded to Megan. "Five, six, seven, eight …"

A solid minute into the dance passed before he remembered to take photos. Anna's elegance gripped him. The grace, the extensions, the sun's soft glow highlighting her natural beauty.

Viewing it from behind the lens doubled the splendor. Once he started, creative drive took over and guided him around the floor to shoot the dance from different vantage points. Each take fanned his assurance that Anna belonged on stage. She always had.

At the end, she swayed with Megan, brimming with joy and radiance. Wisps of hair blew around her hat and against her cheeks. He'd always loved capturing candid moments best. Especially of her.

Recovering, he showered them with applause and made sure to give Megan extra praise.

"You really liked it?" she asked.

"You kidding? Loved it." He tapped Megan's chin. "I think you've got a big dance career ahead of you."

Anna's smile went straight for his heart.

Megan sprang toward her, grabbed her hand, and motioned for her to lean down. On her tiptoes, she cupped a hand around her mouth and whispered something into Anna's ear.

Anna's gaze drifted to him, the corner of her mouth crawling up her cheek. "Yeah," she half-whispered back. "I think he's pretty cute, too."

Megan pinched her bottom lip between two fingers and giggled after confiding something else.

Heat singed the top of his ears.

"I'll see what I can do." Anna tunneled a look of mock seriousness toward Megan. "But I gotta warn you. He's kind of a tough one to catch."

Was that what she thought?

Megan tugged her down one more time.

Still clasping her hand, Anna straightened and glanced around until she spotted whatever she was looking for. Facing Evan, she tipped her head toward a sign for the ladies' room. "Bathroom break."

Girl time. "Say no more." He raised his palms.

They disappeared into the women's restroom a little ways down the hall.

Behind him, a damp breeze off the lake weaseled its way down his collar to his neck. He adjusted his coat. He'd been so caught up in the moment and Anna's contagious love of life, the temperature hadn't even fazed him.

A glance at his camera ended in a shake of his head. She'd even gotten him to remember how to be an artist. He scrolled through the takes until something in the background of one leapt off the image and grabbed him by the throat. A full-length black coat.

Evan shot a glance across the open fixture. No one was in sight, but they had been. Lurking in the distance. Watching.

And he'd missed it.

Evan dropped his fist to the bricks and swore.

Down the hall, the sign for the bathroom twisted a pang of dread in his stomach. *Bells.* Sig drawn, he sprinted across the brick floor and rammed through the door.

At the sink, Megan and Anna both swung their heads toward him, but instincts kept him moving. He kicked each stall door open.

"What are you doing?"

"Stay," he ordered on his way past Anna. Teeth gritted, he stopped in front of the door, let out a breath, and peered behind him. "Please."

Despite the question in her eyes, Anna held on to Megan and nodded her agreement.

Evan slipped back into the hall and slinked against the wall toward shadows flickering around the bend.

Battle mode kicked in. Same as on the field, the adrenaline coursing through him sharpened his focus. Deep breaths relaxed his muscles and slowed everything around him. An exhale brought him around the corner.

He ducked under an incoming swing and nailed the guy's knee with a leg kick. The *snap* echoed across the corridor. Groaning, the guy bent over and went for an ankle holster, but Evan knocked the gun from his hands. It skidded across the concrete, pulling Evan's gaze toward it.

The split second ended in a fist to Evan's mouth. He dropped his Sig. Pain burst from his lip and fed his aggression. He landed an uppercut to the guy's jaw and a right cross to his ribs. The guy stumbled backward, but the sadistic look contorting his features didn't falter.

Evan pinned him against the wall with an elbow to his throat. "What are your orders?"

Blood ran from his smirk. "You think Michelli doesn't know what you're doing here? You can't stop him."

The heck he couldn't. He gripped the dirtbag's coat. "What's he planning?"

The guy's derisive laugh pushed Evan over the edge. He banged him against the wall. His head smacked into the bricks and slumped to his chest, his whole body turning to dead weight.

Evan eased him to the ground. He slid his shirt cuff over his hand, lifted the gun from the ground without putting fingerprints on it, and withdrew his cell. *C'mon, Harris. Pick up the phone.*

"If I run another plate without paperwork, my boss is gonna bust me for unauthorized use of a police computer," Harris rattled off when he answered.

"What about a stolen gun?" Evan reviewed the scratched surface where someone had filed off the serial number. "A Colt 1991 series, from the looks of it."

"Do I even want to ask?"

"Probably not. You got any cops working the beat near Millennium Park?"

"Yeah. Why?"

Evan peered back at the thug hunched against the wall. "Send at least two to pick up one of Michelli's men. Hold him for brandishing an illegal firearm in public."

"O'Riley—"

"I'll text you the location. Make sure your men are fast."

Evan hung up and secured the gun to give to Harris later. Back in the bathroom, Anna stood near the sink with her arms guarding Megan in a protective hold. Her initial reaction at seeing the door fling open transitioned into an exhale … until she zeroed in on the cut above his lip.

He held the door open. "Time to roll."

"What happened?" She shuffled Megan forward.

He prodded them down the hall to grab their things. "Nothing. Keep moving."

Anna gripped his arm and made him stop. "If you say 'nothing' one more time, you're gonna have a nice shiner to go with that busted lip."

A tendon on his neck worked. "Not here." He ushered them forward, but she balked.

"Yes, here." A streak of obstinacy wrinkled her forehead. "I need you to stop acting like one of my dad's overprotective bodyguards and tell me what's going on."

Overprotective? Did she think he'd just brawled with an imaginary person?

He lifted the back of his hand to his mouth and smeared the blood off. "Is this reason enough for you?" he whisper-yelled.

She blanched.

He dug his fingers into his palms. "This is your life, Anna." And protecting her was his. It was the way things would always be, no matter how much either of them wanted to change it.

Looking away, she rubbed her arms. "I know there are dangers, but—"

"There are no buts." She didn't know the half of it. Michelli would go to any length to stay out of prison. The possibilities of what those warped creeps could do if they got their hands on her drilled fury into Evan's bones. He pressed a hand to her back. "We're leaving. Now."

Megan's innocent eyes blinked up at him when he turned. "We're going already?"

Anna slipped around him, with her face wiped of any turmoil, and zipped up Megan's coat. "Don't worry, kiddo. We'll come back another day."

"Mr. Hulk, too?"

His shoulders sagged at the dissonance in Megan's voice. He knew that sound. Knew he couldn't make promises he couldn't keep.

"I hope so." It was the best he could offer. Evan lifted her onto his hip, clasped Anna's hand, and hustled back to the car.

At the parking spot, he closed the door behind Megan and caught Anna's elbow on her way around the bumper. He drew her toward him, but she kept her head down. Everything he wanted to say stayed knotted inside.

"I didn't mean to be short with you. It's just …" His jaw tightened. Eyes closed, he craned his head back. Why was this so hard? He shouldn't have lost his cool earlier. He was supposed to be shielding her from all this. "I need you to trust me."

Her pause doubled his heart rate until earnest green eyes met his. "I do." Without another word, she released his hand and got in the car.

He clenched his keys. How much longer could he do this?

Anna didn't press him on the way to the rec center. In fact, she didn't say a thing. At least, not with her voice. While keeping her gaze out the window and one leg tucked under the other, she let her shoe slip to the floorboard and rubbed her foot.

He didn't want to know what she was thinking, but the silence might've been worse.

Parked along the curb in front of the rec center, his spacious Accord had never felt more compressed.

"I appreciate you protecting me, Evan." Anna unbuckled her seat belt and slowly faced him. "I'm sorry for getting upset."

He lowered his gaze for a moment. "Me too."

She opened her door. "Have fun tonight."

The gala. He groaned at the reminder. Even with a backup plan, the thought of having to leave Anna and Megan right now made his stomach churn.

Something unspoken deepened the corners of Anna's lips. "Make sure you do some dancing while you're out."

Really? After just fighting, she still had jokes? He grunted. "Not happening."

"You wouldn't want your practice to go to waste." A quiet laugh floated outside the car with her. She ducked back in. "And you still owe me lunch, by the way."

He owed her much more than that.

With a quick wink, she closed her door and held out a hand for Megan.

Anna had never been one to hang on to anger. Though for once, he wished she would. At least then, maybe it'd spur her to stay on guard.

Evan walked them to the rec center. After clearing the inside, he stopped in the entryway beside Anna and searched for the strength to pull himself away from this enigma of a woman.

Cool fingertips grazed his hand. "I understand."

Did she?

"Thanks again for looking out for me." She fretted with her coat's zipper as though wanting to say more.

His heartbeat picked up again, words climbing his throat.

Before he could say anything, Anna lifted on her toes and pressed a soft kiss to his cheek. "Good night, Evan." She jogged over to the kids on the basketball court without looking back.

His chest caved. He backed out the front door and waited for the raw wind to drive some sense into him. Anna needed someone in her life who could handle being around her without it clouding his judgment and risking her safety. He might not be able to live up to that, but he'd never leave her unprotected. Failing her again wasn't an option.

Leaning against the cool steel, he withdrew his cell, skipped over Murphy's name since he was out of town, and tapped the only other one he trusted.

"Corporal Harris."

"Bro, I need another favor."

CHAPTER ELEVEN

Pursuit

B etween teaching and paperwork, Anna managed to keep her thoughts away from Evan the rest of the evening. Almost.

Alone in her office, she powered down the archaic computer and strode to a metal filing cabinet in the corner. The whole day replayed in her head as she thumbed through the folders crammed inside the drawer. The guys following her Sunday morning ... the one Evan fought today ... Were they really Michelli's men?

The sad part was, the possibility of Evan hanging around solely because he felt a responsibility to look after her bothered Anna more. It shouldn't. It was his nature. Knowing that shouldn't make her chest feel like someone shoved the filing cabinet on top of her.

Eyes closed, she gave a faint laugh. It was her own fault. Be normal around him? Try to remind him what he left behind? Right. She cringed at how ridiculous she must've come off today.

Here he was, just trying to watch her back, and she'd been … flirting? Ugh. Yeah, flirting. Her internal cringing ratcheted up ten notches and backed her against the wall. What was she trying to do? Drive him out of her life *again*?

Robyn popped her head through the doorway. "You still here?"

Anna leapt away from the wall. "Uh, yeah. Just finishing up." She wedged a manila folder into the drawer and shut it.

Robyn waltzed in with wisps of dark hair frizzing above her glistening forehead. "Girl, what a day." She plopped onto one of the frayed guest chairs, lifted her foot to her knee, and rotated her ankle. "I know running around the courts with these kids isn't as tough on my feet as all that dancing you do. But I swear, some days, this forty-year-old body screams for me to jump off the crazy train."

"It's good for your soul."

"Mm hmm." Robyn tipped her chin. "Spoken by the girl still in her twenties."

Anna's laugh dwindled. Twenties might as well be fifties in the dance world. She'd lose any shot at a career in the next few years. Would lose her edge to teach eventually. Then what? She'd be empty again. And still alone.

She slipped her arms through her coat sleeves and offered Robyn an empathetic smile. "I feel ya, girl. But at least that crazy train has some pretty sweet stops along the way. Including a home with an adorable ten-year-old."

"You mean Miss I-Think-I'm-Already-Eighteen?" Robyn picked at the chipped polish on her nails. "Psh, that stop takes me straight to the psych ward."

"And you love every minute of it."

"You know I do." Robyn's hearty laugh bounced around the office. She mumbled something about her boo, then stood and stretched her back. "Did you find a date for your dad's Thanksgiving party yet?"

Anna tied her scarf in a knot as tight as the one choking back her response. "Don't remind me."

"If you stopped frontin' and asked that O'Riley boy, it'd already be settled."

A series of blinks compensated for Anna's frozen jaw.

"Oh, come off it, sweetie. I saw you two the other day." Robyn leaned against the doorframe with her arms laced. "What's the problem?"

More like what *wasn't* the problem. Glancing at the clock, Anna cracked a laugh. "How much time you got?"

Robyn's arched brow told Anna to spill it.

The truth stretched out in a sigh. "The problem is me. I don't know what my deal is. It's like I can't figure out how to be around him. One minute, I'm over-thinking things, worrying about getting close to him again when he's going to end up leaving. The next minute, I shove all that away and just enjoy time with him like nothing's changed."

She slouched against the corner of the desk. "But when we're being comfortable with each other, it takes everything in me not to show him I want more. If he had any idea how many times I've almost kissed him." She buried her face in her hands. "And then I get all flustered and act like a freaking teenager around him." Gah, it was even worse saying it out loud. "What's wrong with me?"

"Aside from needing anti-anxiety meds?"

Anna glared at Robyn through her fingers.

"I'm just messin' with you." A smile expanded in her voice. "There ain't nothing wrong with you, honey. You're in love."

"Why does love have to be so complicated?"

"It's not."

Anna's hands slid to her sides. "You were ready to send me to the psych ward a second ago, and now you're saying it's not complicated?"

"Loving someone isn't the hard part, sugar. Accepting it in return ..." She shrugged. "Now, *there's* the part most of us struggle with."

Her words pricked a nerve Anna didn't want to expose. "But—"

"Miss Madison?" Megan swung around the doorframe and bumped into Robyn's legs. "Ooh. Sorry." Sweet, uncomplicated eyes looked up at Anna. "Ready to go?"

"Yep." Tucking away her conversation with Robyn, Anna smiled and hopped off the desk. "Sure am."

Robyn locked the door as they all left the office. In the gym, the overhead fluorescent lights magnified her you're-not-off-the-hook expression. "Later," she whispered.

Maybe by then Anna would get herself together.

The echo of a single basketball brought Shaun into view, standing at the free throw line by himself.

Anna squeezed Megan's hand. "Give me just a sec, 'kay?"

Shaun had been quiet all night. From the minute Anna had walked in without Evan, he'd done his best to hide his disappointment, but she knew better. She jogged onto the court and sidled up to him. "What's your percentage now? You beating LeBron yet?"

A flicker of a grin twitched. "Almost." Bending his knees, he aimed for the basket.

Anna scuffed her sneaker over the line. "I'm sorry Mr. Hulk couldn't be here tonight. He really wanted to."

Shaun snapped his wrist to release the ball and shrugged without facing her. "It's cool. Not like we're boys or somethin'."

The fact he'd learned stoicism at such an early age crushed Anna's heart even more. She swallowed the evidence building in her throat, hooked an arm around his shoulders, and kept her tone light. "Well, I guess it worked out. 'Cause I'm not sure I want to share you."

A rosy blush colored Shaun's cheeks. "Aw, Miss Madison, you can't be cramping my style like that." He flicked a glance toward the bleachers, where a cute girl with multi-colored bands around her braids beamed at him.

"Oh." Anna released him from her hug. "Look at you, stud."

There was that blush again. So stinking adorable.

She gave his shoulders a good squeeze and jogged back over to Megan. Robyn met them at the door, and Anna flaunted her an I-told-you-so grin. "Love's easy, huh?" She dipped her head at Shaun. "Tell that to a nine-year-old."

Robyn rolled her eyes. "Mm hmm. This conversation isn't over, by the way." She pulled Megan's hood over her head and opened the door for them. "Be careful going home."

"Yes, ma'am." Anna steered Megan out to the sidewalk, lit up by the streetlight.

Around the corner, Harris pushed off the quarter panel of his cruiser. "Need a lift?"

"Harris?" Anna cast a glance over the quiet block. "What are you doing here?"

"Just doing some rounds in the neighborhood. Figured I'd stop to see if two famous dancers needed an escort home." Offering Megan a wink, he swept an arm inside the car.

Anna cocked her chin. "Evan sent you over here, didn't he?"

"Evan who?"

"Nice try. I was in the car when he called you about that license plate, so I know you know he's in town."

Harris shut the door behind Megan, grin expanding. "Don't know what you're talking about. I'm just a longtime friend, stopping to check on you, like I always do."

"Uh-huh." Anna rounded the bumper but didn't release him from her skeptical gaze, even after she slid into her seat. Inside, the stale aroma of coffee left from one too many stakeouts rose from the Crown Vic's upholstery.

She smiled to herself. Harris had been a good friend to her over the years—giving her rides home, inviting her over for dinner with his family, checking the locks at her apartment. How he had time for all that with such a demanding job, she had no idea.

He and Evan both watched out for her like brothers. If she could get rid of that thing inside her hoping Evan would ever feel differently, she'd make things a heck of a lot easier on herself. But how do you put boundaries around your heart when it won't let you?

As soon as she closed her eyes, the scene at the park flooded in. Getting Evan to dance. Feeling the planes of his back and ridges of his stomach against her palms. Letting his deep laugh wash over her.

She clamped a hand over her face. *Stop. Just stop.*

Streetlights streaked through the car as they turned into Megan's neighborhood. Harris sent a quick glance to the backseat. "Got any fun plans for Thanksgiving?"

Megan raised a shoulder. "My mom doesn't know how to cook."

"Funny. My wife has that same problem."

Anna popped him in the arm. "You better not let Kristy hear you say that."

He rubbed his bicep. "Hey, she's the first to admit it. If it weren't for my mother-in-law cooking each holiday, we'd be carting the whole family to Golden Corral."

The rundown apartments came into view and dragged Anna's heart down the storm drain alongside the curb. "I'm planning to ask if Megan can come to my dad's for the holiday this year," she whispered.

Harris shifted into park and lowered his voice. "That's nice, Anna. I hope—"

The CB radio beeped. "Harris, Twenty-two, code ten on channel one."

Harris grabbed his radio. "Twenty-two, go ahead."

"Armed robbery in progress. Suspect is a white male, five foot eleven, one-eighty, blond. Break."

Harris clutched the wheel with one hand, the radio with the other. "Go ahead."

"Location is 935 North Central Avenue. What's your status?"

"Copy, dispatcher. I'm en route." Deep lines creased his face when he turned to Anna. "I'm sorry, I have to—"

"Go. Don't worry about me. I'm gonna stay and talk with Megan's mom a while."

He didn't look convinced. "Text me when you're leaving. I'll try to send a squad car."

"Thanks." She slid out. "Be careful."

A firm nod similar to the ones Evan gave her told her to do the same. He sped down the street with blue and white lights flashing against the darkness.

Trying to shake off any worry, Anna held Megan's hand on their way up the stairs. Harris had been at this gig for a long time. He'd be fine, just like she and Megan would be.

They'd made this trek hundreds of times, yet the shadows seemed thicker tonight. Darker. She tucked Megan close. Why did Evan have to remind her how safe she felt in his arms and how vulnerable she felt alone?

She knocked on the door. No response. They both shivered in the cold. After another two knocks, Megan fished out a key from the bottom of her backpack. "She's probably not home."

Like usual. It pained Anna to know elementary-aged children had to come home to empty apartments this late.

Inside, the stench of cigarettes assaulted her nostrils.

"You don't have to stay, Miss Madison." Megan toed off her worn sneakers in resignation to the normal state of her life.

Anna cleared her voice of any heartache. "Maybe I should. Just until your mama gets in."

A door down the hall squeaked open. Anna grabbed Megan by the shirt and tugged her near. Her mom stumbled between the walls like a bowling ball against guardrails. She banged into the end table closest to her and swore.

Anna tightened her hold around Megan. "Heather?"

A red-rimmed glare speared through the tangled web of hair hanging in her face. "Get out."

Anna flinched at her harshness. "Um . . . I don't mean to intrude. I came to ask—"

"Now." Heather tottered forward while clutching her torso with shaky arms.

"If we could just talk . . ."

The young woman lifted multiple beer bottles off the coffee table and swayed each until liquid sloshed inside one. She took a swig, dropped it to the floor, and rubbed her temples.

A somewhat coherent gaze roamed toward Anna then. Heather clasped her elbows tighter in a struggle to stand upright. "Look, I know you're trying to do the right thing, but you've already caused me enough trouble."

"We can get you help."

A wheezy laugh quirked the corners of her broken smile. "Please, just go."

Eyes on Megan, Anna backed toward the door with her insides spiraling. Her cell buzzed in her pocket as she turned and gripped the knob. A moment's hesitation caved to the resolution mounting in her gut.

She whirled back around. "Heather, I'd like to invite you both to my dad's for Thanksgiving tomorrow. I understand if you don't want to come, but I'd still like to take Megan. We won't be far away, and it'll just be for the night. I'll have her back the next morning."

"Mom, please."

"Shh." Heather pulled Megan to her side and studied Anna with dilated eyes. "What's in it for you?"

What? "Nothing." Her cell vibrated again.

Heather's gaze wandered to a dark stain on the soiled carpet. "Fine," she said after a moment.

A sigh of relief leveled out Anna's shoulders. "Thank you."

Something she couldn't read moved through Heather's expression. She turned without acknowledging Anna, but it didn't matter. She'd said yes.

Anna winked to Megan and let herself out the door.

It killed her to leave that precious girl each night. And the truth was, Megan may never have the security of a safe, affectionate upbringing. But if Anna could offer her even snippets of the kind of childhood she deserved, she'd never stop trying.

Outside, a stormy wind shook the railing and marched up her body. She overlapped the sides of her coat while hustling down the rusted staircase to the walkway.

A garbage can lid rattled behind her and sent her reaching for her phone to text Harris.

Two missed calls. One from Dad, one from Reese. Just what she needed. A Thanksgiving tag team.

Something rustled in the leaves. Anna spun around right as a bony calico scurried out of the bushes. A long exhale slowed her pulse. She flexed a hand to the wall and clutched her phone to her chest. She seriously had to stop walking around so on edge.

Cautious eyes glowed back at her from under the shrubs.

"It's okay, kitty. You hungry? I bet you're freezing, too, huh?" Poor thing. The thought of it digging in the trash for food broke Anna's heart. "Let's see if we can get you somewhere warm."

As soon as she inched forward, the stray scampered back into the darkness. Evan's comment about Strider roared to mind and steered Anna's gaze up the stairs to Megan's apartment. Maybe she couldn't change the way things were, but she couldn't just stand on the sidelines. He, of all people, should understand that.

Burying the frustration, she turned and froze at the sight of someone lurking in front of her. Gray hoodie. Wild smirk. The guy who'd been in Megan's apartment the other night grabbed a fistful of her coat. Her cell clattered to the ground.

"Look who decided to show up again."

Anna darted a desperate glance from corner to corner until a dark laugh brought her eyes back to his smoke-stained leer.

"Don't you worry. It's just you and me." He snaked a cold finger down the side of her face. "And we're going to have some fun."

She slapped his hand away. "Don't touch me."

"I had a feeling you'd be a feisty one." He rammed her against the brick wall, knocking the air out of her. While her head spun, he tied some kind of twine around her wrists and clucked his tongue. "We could've played nice."

Her stomach convulsed at the look on his face. She elbowed his chest in a fight to break free.

He clutched her jaw so fiercely, the corner of his ring tore into her lip. Pain surged. She spit in his face, splattering blood across his cheek.

His eyes darkened at her resistance.

Shaky heartbeats thundered against her eardrums. Her lungs heaved, but her struggle only fueled his high. With immense effort, she calmed her body. Two could play this game.

"That's it, baby. Just relax."

The second he loosened his hold on her shoulders, she thrust a knee into his groin as hard as she could. He folded in half, and she slammed his head against her other knee. On the ground, nose bleeding, he curled into a ball.

She stood above him. "Should've tied my legs, creep."

Car doors opened behind her and drew her around. A pair of guys in dark clothes stepped out. Adrenaline rocketed her across the property and between two brick walls.

"Find her," the guy on the ground yelled.

Anna edged to the end of the building and poked her head around the corner. The dark alleyway showed no signs of movement. She swung a glance from the building ahead to the path behind her.

Footsteps approached. *Breathe.* Praying no one was waiting in the open, she darted across the road and disappeared between another set of buildings.

Around the corner, she backed into the bricks. Her heart echoed the heavy footfalls still in pursuit. She strained to break her hands free, but the twine dug against her skin without any give. *Come on!*

Dark clouds taunted rain, panic threatening tears. The bitter air clawed down her throat and stung her eyes. Helplessness welled up inside her—the kind she'd vowed she'd never feel again.

"Split up," one of the guys yelled. "You take Fifty-Ninth Street."

The cold bricks scraped along Anna's palms as she moved until a sliver of a main road came into view around the bend. She shrank back and exhaled through her mouth.

"Over here." A dark smirk emerged under the streetlight at the opposite end of the alleyway.

She sprinted through a stream of oncoming traffic and hustled up the stairs to the "L" platform.

She slowed long enough to scan behind her. The rumble of cars zipping below competed with the pulse in her ears. Wind rushed off Lake Michigan into the sweat-soaked collar clinging to her skin.

Anna scoured the platform from every angle. Black coats stood out all over the boarding area. Faces. Conversations. People swishing by in both directions. Any one of them could be the guys after her.

She couldn't stop here. Couldn't afford to assume she'd lost them. A wary glance along the tracks led her back into a jog. On shaky legs, Anna ran down the stairs and to the only place she knew to go.

CHAPTER TWELVE

Pause

At the hotel bar, Evan checked his cell for the sixteenth time tonight. No messages. No reply texts from Harris. Where was he? Evan shoved the phone aside and grabbed his drink. He'd call Anna instead if she hadn't made it clear she thought he was being overprotective.

Maybe he was. A pushover, too, for letting Marissa coax him into coming to this stuffy gala. She'd made a show of him for the first hour until whatever agenda she had got underway.

He lifted the cool glass to the cut on his lip and cracked a grin. Unable to give her the model-escort look she'd hoped for, Evan almost thought he'd unintentionally found a way out of coming. But then she'd ranted about having no last-minute options.

Being a man of his word didn't always lend itself to favorable situations. Evan swirled the ice cubes in his glass and grunted. Story of his life.

Behind him on the crowded floor, Marissa had each guy surrounding her in the palm of one hand and her fifth martini glass in the other. Obviously, she didn't need him here, after all.

He chugged the last of his Coke and banged the glass to the counter. Like it or not, she'd still need him to take her home before one of those high rollers took advantage of her.

Evan worked the knot on his bow tie loose. Between the lingering clouds of cologne and alcohol, he could hardly breathe in here.

"Excuse me?" A silky voice drew his gaze toward a girl approaching. In a dress cut as low as her heels were high, she sashayed up to the empty seat beside him. "I couldn't help noticing how lonely you look over here. Something on your mind?"

He almost laughed at the irony of her asking the same thing Anna had a few hours earlier. How could the same exact question have such different effects?

A curvy grin amplified her seductive gaze. "Why don't you let me buy you a drink? I promise I can make you forget all about it."

An inward shudder rippled down his body. "I'm here with someone."

With a flick of her hair over her shoulder, she peered toward Marissa. "Your date seems a little … preoccupied." Another provocative smile punctuated her point. "Sure you want to waste the night?"

"What do you think he's trying to avoid?" someone said from behind him.

He swiveled around. Kate? He hadn't seen her since high school graduation. She shot him a go-with-it expression to which he nodded in reply.

The woman beside him ran a glare up and down Kate's profile before stalking toward her next target for the evening.

Evan nabbed his drink again. "Thanks. I didn't want to have to get rude."

Kate took the chair beside him. "Good thing for you, blunt's still my middle name." She leaned an elbow on the counter, sank her chin onto her hand, and slid a glance at his cell. "Must be a lucky girl."

He scratched his cheek and jutted a thumb behind him. "I'm here with—"

"The wrong person. Yeah, I gathered."

Shifting in his seat, Evan loosened his tie a little more.

"Don't worry. Most people aren't observant enough to pick up the subtext."

"Except you."

She laughed. "Yeah, well, years of working as an auditor will do that to ya. Details matter." Laying a black clutch on the counter, she flagged the bartender for a refill of her drink. "What I really want to know is what you're still doing here."

He blinked at her.

She stirred the ice left in her glass with her straw. "Hey, I just call it like it is."

Obviously. "Then you know my date is about two drinks away from being a sloppy drunk."

"And you're hiding behind the chivalrous knight role, waiting to take her home. Yeah, I caught that part, too."

Another long blink. "I see you still haven't found a filter."

She almost spewed a sip of her fruity-smelling drink. "A lot of things might've changed since high school, but needing sarcasm to survive isn't one of them."

They shared a laugh. "It's good to see you, Kate."

"Ditto. Now, get outta here, already. I'll make sure your *date* gets a taxi home." She shoved him in the arm. "And just because I don't show empathy most of the time, doesn't mean I don't have any. I got ya on this one."

Evan rocked the bottom of his glass back and forth against the wooden counter.

Sighing, Kate pulled the napkin out from under her drink and laid a pen beside it. "Leave me your number if it makes you feel better. I'll text you when she's getting ready to leave."

It wasn't a bad plan. From what he'd seen from Marissa this week, she'd be milking the night for hours yet. There'd be enough time for him to check on Anna before Marissa was ready to leave.

After jotting down his number, Evan snagged his tux jacket off the back of the chair, turned, and stopped a foot away. He pivoted around with a grateful smile. "Thanks."

Kate offered a nonchalant shrug. "I'm stuck here as a favor to my boss. One of us might as well get to escape. Besides, I'm sure I'll need a return favor at some point."

"Just say the word." He pushed his arms through his jacket sleeves on his way toward the door without glancing at Marissa.

Slow, icy rainfall greeted him in the parking lot with a reminder of the upcoming storm the news had been cautioning about. In his car, he jabbed the button for the seat warmer, cranked the heat, and rubbed his hands together. They were almost as cold as Anna's usually were.

Images of her monkey gloves and owl slippers garnered a laugh, but the thought of Michelli's hired guns lurking around crowded out any humor. He called Harris and pinned the phone to his ear with his shoulder while backing out of the parking space.

"C'mon, man, pick up."

Voice mail. Again. Evan dropped the cell and veered onto the main street. He'd go home, change, and do a quick sweep around Anna's place. She'd never have to know he was checking up on her.

Almost to his hotel, he glanced at his phone. "Screw it." With a gruff exhale, he scrolled to Anna's number. She could be mad if she wanted. He needed to know she'd made it home safely.

Each ring stretched into the one behind it. Okay, if she didn't answer either, he'd—

Her voice mail clicked on. Swearing, he tossed the phone onto the passenger seat and turned into his hotel parking lot. Five minutes to change and grab his Sig, and he'd be out of here. Something wasn't right.

An incoming ring struck the silence. He slowed beside the curb and scrambled for the phone. About time Harris called back. "You better have a good reason for not answering my calls, bro."

The pause from Harris's end of the line caught Evan in the gut. "Harris?"

"Sorry, man. I got called in. Armed burglary. The suspect took a bystander, and things got ugly. I'm just now catching a breather."

The Accord stalled in front of the hotel's side door. "What about Anna?"

A second pause thrust the first one in even deeper. "I dropped her off at Brookfield. She said she was going to stay a while. I'm sorry. I had no choice."

Evan gritted his teeth. Why did Murphy have to be out of town tonight? He would've been the one Evan asked to stand in his place.

A long breath filtered through the line. "I sent Officer Adams as soon as I could, but ..."

Evan let go of the wheel. "Harris, I swear, if you pause one more time—"

"He found her cell in the grass ... along with traces of blood. Looks like a fight went down."

Fury assailed Evan's veins. "Where is she?"

"I'm headed there now. Adams is already canvassing the area." Harris exhaled again. "We'll find her."

That was Evan's responsibility. He jerked the car back into drive and started to back up when someone inside the stairwell caught him short. *Bells.*

He threw the gearshift into park and jumped out. "Harris, she's at my hotel. Have uniforms fan out. Chances are the perps are still on the prowl."

"Ten-four."

Evan pocketed his cell and blew through the door right as Anna was coming down the stairs. Relief rushed over him until his gaze flew from her bound hands to a bloody cut on her lip.

A dozen emotions wrestled behind her eyes. "I'm sorry. I didn't know where else to go."

Sorry?

"What happened?" He sawed through the twine with his pocketknife.

"That guy from Megan's apartment. He was waiting for me."

Fingers balled, Evan prayed for self-control. Anna needed strength right now, not anger.

"I got away, but he sent two guys after me." She gripped his sleeve. "I ran as hard as I could. I don't think they followed me, but I—"

"Come here." He closed her in his arms, and she quivered against him—cold, shaken. He held her tighter, rested his chin over her head, and willed his embrace to absorb every fear. "It's okay. You're safe."

Minutes lapsed inside the stairwell as she clung to him. Every stupid justification he'd had for backing off earlier burned in his chest.

Once she calmed, she lifted away. He followed her apologetic gaze to a bloodstain on his white shirt. She touched a hand to her lip and backed up. "Your night ... I didn't mean to ..."

He cupped her cheeks with both hands. "Anna, look at me. Don't ever hesitate to come to me. This is home, okay?" He pulled her close again. "Right here. I've got you." He pressed a kiss to the top of her hair. "Always."

One day, he'd make up for every reason she had to doubt that truth.

The door whisked open behind them and ushered a frosty breeze inside. He shielded her and turned. A pot-bellied man with his tie halfway undone stumbled past them, glaring.

Evan secured an arm across Anna's back and led her upstairs to his suite. They needed to get out of view. Painter and his punks might be stupid, but they'd be persistent. He'd take care of them later tonight. Right now, Anna needed him.

"You'll have to give your statement to Harris." Evan locked up behind them. "But let me take care of that cut first. You could use some time to let things settle."

"I'm fine." She rested a consoling hand to his, as if he were the one who needed to be comforted instead of her. "Really. I panicked for a minute, but I'm okay now."

And as brave and stubborn as ever. Her eyes beseeched him to downplay it. Knowing that was how she coped, he'd do his best.

She wandered around the living area while he made his way to the kitchen.

"Sorry for the mess."

Anna looked from the couch to him, the corner of her mouth tipping. "You mean the one throw pillow that's out of place?"

Along with his open duffel bag beside the couch, the folders covering the desk, and the two framed pictures taking up most of the coffee table. Apparently, neatness was relative. A chuckle trailed the thought as he dumped a handful of ice into a Ziploc bag and searched the drawers for a dish towel to wrap it in.

He left it on the kitchen table, beside a washcloth and a bowl of warm water, and sifted through his bag for the first aid kit.

Anna settled on the couch and lifted one of the pictures from the coffee table. "You had it framed."

A peek in her direction turned into a wistful smile. The photo wasn't on his top ten list, but the night he'd taken it always would be. The summer between their junior and senior year. A week at her dad's vacation home in the Outer Banks. He'd never felt more a part of their family. One he'd almost believed he could belong in.

Until his dad's derisive laugh reminded him he'd never measure up to the Madison's standards. *"You think that family accepts you? It's called pity, boy. Save yourself some heartache, and stop trying to be more than you are."*

Evan fisted his hands, clenching back what he couldn't change. It didn't matter. Whatever miniscule chance he had of proving his dad wrong died with Anna's mom.

He swallowed his failures and focused on what Anna needed right now. At least reminiscing might take her mind off what'd just happened. "You like that one?"

"It's one of my favorites. Well, all your work is, really." She propped the frame against her knees. "But this one comes with some pretty great memories."

"You remember that trip, huh?" He sat beside her and scratched his jaw.

"You kidding? I crack up every time I look at the starfish on my shelf."

He pressed his tongue to the inside of his cheek. "You weren't laughing when I tossed you off that pier."

"But I was when I got you to dance on it that night."

He raised a finger. "You were sworn to secrecy."

Lips zipped together, Anna's wry look sent his heart rate climbing. "Don't worry, Sarge. All your secrets are safe with me."

Except for the one he could never tell her.

She must've noticed his reaction. Looking away, she redirected her attention to the picture. "I'm glad you had it matted. Makes it feel like it's freeze-framed in history that way."

"You can thank my mom for that. She kept all my work." Evan returned the frame to the coffee table and motioned to the other one. "They were in her apartment. I thought I'd have these two reframed for her while I'm here."

"She'll love that." Anna set a gentle hand on his knee. "I mean it. Your work is special. You should take your portfolio to a gallery. They'd carry it in a heartbeat. I'm sure of it."

"Doubt that."

"You didn't used to."

She'd just experienced a traumatic situation, and yet the only concern she showed was for him. She had no idea what the ache in her voice did to him.

He picked at the corners of the first aid kit and cleared his throat. "We should get you cleaned up."

Anna followed him into the kitchen without saying anything.

At the table, he dragged a chair in front of hers and tended to her cut. Anger at Painter boiled each time she winced at Evan's touch. That lowlife better hope Evan kept his cool when he found him. As if Michelli's men weren't enough to deal with. Anna shouldn't have to worry about dodging Painter, too.

Anna peered back to the living room. Her brow creased with whatever she was thinking.

Evan lowered the warm washcloth, now coated in crusted blood. "What?"

"I'm just trying to make sense of it …" She turned her green eyes on him, equal parts soft and piercing. "I mean, when I think about it, it's obvious you'd make a great soldier, but why didn't you pursue photography?"

Was she serious? "Carrying a camera around as a kid didn't make me a photographer. It never amounted to anything."

"Don't you dare discount your talent as some worthless hobby." She squeezed his arm and let go. "You have what it takes."

"To be a starving artist the rest of my life?"

She winced again. This time, from his words.

"That didn't come out right. You're talented enough to succeed in that field. I'm not."

She squared her shoulders. "That's your dad talking."

He grunted. "The old man was bound to get at least one thing right."

"How can you say that?" Visible heartache streaked her face. "What happened to our plans?"

Her voice cracked on the last question, right along with Evan's insides. He set the rag aside and squeezed some antiseptic cream onto his fingertip. "They were a kid's daydreams. An escape from things I couldn't change back then. Thinking it'd ever be more only breeds disappointment."

"Art isn't a disappointment, Evan. And neither are you. The only thing that's disappointing is seeing you believe that."

Conviction and belief brimmed in her eyes until he couldn't take it. Why did she have to stir things better left forgotten?

He straightened the chain to his dog tags along the back of his neck. "Wishing for that life wasn't going to keep me from ending up like my dad."

"You could never be like him."

"Not a drunk, maybe, but still a deadbeat mechanic with no future." He released a hard breath. "C'mon, Bells. I would've stayed the town joke."

A flare of indignation stormed the sadness in her eyes. "You're the only one who ever saw yourself like that."

"More like you were the only one who didn't." He scooted forward and dabbed the ointment on her cut. "You were my best friend. I think you might've been a little biased."

Her heart-wrenching stare didn't waver. "No. I just saw what you couldn't." She brushed a cool hand to his cheek. "Still do."

Heat spread through him. Her green sweater brought out depths in her eyes he couldn't tear himself away from.

She grazed her thumb across the bruise on his lip. "We make quite a pair, don't we?"

Her hand drifted from his cheek and trailed the length of the dog tags tucked under his tuxedo shirt. His body quaked against the failing war inside him. Her touch, her voice, her belief in him.

He didn't deserve her affection. And whatever she thought she felt for him would change if she knew why. But when her lips parted just enough to draw his eyes to her mouth, he couldn't mask what he felt, what he wanted. Not when he was this close to her.

Evan's pulse echoed the one beating through her palm against his chest. Adrenaline teemed across his muscles, every part of him hyperaware of her. She swept her lashes toward him and broke the last barrier holding him suspended.

An abrupt ring blared from his cell on the table. They both flinched. Finding his voice again, he grabbed the phone and swiped the screen. "O'Riley."

"Evan, it's Kate. I stepped out for two minutes to use the ladies' room, and when I came back, your date was leaving with some dude. They headed toward a blue Lexus. Both looked pretty wasted."

Evan craned his neck to the ceiling to keep the string of words neither she nor Anna needed to hear from coming out. "Thanks for letting me know." What else could he say?

Anna sat back when he hung up. "What's wrong?"

"We have to take a ride." He handed her the wrapped-up bag of ice. "Keep this on your lip. It'll stop the swelling." He jogged into the bedroom, checked the mag on his Sig, and wedged it into the holster at his back. After the night he'd been having, all he needed was one more excuse to use it.

CHAPTER THIRTEEN

Boundaries

Evan pulled into the gala hotel's lot. If Marissa was with one of the guys she'd been leading on all night, they probably hadn't left their parking space yet.

He choked back an image he didn't want to think about and braced himself for her impending wrath. The rain might've stopped, but he was about to unleash a whole other storm by interrupting.

Marissa didn't need a babysitter. But they'd traveled here together, and while she was on his watch, he'd look out for her.

Anna turned from the window and lowered her ice compress.

Evan raised it back up to her mouth. "Keep pressure on it for another ten minutes." He unbuckled his seat belt and opened the door. "Stay here. I'll be right back." She didn't need to see this confrontation.

This late, the parking lot had thinned out to only a few dozen cars. He approached the only blue Lexus. Tinted windows. Figured. He banged on the passenger window in the back and opened the door. "Marissa, let's go."

Two pairs of feet stretched out from the seat. Evan's lip curled. Getting close to a lead on a story was one way of putting it.

The guy fell onto the floorboard and hustled to button his shirt while Marissa's biting glare skewered Evan from the backseat.

"What do you think you're doing?"

"Sparing you from regretting a bad hangover more than you already will. You're loaded. You need to go home."

She shimmied out of the car and resituated her dress. "I don't *need* to do anything. I'm a grown woman. I'll do what I like."

Jaw twitching, Evan pointed at the loser still crouched on the floorboard. "I'm not leaving you here with some guy who's too plastered to know he shouldn't get behind the wheel."

"Just because you have a soldier complex doesn't mean everyone else needs you to protect them."

The anger he'd anticipated sank straight to his gut. He swallowed the sting. "You're a lousy drunk, Marissa. Anyone ever tell you that?"

"And you're a lousy... boyfriend," she sputtered, as though unable to come up with a better insult. Her cutting gaze skimmed past him. "You certainly didn't waste any time moving on."

Anna shrank behind another car when he turned. Why did he ever bother telling her to stay put?

He prodded Marissa forward.

She dragged her heels. "What are you doing?"

"Hailing you a cab." At the curb, Evan whistled through his fingers, and a taxi whipped out of traffic. Sometimes, he loved Chicago. He paid the driver. "The Hilton on South Michigan. No matter what she says."

The street's Christmas lights shimmered over Marissa's irate expression from the backseat.

Without wasting another word, Evan closed her door and tapped the cab's trunk. A gust of exhaust clouded him as the taxi merged back into the fast-paced traffic.

Evan turned to apologize to Anna, but she must've gone back to the car. Hard to blame her. She'd probably heard enough. He certainly had.

Still fuming, he sank into the driver's seat but couldn't bring himself to face her yet. Instead, he zipped the car out of the lot and punched the gas.

Speed. Pavement. Space. He drove until the road absorbed the hurt and frustration of what he didn't want to admit. Marissa was right about him.

After stopping by the precinct for Anna to give her statement about the attack, Evan slowed the car on a side street leading to her neighborhood. His blood pressure had leveled out over the last two hours, but the embarrassment of what'd gone down with Marissa hadn't waned.

"Anna, about earlier … I'm sorry you had to see that."

"Which part?" She set her icepack in the cup holder. "Marissa being a real you-know-what or you being an honorable guy?"

"I don't think that's what she'd call it."

"She will. Eventually."

He eased into a parking spot beside Anna's building. "Glad you're confident of that."

"I may not know her, but I know you." She unbuckled her belt. "Your intentions are upright, Evan. They always are. Marissa will realize that after she has time to accept it."

He cut the ignition and rubbed the back of his neck. "There's that friendship bias kicking in again."

Her chin drooped slightly as she mumbled something he couldn't hear.

He pulled the keys from the ignition. "Marissa wasn't like this when I first met her."

"You don't owe me an explanation."

After what she just saw? "Yeah. I do." Fidgeting with the keys, Evan stared out the windshield. "She lost her job. Layoff. She's too proud to tell me, but the signs were hard to miss. That's why she asked to come on this trip. Hoping she'd sniff out a story or some kind of lead to a new job. And apparently, she'll do whatever … or whoever," he muttered below his breath, "to catch a break." He scoffed. "Nothing like a little pressure to show you who someone is underneath it all."

Anna set her fingers over his sleeve. "Which is exactly what she saw, too. The real side of both of you. That's why she said those things." She waited for him to look up. "Because she knows she doesn't deserve you."

The compassion in Anna's eyes took over the inside of the Accord until he felt nothing else.

She blinked and reached for the icepack and the door handle. "And it has nothing to do with bias."

It took him a minute to move. He got out, skirted around the bumper, and jogged up to the building with her.

A draft snuck into the stairwell and fluttered a piece of paper taped to her apartment door.

He stopped her on the top step and approached it first. A handwritten note in black magic marker read, *Rent's due in 8 days. Clock's ticking.* Evan yanked it off. What a world class—

"It's okay." Anna unfolded his hand and took it from him. "Mr. Reyes is just doing his job."

"That doesn't mean he has to be a jerk about it."

She shrugged like she was the problem instead of him. Even if her landlord had the right to press, she didn't need that reminder on top of everything else she'd faced today.

In front of the welcome mat, Anna toyed with her key ring. A look of fatigue joined the exhaustion already plaguing her movement. And when she lifted her gaze from the tiles, a trace of her earlier fear escaped her tired eyes. "Would you mind checking out the apartment before you go?"

He hid a smile. As if he'd leave without making sure she was safe first.

Evan withdrew his Sig and motioned her behind him after she unlocked the deadbolt. Once he cleared the initial area, she followed and locked up while he checked the remaining rooms.

"All clear," he said on his way back down the hall.

"You been carrying that thing around this whole time?" She flicked a glance at his gun.

No way to hide it now. He nodded.

Looking away, Anna dropped the icepack on the end table. "Any word from Harris?"

Evan swiped his cell screen. "Not yet."

She hung up her coat and ran her hands over her arms. She had every right to still be scared.

Knowing her, she was probably fighting the urge to ask him to stay. One of these days, he'd convince her needing help wasn't a sign of weakness.

Evan motioned to the outdated, undersized TV in the living room. "Mind if I stay and watch the game replay for a while? Your TV is way better than the one in my hotel." He took off his tux jacket and reclined on the couch, straining to keep a straight face.

Anna tossed a throw pillow at him. "Dork." She strode down the hall, shaking her head.

Bailey lunged onto the cushion and pawed over his lap. Purring louder than a Humvee, she nestled into the cramped space between the armrest and his legs. Evan rubbed a finger to her cheek. She pushed against his hand and curled her whole body into him until her legs ended up in the air.

"Make yourself comfortable." He ruffled her gray and white speckled belly. "You just stay right there and keep me warm, 'kay?"

She answered with a purring rumble. Worked for him.

A few minutes later, Anna returned in a long-sleeved T-shirt, camo-patterned flannel pajama pants, and glasses that shouldn't look anywhere near as attractive as they did on her.

He tried to play it off. "Nice outfit."

"Hey, consider it a compliment. I don't let just anyone see me like this."

Only someone she considered a brother. An inward grimace twisted inside.

Anna shuffled into the kitchen while whirling her hair into a messy half ponytail. "Hot chocolate?"

"You read my mind." He flipped on the TV at the same time she snapped on the burner under the teakettle.

The sound of the front door opening drew his gaze. "What are you doing?"

She held the door open with her back and waved a food container at him. "I'm taking Mrs. Santos's dish back to her."

He splayed his hands to his sides. "You were just attacked, and you're worried about returning a dish to a neighbor."

She made a face like it was a perfectly normal response. "I want to check on her. It'll just take a minute." Halfway over the threshold, she stopped and peered back at him. "Stay put," she said with the same tone he usually used on her.

The door shuddered into its metal frame and set off his already-live nerve endings. Images passed on the TV, but he might as well have been staring at a blank wall. He lifted off the cushion to straighten out his wrinkled dress pants and sat back down.

Bailey twitched awake and glared at him for disturbing her.

Evan flung his palms up. "Sorry." He shifted again, ginger-ly this time. If Anna didn't return in thirty more seconds, staying put would no longer be an option.

Right as he started to get up, she breezed back in with the container still in hand. "No answer."

Evan sank into the back of the couch and pretended to be engrossed in the game. She'd have a fit if she thought he couldn't handle letting her out the door by herself.

After a few commercials, a mint chocolate aroma billowed into the living room and relaxed him even more.

Anna shuffled across the carpet with two mugs and a bag of popcorn tucked under her arm. "I'm sorry you didn't get to change."

He followed her stare to his dirty white tux shirt and gave a small shrug. "I'm used to uniforms. It's not much different." He pulled his flattened bow tie off and undid the top button.

She handed him one mug and steadied the other as she sank onto the cushion. Bailey crossed over Evan's legs and snuggled into a ball on Anna's lap instead. *Little traitor.*

With the empty space now cooling his leg, he sipped the hot chocolate Anna made perfectly every single time. "I didn't hear you making popcorn."

"That's 'cause I made it three days ago." She pulled open the bag. "It's best when it's stale."

Brow cocked, he tipped his head at her.

"I'm serious." She tossed a handful into her mouth and formed a contented smile. "Stale snacks are my favorite."

"You need help."

"Whatever." She flicked a piece at his face. "It's better than those nasty peanut butter and mayonnaise sandwiches you used to make."

He laughed. "Don't knock it till you try it."

"I'll pass. Thanks."

Anna jutted her mug at the screen when the game came back on. "Ooh, perfect," she mocked. "I'll be asleep in no time."

He extended an arm toward the TV. "You kidding me? It's the Bears."

She raised a nonchalant shoulder, visibly fighting a grin.

"And you say *I'm* not a true Chicagoan." He set the remote down.

Exaggerating a yawn, she curled her feet onto the couch. "If I had a VHS player, we could watch my old *Pretty In Pink* video instead."

A sip of hot chocolate almost came back out. He held the mug away. "You trying to run me out?"

Still smiling, she leaned into his side. "Never."

Evan drank in the feel of her body cozied up to his. Who needed the cat? Anna warmed every inch of him. She may have thought he'd only stayed because she needed him. But truth was, he needed her more. No matter how much in life spun off its axel, she was his anchor. Calming, reassuring. Right here was the only place he wanted to be. Ever.

"I know it's not much to most people, but I'm gonna miss this place," she said out of nowhere.

A sideways glance caught her taking in the corners of her tiny living room.

She breathed in as though drawing from a depleting reserve of courage. "It's the first real thing I did on my own." She set her mug on the carpet. "Stepping out in faith … I thought I was really doing something. Thought Mom would've been proud of me."

"It's not over, Anna."

"But if this audition doesn't—"

"It will." He covered her fingers with his. "You're gonna rock it."

Turmoil he didn't understand touched her eyes. "I wish it were that simple."

"Why isn't it?"

Chin lowered, she twisted the drawstrings on her pants. "I gave up dance for a while. After Mom died and you left—I don't know—it felt like art lost its meaning. There was just this emptiness." A shudder followed her words. "Until I got on the floor again. Dance kept me going. It was like this safe place where I could come alive again."

He squeezed her hand, desperate to take away every ounce of pain she'd experienced—pain he'd been a part of causing. "You're not going to lose that."

"But what if I should? The rec center, helping the people in this community … I can't abandon everything Mom wanted me to live for."

Evan angled toward her. "What are you talking about? She always believed in your dance career."

"No, she believed in using art to bless people. It's supposed to be about giving, not receiving."

"Why can't it be both? You used to think you could make a difference on a company."

She scoffed. "Maybe I was wrong."

"Or maybe you're scared."

"Of what?" She drew herself up.

"You tell me." He held her gaze until her defensive pose withered into a torn expression.

Instead of answering, she nestled closer to his side. "You sound like her, you know? My mom. She always made it feel like there was nothing to be afraid of." She exhaled against him. "But after training your whole life for something, what happens if it's not enough?"

Evan bristled at the question cutting to his core. With a slow breath, he rested his cheek to her hair and prayed the truth her heart needed to hear right now would one day penetrate his own. "Then you find the faith to believe the journey was still worth it."

Her hold tightened around his arm. But rather than respond, she let the even tempo of her breathing stand in for words.

Minutes faded with the steam rising from the mugs on the floor until Anna finally stirred again.

"Thanks for making an excuse to stay." She sat upright and yawned, once again tucking away any hint of angst. "I mean, it wasn't your smoothest act, but I'll cut you some slack since it's been a draining day."

His lips pulled to the left. "I think I should at least get some bonus points for keeping your icy hands warm."

Her eyes shot ice darts of their own. "You wanna feel cold?"

He squirmed away from her fingers reaching for the back of his neck.

Bailey catapulted to the floor and cast them both a Gollum-worthy glare before trotting to her well-worn spot on the purple easy chair.

Anna didn't miss the diversion. She stretched to the end table for the diluted icepack, tackled him on the cushion, and slipped it down his shirt. "How's that for cold?" Patting the bag as it drifted down his back, she lit up in satisfied laughter. "Now who's got bonus points?"

He jumped up and fanned out his shirt until the bag landed on the carpet. "Real cute." He flopped back down. "Just wait until you fall asleep."

"Right back at ya." She slid her legs out from under her and brandished her toes. "I haven't busted out my greatest weapons yet."

"Death by ice. You should contract for the army."

She gave him a good whack with the pillow. He caught it and drew her close. Relenting, she nuzzled up to him again. A palpable silence took the place of her laughter. What was going through her mind?

Delaying whatever she wasn't saying, she picked cat hairs off her pajama bottoms one at a time. "I'm sorry I've been … difficult lately. I really appreciate you being here for me."

He brushed his cheek over her head and inhaled her natural fragrance. "I wouldn't be anywhere else."

"Until you go back to Georgia." She spoke so softly, he almost didn't hear it.

"I haven't decided that yet," he whispered back.

Another weighted pause hung between them. She drew her legs in, curved a hand over her toes, and bent her foot back and forth.

"What are you thinking?" Was it fair to ask?

She released her foot and a sigh. "Are you here because ... I mean, I'll understand if you are, but I need to know ... Are you only hanging out with me this week because you feel like you have to until this case blows over?" Her voice dwindled to a whisper by the end of her question.

His pulse sprinted in a race to suppress the words he had to keep buried. He wanted to tell her, wanted to be honest, but not at the risk of forfeiting the only place he had in her life. He couldn't lose her for good.

"It's fine." She pulled back, leaving a cold draft billowing down his arm. "I know we've lost touch and aren't as close anymore. I understand if—"

"Anna, please." He faced her but stopped himself from lifting a hand to her cheek again. He'd already crossed enough boundaries tonight.

Drawing from his military training, Evan leveled his gaze with as much candor as he could offer. "I'll always do what I can to protect you, but it's never out of obligation."

She batted away the slightest gleam coating her eyes.

A garbled sound sawed from the easy chair. He peeked over the arm. "Is that ...?"

Another snore.

Anna laughed away any trace of tears, clearly grateful for the interruption. "It's Bailey. She snores when she's over-tired."

Evan made a face, and she shoved him. "Don't make fun of her."

"So, it's true what they say." He winked. "Pets eventually become one with their owners."

"I don't snore."

"Yeah, right." He dared her to deny it. "Camping trip. Seventh grade."

That got a rise out of her. "I wouldn't have been out cold like that if you and Bobby Fenson weren't up to your stupid pranks, slipping me Benadryl. I don't usually sleep that hard."

A strand of hair that'd fallen loose from her ponytail dangled over her eyelash. She huffed it away, keeping her stance but crippling his. She shouldn't be allowed to look so sexy when she wasn't even trying.

He tried to pass off his groan as a barb. "If you say so."

Arms crossed, nose and eyes scrunched, Anna stared him down. But another drawn-out snore sent the corners of her lips twitching until she caved to a laugh.

Her soft gaze lingered on him. "How do you do it?"

"Do what?"

"Always know how to make me feel better?" She twisted her pajama pants' strings again. "Especially when I should be the one being strong for you."

He swallowed and hugged her to his side. "You are." She had since they were five.

"Thanks for putting up with me, Evan," she whispered against his arm. "You don't know how much I've missed having my best friend here."

A pang of mixed emotions sank into him. Raking a hand through his hair, he clung to the only thing getting him through this right now. Humor. "As long as you keep your cold feet off me, we'll call it even."

"Always got jokes. I'm glad you find yourself amusing. You're gonna need it if you come to dinner tomorrow."

"Why? 'Cause Reese is gonna kill you for showing up with me instead of a real date?"

Anna sat up and gawked at him.

"What?" He cocked his chin. "This *is* Reese we're talking about, right?"

"True. But how'd you know she doesn't want me to bring you?"

The innocence in her eyes wedged guilt into his rib cage. "I hurt you when I left, Anna. The only one pretending I didn't is you."

She rubbed her foot but didn't look away. "It's in the past."

"How can you be so forgiving?"

Her fingers stilled over her toes. "Guess our hearts have minds of their own." Her faint smile gave way to a look of sobriety. "You don't have to go with me, you know."

He smoothed back the wisps of hair curling around her forehead. "I know." Withdrawing his hand, Evan cleared his throat and turned on a playful tone. "But after all our escape routines, I have lots of practice acting, remember? I'll play whatever role you need. It'll be fine."

"Right." She lowered her chin and her voice. "Reese is a tough one to fool, though."

No worse than himself.

He summoned a lighthearted composure and draped an arm around her. "How about you just focus on getting some sleep right now? Tomorrow will take care of itself."

"I hope you're right."

You and me both. But he couldn't get caught up worrying about that yet. Tonight, he had other business to take care of. As soon as Anna fell asleep.

CHAPTER FOURTEEN

Restraint

Evan eased up from the couch and set a pillow in his place for Anna to rest on. He slid her glasses off, stretched a fleece blanket over her, and leaned down to press a light kiss to her temple.

The swelling on her lip had gone down, replaced with the beginning of a small scab he prayed wouldn't leave a scar. She carried enough from life already.

He stalled in the open doorway and swept one more glance over the girl he'd do anything for.

In the stairwell, he locked the deadbolt with her key and pulled up Murphy's number on his cell. Three rings went unanswered on his way down the stairs.

"It's after midnight," Murphy said. "You out on bat patrol or something?"

And Anna thought Evan always had jokes. Wait till she got to know Casanova. "You back in town yet?"

"Just crossed the border."

"Good. Meet me at Brookfield Apartments in forty-five."

"Why?"

179

Evan stopped in front of the glass exit door and surveyed the motionless street corner. "You're the one who wanted to play Robin."

An audible swell of intrigue built in Murphy's pause. "I'm in."

Good thing. Because Harris would want this clean and quiet. With Casanova there, Evan had a chance of not killing Painter.

Climbing into his Accord, he glanced from his stained tux shirt to the hoodie in the backseat. A quick thought of changing ended in a shrug. What was a little more blood? He had to get it dry cleaned anyway.

Evan pulled up to the curb in front of Megan's apartment. No sign of the police. But he knew as well as Painter, the cops were nearby, still searching for him.

He pressed the lock button on his key fob while hustling up the staircase. At this hour, hopefully Megan was fast asleep. Still, he gently rapped a knuckle on the door.

It cracked open. A sliver of dim light cut into the darkness and released the sharp smell of neglect from inside. Dilated, watery eyes stared him up and down. "What do you want?"

"We need to talk."

Scoffing, Megan's mom started to close the door, but he stopped it with his hand.

"It's about Painter."

She ran a stained sweatshirt sleeve under her runny nose and clutched her shaky arms to her stomach. "You here to give me cash to pay him? If not, you can leave. I don't need any more problems."

He'd almost forgotten she owed her dealer money. No wonder she looked like death. The poor girl was probably going through withdrawals.

Evan nudged the door open far enough to let himself in. "It's past time you got this guy out of your life."

A mix of anxiety and agitation twisted her features.

He scanned over the living room to a disheveled pile of mail on an end table. "Heather," he read from the top envelope. "This isn't just about you. Think of your little girl."

Her goose-bump-covered arms unfurled and sagged to her sides. "Don't talk to me like you know *a thing* about what it's like to be a single parent in this neighborhood."

"Maybe not, but I know what it's like to live in Megan's shoes, growing up around addiction. Never knowing what you're coming home to and feeling helpless to change anything."

Memories edged past his defenses. "I know what it's like to call Social Services and find out your parent isn't the only one who thinks you're not worth their time."

Slow, off-balance steps moved Heather backward. She averted her eyes but couldn't mask the torment pouring through them.

He softened his voice. "Heather, don't keep doing this." He waved a hand over the collection of drained alcohol bottles, ashtrays, and empty syringes strewn across the room alongside Megan's toys and clothes. He lifted up a grungy Barbie doll. "Please. Give her the life she deserves. The life you both do."

Tears stormed her bottom lashes. Her legs gave way, and she folded onto a tattered armchair. "What am I supposed to do? This *is* my life."

"It doesn't have to be." He knelt beside her on the dingy carpet. "We can put Painter away. You can start over."

Her chapped lips formed a hollow smile. "There'll always be another dealer."

"And there'll always be a choice." He couldn't give her the courage to make the right one, only the encouragement to believe she could.

He rested a hand over her clammy fingers. "You're almost there already. You just gotta fight a little longer. And I promise. You're not in this alone."

Heather buried her face in her hands. Evan sat back on his heels to give her space. Stillness hovered inside the rundown apartment, minutes passing.

Once her bony shoulders stopped shaking, she uncovered her bloodshot eyes, drew in a stabilizing breath, and fixed a determined gaze on him. "What do I have to do?"

He hung his head in a sigh of relief and retrieved his cell. "Tell me how to find Painter."

With another long inhale, she grabbed a pen and jotted something down on the back of an envelope. "He stays in Englewood. Deals at Sherwood Park."

That was all he needed. Evan tapped the info into his phone and jimmied the envelope into his pocket.

She grabbed his forearm as he rose. "What are you gonna do?"

He gave her fingers a gentle squeeze. "I'm gonna take care of you guys." His focus gravitated toward Megan's bedroom, his thoughts back to Anna. "All of you." He hurried to the door.

"Wait." Heather tottered up from the chair and clutched her stomach. "Thanks," she whispered.

He dipped his chin. "You're braver than you think you are." His gaze slanted past her to the hallway. "Don't lose sight of what's worth living for."

Still trembling from withdrawals, she brought her sleeve to her nose again and raised her head with what he hoped was the beginning of belief in herself. Nothing ahead would be easy. He knew it as much as she had to. But something broke in her spirit just now. He sensed it. And if he could play a small part in her road to recovery, he'd do what it took.

Outside, Evan hustled down the stairs and spotted Casanova's Jeep. Right on time.

Murphy hopped out and gave Evan's tux an impish once-over. "I thought Bruce Wayne only held up his cover in the daylight. Your party run a little longer than expected?"

Evan clapped him on the back on their way to his Accord. "Long story."

He brought him up to speed on the ride to the park.

"So, how's this gonna go down?" Murphy asked as Evan parked on a back street and killed the headlights.

"By the books as much as possible." He couldn't afford any mistakes. Evan stretched behind the seats for his camera bag. Something had told him to leave it in the car after his outing with Anna and Megan earlier. Now he knew why. He swapped lenses and scanned the park until he found Painter. "Bingo."

If the loser had half a brain, he'd be lying low right now. But he was probably out here, licking his wounds after Anna showed him up. Again. Evan cracked a grin. She was one girl Painter shouldn't have messed with.

With his hand cupped under the telephoto lens, Evan zoomed in to scope out the scene. Painter and a meth head, if he read the cues right, huddled in the shadows with two backup thugs standing guard.

Evan didn't need to hear the conversation to tell it was getting heated. The junkie probably didn't have the cash. Painter grabbed the guy by the shirt, brandished his gun, and got up in the dude's face like he had with Evan at Megan's apartment.

Evan shot a handful of photos.

"That the guy who took a swing at Anna?" Murphy already had his hand on the door handle, jaw clenched.

Evan couldn't blame him. It took massive restraint to stay in the car right now. He nodded while pulling out his cell.

"We're still canvassing the area," Harris said on answering.

"Send all units to Sherwood Park. Ten minutes. Painter's all yours."

"How'd you find him?"

"Not important." Evan scrolled through the shots he'd taken. "I just witnessed him pulling a gun on someone. We'll hold him till you get here to make the arrest."

"We got movement." Murphy gestured to Painter and his boys hustling toward the left side of the park.

Evan pinned the phone to his shoulder, raised his camera again, and zoomed in on the Impala at the curb. "Make it a fast ten minutes, Harris."

Sirens clipped on in the background, followed by tires screeching. "O'Riley, don't do anything stu—"

Evan hung up and arched a brow at Casanova. "Ready?"

Murphy flexed his laced hands. "Let's do this."

They crept out of the car and slinked along the park's perimeter. The stench of urine rose from the shadowy corners with crude reminders of the life drug addictions drove people to.

Not slowing down, he and Murphy came up behind Painter and the two guys lagging five paces back. Three against two was nothing, especially with these punks.

Evan motioned for Murphy to take the one on the left. "On my mark," he mouthed. He signaled with three fingers. On the last, they each locked the guys in a sleeper hold until they went limp enough to drop.

Painter whipped around, gun raised. One shot. Two. *Pops* shuddered across the open yard. All that pride in waving his Glock around, and he couldn't hit a target if his life depended on it.

Evan disarmed him and nailed a blow to his jaw. He twisted Painter's arm around his back and butted him against the hood of the Impala, face down. "One busted lip for another."

"Get off me." He shoved back, and Evan ground his cheek harder into the hood. Just the thought of his hands anywhere near Anna sent a dangerous level of adrenaline through Evan's veins.

"Easy." Murphy cast Evan a warning glance and took over securing Painter.

Evan backed up, palms lifted. Probably better that way.

Sirens neared. Blue and white lights circled the shadows as a cruiser pulled up beside them. Harris and his partner got out with weapons drawn. Harris's gaze swept the scene, skimming over the two guys down in the grass. "O'Riley, what the—?"

"All by the book, Corporal. Promise." He jutted his chin at the Impala. "There are your stolen plates to go along with the illegal gun Painter's been brandishing. Not to mention whatever drugs you find on him. Take your pick which charge to bust him for first."

Harris holstered his gun and motioned for his partner to cuff Painter.

Murphy handed him over with an extra shove.

While Harris grabbed his shoulder mic to radio in the call, Murphy leaned over to Evan. "That was too easy, bro. Next time, you at least gotta let me wear a cape to make it interesting."

Harris shook a blank face at them. "Just a couple of vigilantes. You got a bat signal I can use next time I need it?"

Murphy took one look at Evan and busted up. Like he needed any more ammo to keep riding this Batman joke he enjoyed way too much.

"Now that you mention it," Murphy said. "It's not a bad idea."

Evan pushed him in the opposite direction and scowled at Harris. "Don't encourage him."

"Looks like you do that all on your own." After his partner steered Painter into the back of the squad car, Harris pulled out a pen and notepad. "Which of you wants to give me their statement first?"

Murphy deferred to Evan. "You're the one with the photos."

"Photos? How did you …?" Harris raised a hand. "On second thought, never mind." He flipped open the pad. "Okay, give it to me from the top."

His partner cuffed the other two guys, still on the ground, while Evan and Murphy each gave Harris the lowdown on what happened.

"Good work, O'Riley." Harris planted a hand on Evan's shoulder. "But do me a favor and leave the police work to me, huh, tough guy?"

Evan refrained from pointing out the PD had been looking for Painter for hours with no leads, while he found him in less than one. Didn't matter. They had the perp in custody. And with a list of offenses to add to his record of priors, he likely wasn't getting out for a while.

Evan wiped his brow across his sleeve. One threat down. Painter didn't have the kind of loyalty to warrant worrying about who he left on the outside. Michelli on the other hand …

His men had been lying low, loitering in the distance. Why hadn't they made any moves? Whatever game they were playing, it unnerved Evan. Something didn't feel right.

He clenched Anna's keys in his pocket and released them just as quickly. Even with her dad's men staking out the apartment, he had to get back to her.

Once he wrapped things up with Harris and dropped Murphy off at his Jeep, Evan returned to Stonybrook. He tiptoed inside Anna's apartment and knelt beside her. An unconscious rhythm moved her chest as she slept. Peaceful and safe. Unaware of the dangers stalking her as much as the ones stalking his heart.

He lifted a strand of hair from her cheek and left a kiss in its place. As much as he wanted to sleep with her in his arms, he took up post in the armchair facing the door. She still looked to him for safety, despite the ways he'd failed her in the past. Keeping her alive and in his life were the only things that mattered. He wouldn't jeopardize that. Not now.

He craned his head toward the ceiling. *One more shot. Just give me one more shot to keep my promise.* He closed his eyes and released a long breath. *A little grace to make it through tomorrow wouldn't hurt either.*

CHAPTER FIFTEEN

Surrendered

Showered and dressed to hit the studio early, Anna squatted in front of the chair Evan had fallen asleep on. Neck down, arms limp, legs hanging off the side. He really could sleep in any position.

With the slightest nudge to his shoulder, he jerked awake, gun raised.

She teetered backward on her feet. "Whoa, Sarge. Easy."

His sleep-covered gaze ricocheted off all four corners of the room before his arms so much as twitched. "Sorry." He hobbled up to his feet and rotated his creaky neck. Knowing him, he probably hadn't meant to fall asleep at all.

"I hope it's all right I stayed."

If he only knew what she was really thinking. "Of course. The couch would've been a lot more comfortable, though."

Flushing, Evan secured his gun and combed his fingers through his messy hair. His rumpled shirt stayed caught above the holster, revealing a sliver of skin beneath his hip.

Wow. What she'd give to wake up to this sight every day, to relive last night again and again. The way he'd held her in his hotel stairwell, told her he was home. She'd never felt more safe, more cherished. Right then, she'd surrendered her heart. The war was pointless, anyway. It always had been.

Maybe it was dangerous to hope his comfort had been more than just his protective nature. She couldn't prevent the clock from ticking and separating them again, and he belonged in Georgia with his team. But what if he'd be willing to leave his heart here with her? Could she take the risk to find out?

Anna pulled in her bottom lip, words not coming. Maybe if she showed him …

As if reading her thoughts, Evan matched her steps, drawing them closer. His eyes traveled over her damp hair and fitted shirt before darting to the kitchen. "We should—" He cleared the raspy inflection in his voice and tried again. "We should get some coffee."

She didn't need any help staying awake … or hot. Sleeping in the same room with him sparked a live wire down her body all the way to her toes. He had to feel it too, didn't he?

He blinked from her to the bag by the door. "You, uh, going to the studio?"

Or maybe he didn't feel anything.

"Yeah. With all that happened, I missed my contemporary class last night. I can't afford to spend a full day off the floor."

Evan pinched the back of his neck, still looking disoriented. Poor guy was probably exhausted.

Anna tamed her cravings as best she could. They had other things to think about. "Make sure you grab breakfast. You're gonna need energy for today."

He flung a questioning gaze at her.

"My dad's. It could get … interesting."

The corner of his mouth tipped sideways. "We could always escape to the attic."

Their childhood secret hideout. She slid him a playful smile. "Not sure you'd fit up there anymore, Mr. Hulk."

He bounced his pecs but skirted to the kitchen before she could react. "It's probably covered in dust, anyway."

"Time has a way of doing that." Anna swiped a picture frame tucked in the back corner of her bookshelf and joined him by the fridge. "But some things never change."

He brushed his fingers over a black and white selfie he'd taken of them in the attic during the ninth grade. "Two artists ready to take over the world."

She grinned. "We were total dorks, weren't we?"

"Hey, speak for yourself."

"Yeah, right. Sorry to break it to you, but carrying that antique camera of yours around school every day didn't exactly land you in the popular crowd."

"Must be why I could never get a date." He laughed. "Good thing you took pity on me so I didn't have to go to dances alone."

"Please. If you weren't blind, you would've noticed the line of girls pining away for you." Including herself.

"Whatever. Thought you just said I wasn't popular."

"That doesn't mean you weren't attractive." She didn't really just say that out loud, did she? Blood raced for her cheeks.

"What about you?" His husky voice was all but a whisper.

"What *about* me?"

"You telling me you didn't carve a few more names in those trusses after high school?"

Chin lifted, she crossed her arms. "I've never taken anyone else up there."

"Never? Why not?"

"Because …" She twisted her hair over her shoulder. "It's our spot." Fabulous. If there'd been any doubt she was *still* a dork, hanging on to the past like it hadn't changed, she definitely just obliterated it.

Evan tapped the tip of his shoe against the linoleum. "Not even Jack?"

"Calloway?" She tripped over her ex's name. If she could even call him that. "Wait. How do you know about him?"

Evan slipped his hands in his pockets and pulled them right back out like he was scrambling to backpedal. "The guy had a crush on you all through school."

She tried not to snort. "More like he had his eye on someone else."

"What are you talking about?"

"He works for my dad, Evan. It only took two months into the relationship to see he was working an angle. Get in with the daughter, score with the boss." It was the same tired song stuck on repeat. "If guys aren't trying to get in my pants, they're trying to get in my dad's pockets. I'm honestly not sure which is worse."

His fists clenched at his sides. "You're worth more than that. You're—"

"The DA's daughter. I know."

His brow furrowed. "That's not all you are."

She stared at a knot in the cabinet, the one in her throat returning. "But that's all everyone sees."

"Not everyone." The floor creaked under his footsteps.

"C'mon, Evan. You're the only guy not on my dad's payroll who's interested in hanging out with me for me. And even *you* eventually left." She froze, kicking herself for letting those words escape. That wasn't fair. He had his reasons for leaving. Even though it killed her, she had to respect that.

Sunlight from the window flickered shadows across a broken expression a foot in front of her.

"You'll find the right guy, Anna. Someone who deserves you."

I already have. Looking down, she rubbed her arms. If she'd pushed Evan away, how could she possibly expect anyone else to stay with her? Not that it mattered. She'd always want the one person who didn't want her back.

Unless that'd changed.

Last night flooded in again. A mix of hope and fear picked up her pulse. "You don't know how much I wish you were right."

"And you don't know how much I want to prove to you I am." His soft voice followed another slow step to her.

This close, the unrelenting drive calling her to him roared against the insistent one pleading with her to let him go. Faded scents of soap and pure masculinity wrapped around her until she couldn't think straight.

His Adam's apple bobbed and drew her eyes from his mouth to a tendon pulsing on his neck. He didn't move, but she felt his presence all over. What if it could be real?

A breath stood between them.

"Why does it matter?"

"Because." He edged in another inch, swallowed. "Bells, I—"

A stark ring pierced the air. With a look of what Anna would've sworn was relief, Evan reached for his cell. His face creased at the screen. "It's my buddy, Hernandez. He can wait."

"No, take it. Please." She sidestepped around him. "I need to leave, anyway." Before that look on his face reminded her any more of the last time she'd messed up and almost kissed him.

"Give me a minute, and I'll drive you."

At the door, she steeled herself, pasted on a smile, and turned. "Don't worry about it. Go home and get cleaned up. I'll meet you in two hours. I'm taking you somewhere before we go to my dad's."

Evan's brows knit together above a wary stare.

Why did he have to pull off the tousled sexy look so well? Giving in to a grin, Anna ruffled her fingers through the hairs sticking up in three different directions over his forehead. "Relax, Strider. What's a little spontaneity to a Ranger? You should be used to it."

He stood in the entryway, looking lost for what to say.

She inched her scarf up her neck, her gaze sloping in the opposite direction. "Thanks for being a good friend to me." She gave his shoulder a gentle shove. "Now, take some advice from someone returning the favor. Don't stop anywhere till you hit the shower first."

His smile curled around her like her favorite sweatshirt. Warm, soothing. It took all her strength to let go of it and turn to the stairs. "See you in two hours. And don't forget to pack an overnight bag."

"Anna—"

"I'm taking the green line," she said before he could insist on driving her. Somehow, she doubted thugs—professional or not—would try anything at eight in the morning. Like orcs, they moved in the shadows of night. Besides, she had more dangerous things to conquer.

Starting with her heart.

Outside, deep clouds shrouding the sky made it feel later than it was. Keeping her headphones on during the train ride failed to tune out the questions she wanted to ignore. A few strides away from the studio door, her cell rang. Reese. Even worse.

Anna's thumb hovered over the end button but swept to answer instead. "I'll be on time. And yes, I have a date," she said, working a light tone into her tension-plagued voice.

"Hello to you, too."

Anna pinned the phone to her ear with her shoulder while unlocking the door. "Sorry. I'm trying to get a solid rehearsal in before my audition tomorrow." She strode to the locker room to change.

"Okay, but back up a sec. You have a date?"

"Uh, yeah." She shucked off her coat. How much could she say without giving it away?

"And...?" Reese prompted.

"And what?"

"Do I have to pull everything out of you? Spill it."

Anna stared at the mirror as if her reflection would come up with some plausible reply. "He's ... ruggedly handsome, resourceful, and capable of handling himself." And completely off limits.

"And you met him where?"

Memories of building sandcastles with Evan in the sandbox as five-year-olds zipped through her mind. "At the beach, years back." She unwound her scarf. "Art show." Sort of.

"Does Mr. Perfect have a name?"

"Um ..." Anna unzipped her boot.

"You're making this up, aren't you?"

"Not exactly."

"Anna."

Her shoulders drooped. Probably better to tell her ahead of time, anyway. "I'm bringing Evan, all right? And no, he's not dating that girl anymore. And yes, we're just friends."

Reese's silence might as well have been a screaming reprimand. "I can't talk about this right now."

Good. That made two of them.

They both hung up. Anna leaned against the sink, her chest deflating with a sigh.

She dabbed a finger over the tender scab above her lip. Thanks to Evan's ice treatment, it wasn't as bad as it could've been. Maybe no one would notice. Yeah, right. The thought of explaining this to Dad and Reese made her stomach churn.

A weak smile pulled at the edges of her cut. If Mom were here, she'd give Anna props for kneeing that dealer in the groin. She'd probably make some crack about it at the dinner table tonight. The ache of missing her heightened Anna's already-wired emotions.

Shaking it off, she stretched her neck and ambled out of the locker room. She'd deal with that later. All of it. Right now, she needed to leave her heart where it belonged. On the dance floor.

Mr. Jamison's expectant smile met her from across the room. "Ready?"

"I hope so." Her future hinged on it.

Two hours in the studio had worked its therapeutic magic. By the third run through her audition piece, all aggravation dissipated behind the peace of being at home on the floor. The music and choreo, the familiar stretch of her muscles, the lapse in time when everything else faded ... Too bad the rest of life couldn't be as uncomplicated.

All bundled up, Anna backed open the front door and stopped short. As if the icy air didn't strip enough breath out of her, a view of Evan—cleaned up and unfairly gorgeous with an arm lounged against the hood of his car—finished her off.

In dark jeans and a hunter green button-up under his leather jacket, he smiled at her lingering stare. Heat tinged her ears. Thankfully, her hat covered them. And at least she could pass off the flush in her cheeks as a reaction to the cold, right?

His unabashed grin widened.

Okay, maybe not. She'd be lucky to remember how to speak, forget pulling anything else off. Seeing him this casual shouldn't make her heart stagger worse than seeing him in a tux had.

She swallowed the lump that had no business terrorizing her throat. "I thought I said I'd meet up with you later."

He pushed off the car. "It *is* later."

The breeze rustled damp bits of brown hair over his forehead and swirled hints of his recent shower around her. And she was supposed to hold herself together around him ... right.

Somehow managing coordination, she held out a hand. "What?"

"Keys." Anna motioned for him to surrender them. "I'm driving."

"Should I be scared?" He retrieved his keys from his jeans pocket.

She swiped them, circled the bumper, and let a mischievous grin suffice as an answer.

Evan chuckled while getting in the passenger side. "Okay, but go easy on her."

"Her?" Anna started the engine. "Don't tell me you named your car."

He flaunted a sworn-to-secrecy expression.

"Mm hmm." After a quick check in the mirrors, she pulled away from the curb. "Next, you'll tell me it's classified, right?"

An awkward silence ensued. He drew back his seat belt and resituated positions.

She hadn't meant to make him uncomfortable. "I'm just teasing, Evan. I understand your job prevents you from telling me things. We both need to let it go. It's the way things are."

With his elbow on the door panel, he kept his gaze out the passenger window and his voice a shell of its normal tone. "That doesn't mean it's easy."

Anna wrestled to shake off the uninvited tension. They should be celebrating the things they were grateful for today, not dwelling on the ones neither of them could change. They'd be apart again soon. It was time to stop messing this up.

She smiled across the console. "How about we retire from adulthood for the day? Pretend we're kids again, back when things were simple. Just friendship, family, living in the present."

He nodded away a hint of sadness shading his eyes. "Copy that."

Hopefully, he'd still agree once he found out where they were going first.

"You saved room for dinner, right? 'Cause you know Ms. Riza's gonna go all out with her spread. Which reminds me." She feigned an apologetic frown. "No recyclable dinnerware tonight. You gonna be able to handle that?"

"Think I'll manage." His laugh stretched into a yawn. Visible exhaustion pulled him deeper into the seat.

He never did tell her how late he stayed up last night. She needed to convince him to lower his guard long enough to get sufficient rest. At least she had the turkey conspiring with her today. As long as Reese actually let him in the house.

Several miles down the road, Anna sent a glance his way while turning into the hospital parking lot. Eyes closed, he didn't even startle when they rolled over a speed bump. A silent laugh shook her shoulders. The man could fall asleep at the drop of a hat in any location. Pure talent.

Parked in the garage, she cut the engine but left the heat on. They could spare a few more minutes. Honestly, he'd probably need all the strength he could get. Had she made the right decision bringing him here?

Questions circled as she twisted the strings hanging from her hat and let them unwind. Grabbing on to conviction, she leveled her shoulders. No, he needed to be here. She was sure of it. Getting him to believe it, on the other hand, was another story.

True to his power-nap-taking self, Evan stirred ten minutes later. He wiped a hand over his eyes, yawned, and stopped mid-stretch when his gaze landed on her. "Sorry. Long night."

"I can imagine."

He looked around and froze again. "The hospital?"

"There's someone waiting to see you."

"Anna …"

Trying to thwart an argument, she met him on the opposite side of the car. He leaned against the panel with his head angled in resistance, but she wasn't backing down. She curled her fingers under his. "Trust me."

He wasn't alone in this. Even if he didn't reciprocate her feelings, she wouldn't stop being the friend he'd been for her.

His warm breath clashed with the frigid air until soldier-mode kicked in. He nodded, pushed off the car, and approached the entrance.

Inside, a gust of heat fanned an antiseptic-scented greeting over them. Evan's confident strides led them to the Cardiothoracic Unit, where they stopped to wash their hands and pick up masks and gloves.

His feet slowed in front of his mom's door, as though settling into a worn spot they were forbidden to pass. How many times had he come and stood on the fringe, trapped in unwarranted guilt?

"She looks much better than she did in ICU." He stared ahead. "Seeing her after the surgery... The breathing tube... I couldn't ..." A slow exhale veered his gaze to the floor.

"She loves you, Evan."

He balled his fingers at his sides. "But my dad—"

"Is gone." Anna rested a hand to his lower back and dipped her head forward. "Don't lose any more time with someone who's still here."

A deep breath freed his feet and pushed him across the threshold.

The blood pressure cuff around his mom's arm compressed while heartbeats pulsed on the echogram. Mrs. O'Riley's eyes fluttered open as he approached her bed. One look at her son, and a wave of emotion overrode her expression.

Anna couldn't see Evan's face with his back toward her, but the slight tremor in his shoulders said enough.

Mrs. O'Riley's mouth quivered. "Evan?"

Head down, he closed her hand in both of his. "I'm so sorry ..."

Without the slightest hesitancy, his mom tugged him close. And in the arms of complete acceptance, the undaunted soldier he'd become gave way to the tender boy Anna had never once stopped loving.

Mrs. O'Riley's frail hands rubbed circles over his back. "You're here," she whispered. "That's all that matters."

Monitors continued to beep. Foot traffic carried on outside the room. But the image of a mother's love for her child superseded everything surrounding Anna. A stinging sensation constricted her throat and backed her out of the doorway. She lowered her mask beneath her chin, needing to breathe.

Maneuvering through the halls, she fought a riptide of memories with her own mom. Her laughter, her encouragement. Every rehearsal, every recital. She'd always been there, always rooted for her. Until that night. When a single moment branded the rest of Anna's life with the scar of loss.

She jogged harder, faster—afraid to let go of the memories but equally as afraid of holding on to them. Along a quiet hall, Anna braced a palm against a vending machine and waited for the waves to subside. *Don't fall apart. Not here. Not today.*

Something dark stirred in the periphery. A glance down the hall caught a sliver of a black trench coat shrinking behind the corner. Heat pricked the back of her neck, the same panic from last night closing in. Was someone watching her?

Goose bumps multiplied down her arms. She spun in the opposite direction and ran until her momentum drove her smack into someone hastening in the other direction.

"Whoa." Evan steadied her.

The sound of his voice collided with her yearning for safety. Anna clutched his arms without thinking.

"Hey, you okay?"

What was she doing? She had to stop letting him see how afraid she was. "Yeah." She stepped back and dragged a finger under her eyes. "I was just, um, thinking of my mom. It's nothing."

He lifted her chin. "You look scared. What happened?"

Why did he have to be so good at reading her? She peered behind her. "I thought I saw something."

"Saw what?" Concerned eyes searched hers.

"It looked like someone was ..."

Footsteps echoed from down the hall. They both glanced up as a doctor with a charcoal coat draped over his arm rounded the bend.

Anna's pent-up breath oozed out in a silent scolding. No way she was going to let that creep from last night hold the fear of paranoia over her. She wouldn't live her life like this, especially with Evan watching.

"Anna." He angled in front of her. "If you're worried about Painter, he's not coming near you again. Harris locked him up last night."

"They found him?"

Evan ran a knuckle above his brow and scuffed his Skecher over the tiles. "Yeah."

A swell of relief quaked through her. "Sorry. I shouldn't let stuff freak me out so easily. Everything going on has me overly emotional right now."

His gaze hardened. "Don't ever apologize for listening to your gut."

But what if he knew her gut was telling her to run right now—away from him, from her heart? Or worse, that it was begging her to stay—to give in and show him how she really felt?

The shuffle of footfalls behind her pulled Evan's gaze past her shoulder. A pair of nurses glided by, carrying charts in their hands. "Happy Thanksgiving," one said with a warm smile.

Thanksgiving at Dad's was the last thing Anna wanted to deal with right now. No wonder she was such a mess today. Holidays without Mom always hit her the hardest. If she couldn't get a hold on her emotions, maybe it'd be better if Evan didn't go.

She untied her mask from behind her neck, folded it in her hands, and grappled for some semblance of a composed tone. "You don't have to come with me today. You could stay here. Spend time with your mom."

His jaw rippled. "She needs to rest. I'm coming back tomorrow."

Anna's inner turmoil succumbed to a smile. "I'm glad." It'd be good for him and his mom both. The short time he'd shared with her a moment ago had opened the doors for healing, but they still had a long road ahead.

Shoulders slack, Evan tinkered with his keys a moment before meeting her eyes again. "If you're not comfortable with bringing me today, at least let me drive you."

What? No, it was the other way around. "Of course I'm comfortable. You're like our surrogate brother. I just didn't want you to think I was pressuring you into making it a date or something." Why didn't she know when to stop talking?

A tendon on his neck flexed, but he didn't retract his stoic gaze. "I know where we stand, Anna. I always have."

And now, that made two of them.

CHAPTER SIXTEEN

Border

After picking up Megan and making the thirty-minute drive north to the Gold Coast, they pulled into one of Dad's private parking spots beside his black town cars.

Two streets away from the lake, the home Anna essentially ran away from stared back at her through the window. Muddled memories rained down with the wintery mix dotting the windshield. She grabbed the door handle and inhaled slowly. *Please help me get through this night.*

"Hey." Evan reached for her. "Before we go in, I want to say thanks."

She twisted in her seat. "For what?"

He dragged his pointer finger along the bottom of the steering wheel. "For pushing me to see my mom."

"You're welcome. And I didn't push. I nudged," she corrected.

His raised brow begged to differ. He nodded at the house. "Well, just so you know, I'm here to do the same."

But he wouldn't always be. He'd be leaving soon ... unless she gave him a reason to stay. After last night, she thought she had. Thought he might even want to share a life with her. But maybe it wasn't enough. Would being back in this house together change things?

Something beneath his dauntless exterior held her a moment longer. He hadn't said more than a few words on the drive here. What was going through his mind?

He broke eye contact and diverted his attention to the backseat. "Ready, kiddo?"

"For pumpkin pie?" Megan opened her door. "Oh, yeah."

Thank goodness for levity. Anna followed suit and climbed out. All three jogged through the sleet to the front porch, where one of Dad's long-time guards stood post.

He moved his umbrella over them and dipped his head while opening the door. "Miss Madison. Mr. O'Riley."

"Hi, John." Anna stretched on her tiptoes to peck him on the cheek. Unlike most of the Secret Service wannabes Dad had on his detail, John had an actual personality. He'd been in her life long enough to be an adopted uncle. "You joining us for dinner?"

"Wouldn't miss it. My shift ends in ten." He stopped short on closing the door when his gaze fell on Megan. Arching a bushy eyebrow toward Anna, he lowered his umbrella and stepped out of the slushy rain. "And who do we have here?"

Megan bunched her lips to the side, tilted her head to her shoulder, and shrugged.

Anna rubbed Megan's arms from behind. "Mr. John, I'd like to introduce you to Megan Allison."

"A soon-to-be famous ballerina," Evan added.

A gigantic smile lifted Megan's rosy cheeks.

"Is that right?" John rubbed his chin. "Well, now, I bet you'd enjoy watching some of Miss Madison's old dance recital videos. "

Her high-speed nod sent her red braids bobbing against her shoulders.

He winked at Anna. "I think I can arrange that."

"Careful, mister," Anna teased. "I'm pretty sure there are some clips of you attending my tea parties, too. I seem to remember there being aprons and dollies involved."

A hearty laugh trailed him outside. "Well played."

With the door closed, the savory aromas of Ms. Riza's cooking mingled with the scent of the wood-burning fireplace and a hint of fresh pine.

A tinge of anticipation butted into Anna's apprehension and blindsided her with a wave of nostalgia. Until Reese's voice bubbled from down the hall, along with the *pop* of a champagne bottle opening.

No backing out now.

Evan offered a reassuring nod. If anything ever flustered him, he did a solid job at hiding it.

He helped her with her coat, did the same for Megan, and finally shed his own. Anna stashed their bags in the corner beside the coat rack and straightened her spine.

A gentle, yet confident hand to the small of her back led her forward into the dining room. As soon as they crossed the open doorway, Evan slid his arm to his side, taking his warmth and security with him. After that short amount of contact, the loss shouldn't have left such noticeable emptiness in its wake. She focused on the dining room instead.

In the center, a flicker of candlelight cascaded over the elaborate place settings garnishing the oblong mahogany table. Ms. Riza's touch of elegance, no doubt. Dad had done well hiring such a talented cook. How he'd managed to keep her on staff after Anna and Reese moved out, she had no idea.

Megan tightened her grasp around Anna's fingers when Reese and her husband, Mark, turned in their direction. Dressed to the hilt, they could've been extracted from a holiday-themed magazine. The pregnancy glow only added to the lovebird aura they always carried.

Anna tugged off her hat and sent a peace offering smile in Reese's direction. "Told you I'd be on time."

Reese set a water glass on the table. "Early, actually."

"And with such a handsome date." Ms. Riza sailed around the corner from the kitchen with a scalloped apron on and a red dish towel draped over one arm. "Look at you. All grown up." She kissed both of Evan's cheeks. "Did I hear right that you're a soldier now?"

"Yes, ma'am." The slightest shade of pink dusted his cheeks.

"A Ranger," Anna clarified with a pointed glare at Reese's stone cold stare.

Looking impressed, Ms. Riza patted his bicep. "I bet you have a few stories to share."

"I bet he does," Reese mumbled. Her wary gaze zeroed in on the cut above Anna's lip and then on to Evan's. The smallest grin tipped her mouth sideways. "Don't tell me you two head-butted each other trying to kiss."

Anna's jaw came unhinged.

"What?" Chuckling, Reese hurled Anna's gaping stare back at her. "The guy never dated in high school. Maybe he never learned how to be smooth. Just sayin'."

Oh my word. They weren't actually having this conversation. In. Front. Of. Everyone. Had the girl ever heard of a filter? Jeez.

The flush already coating Evan's cheeks streaked down his neck.

Anna twisted her hat into a tight spiral. She was two seconds away from dragging Reese out of the room by her elegant updo.

Mark defused the electricity with a mollifying cough while strolling toward Evan. "Mark Falloway, Reese's husband."

Evan clasped his hand. "Evan O'Riley. A family friend. Well…" He zipped a glance at Reese. "To most of them, anyway."

"Be nice," Anna mouthed to her sister.

A dramatic sigh lowered Reese's defenses. "Fine." She waddled over and rested her arms across her baby bump. "I'll cut you some slack since it's Thanksgiving. But tomorrow…" She wagged a finger at him. "You and me, we're having a little heart-to-heart. This house isn't as big as it looks, so don't think you can hide from me."

Evan scratched his smooth jawline, smile quirking. "Wouldn't dream of it."

"Okay, then. Now, come here, Pipsqueak." Reese pulled him into a hug. "You might be twice my size now, but I'm still older."

"And you still kinda scare me." Evan laughed.

"I think that goes for all of us." Dad winked at Reese while striding in behind them. He curled an arm around Anna's back and squeezed her to his side. "It's good to have you home, sweetheart." He kissed the top of her head.

Anna leaned into him, longing for his embrace more than she realized.

Dad cleared his throat and strode behind the chair at the head of the table.

Everyone's gazes banked around the walls like pool balls. On instinct, Anna inched closer to Evan. Not that he couldn't hold his own. Shoulders back, he stood at attention as though ready to salute a general, but Dad barely acknowledged him. The silence plunged past awkward.

"Dad," she squeaked out. She swallowed the knot barricading her voice and tried again. "Dad, you remember Evan."

Toying with the top of the chair in front of him, Dad swerved an uncertain glance between the two of them. "Of course." He stretched out a hand. "Evan."

"Sir." Evan returned the firm handshake.

"Good to see you again."

"Likewise."

Mom's Irish Setter hobbled in on arthritic legs with his impossible-to-turn-down brown eyes scouting the tabletop.

"Aye, Hunter." Ms. Riza fanned her dish towel at him. "Shoo. Out of the dining room. Go on."

Megan released Anna's hand and scurried over to him. On her knees, she rubbed Hunter's face, red hair going everywhere. High-pitched laughs trailed each sloppy kiss to her cheek.

Evan leaned close enough to Anna to whisper. "Looks like she just found a new best friend."

One of the many childhood experiences she deserved to have. Warmth from seeing Megan so full of life and joy spread across Anna's chest and sprawled into a smile.

Ms. Riza didn't seem to miss it. "I'll keep an eye on her." She patted Anna's arm. "There are hors d'oeuvres in the kitchen. The main course will be served after the tree trimming," she called behind her while prodding Hunter and Megan into the living room.

Mark tipped back the last of his drink and jutted his empty glass at the kitchen. "Don't have to tell me twice." He strolled around the table.

Reese arched a brow at her husband and rubbed a hand over the silky fabric covering her belly. "Seriously, guys, you better get in there before it's all gone. And be sure to have some champagne for me." She snagged her water goblet as she turned. "Just don't tell me how good it is."

Alone with Evan and Dad, Anna dawdled in front of the table. A blast of heat from the ceiling vent stirred another round of awkward silence throughout the room.

Did seeing Evan catch him off guard, or did this have to do with the last argument she'd had with him? Either way, couldn't he drop it, just for the night?

She folded her hat back and forth enough times to perforate it down the middle, trying to think of something to say.

Dad pressed off the back of the chair he'd been leaning against and gestured toward the kitchen. "Please. Help yourself. I need to take care of a couple things in the office first."

Evan's stance relaxed once the *whoosh* of Dad passing by settled.

"Sorry."

He stared at the shirt cuff he was unbuttoning. "For what?"

"For that." Anna waved between the two doorways her family had just exited.

His lips thinned as he rolled up his sleeve. "It's nothing less than expected."

Did he really think that? "Evan—"

"Shall we?" He splayed a hand toward the kitchen.

The decorative mirror on the wall caught a flicker of her reflection. She choked back a grimace. "Um, actually, you go ahead. I'm gonna run upstairs for a sec."

He studied her, always reading between the lines.

"It's nothing. I just want to change before we eat." *And tame this massive rat's nest of hair.* She shouldn't have worn a hat today.

A *clank* from the kitchen drew Evan around.

Taking advantage of the distraction, Anna headed into the entryway, swiped her bag from the floor, and made a beeline upstairs.

At the top of the steps, she slowed around the banister. The attic door's cord swung in front of the vent. Memories trickled over her until a dim light fanned across the carpet from Mom's study.

A pull Anna could neither explain nor ignore drew her to the door that'd stayed closed for most of the last five years.

Inside, the subtle fragrance of vanilla scented candles and the faintest smell of acrylic paint triggered such specific memories, she could almost feel the paintbrush in her hand.

Dad left the room exactly as Mom had it—easel propped open in the corner beside a bay window, a slew of scrapbooks lining a bookshelf above a daybed, Anna's old dance uniforms sprawled across a sewing table on the left. All of it here.

Except for Mom.

Anna traced her fingertips over an unfinished project lying in the glow of the streetlight.

Unfinished. No notice. No preparation. No chance to say good-bye. Life had stopped that night. And somehow, Anna's world was supposed to carry on as if it hadn't.

Her knees found the soft berber carpet. The same burning sensation from the hospital seared around the hole in her chest.

A week before she died, Mom made Anna promise to pursue her dreams without losing herself. Almost as if she'd worried she wouldn't be around to help. "I'm trying, Mom. I swear. Don't give up on me yet. Please."

Metal jingled behind her right before Hunter's wet nose nudged its way to Anna's cheek. She held him down by the collar. As if there were any point. He slobbered her face, anyway.

"Okay, boy. I missed you, too." A soft chuckle chased away the tears. Anna sat back on her heels and ran her hands down his floppy ears. "We gotta be strong, though, buddy." For Mom and Evan both.

Hunter tilted his head, tongue out. He didn't need a voice to let her know he understood. His round brown eyes held enough memory of Mom to make Anna's heart weep all over again.

"No sadness tonight. Deal?"

He rose when she did and wagged his tail expectantly.

Smiling, she patted her leg. "C'mon."

Hunter moseyed into her old bedroom, probably to escape under her bed away from all the activity rumbling downstairs. Hard to blame him.

In the bathroom, Anna changed into her newest pair of dark jeans and a cozy scoop neck sweater. Mom always told her red brought out the color in her cheeks. As if she ever needed much help with that.

A quick touch-up to her makeup made a world of difference. Her hair, however, might be beyond rescuing. If she could patent some way to tame static electricity during the winter months, she'd never have to worry about another unpaid bill.

She rummaged through her bag for the bottle of Miracle Leave-In Mist that Reese had given her for her birthday. "You better live up to your name, Wonder Bottle. That's all I gotta say." She spritzed it over her hair and worked it in with her fingers.

After snapping on a pair of dangling earrings for a finishing touch, she smoothed out her sweater. At least she looked presentable. Maybe even attractive? She hoped. This might be one of her last nights with Evan. Time was running out.

Leaving her bag for later, she ambled down the steps and into the kitchen in her socks.

Beside the fridge, Evan looked up and stared, wide-eyed. The Coke he was pouring ran over the top of his cup. He held it away from him, huffing something under his breath.

Anna scurried over to grab a rag from the sink.

"I've got it." He tore off a paper towel and bent down at the same time she did.

Another open gaze lingered over her features and fanned a tingle of self-awareness through her. She curved her hair over her shoulder. "What?"

Mopping the towel around in mindless circles, he blinked but didn't look away.

"Is my hair still a mess? I tried to fix it. And I probably should've worn a dress like Reese, but—"

"Bells." Evan set a solid hand on hers and lifted his gaze so slowly, her heart raced in his pause. "You're beautiful."

Enough to see her as more than a friend?

"Just like her mama." Ms. Riza hurried around the corner on a path to the stove. She flipped on the light and peered inside at a dish of what looked like sweet potatoes. "I always knew one day you'd figure that out, Mr. Evan."

Apparently, the entire household was short on filters.

Heat soared up Anna's face, clear past her hairline.

Ms. Riza sent a completely unassuming glance from them to the spill on the floor and waved them off. "Go have fun. I'll take care of this."

"No, it's my mess." Evan tossed the sopping paper towel into the trash and rose to grab another one.

"Out of my kitchen. Both of ya." Ms. Riza marched them backward to the edge of the tiles, her smile betraying her firm expression.

"Yes, ma'am." Palms raised, Evan tossed Anna a knowing glance.

He didn't have to prod. She knew better than to get Ms. Riza on a roll.

Down the hall, Anna leaned a shoulder against the doorway leading into the living room. Reese sat beside Mark on the ottoman in front of at least five tubs of Christmas decorations she'd already started sorting through. Dad lounged in his Lazy Boy with a mug of coffee while Megan hustled Mr. John in a game of pool.

"Aww." Reese lifted up a handful of white snowflake decorations Mom crocheted back when they were around Megan's age. "I'd almost forgotten about these."

Evan and Anna joined her in front of the massive pine Dad had set up in the corner of the room. The biggest and best—Dad's style all the way. At least they got to temper it with Mom's softer influence.

"I can't believe you still have this." Evan lifted a round piece of wood they'd cut from the base of one of their Christmas trees ages ago. He'd sanded and stained it, so proud of the little art project Mom had prompted. Clutching his strong hands around it now, he ironed out another indecipherable look from his face.

"You made it for me. Of course I still have it." Anna glided a thumb over the carving. *A. M. + E. O. Friends Always.* It was as true now as it had been when they were thirteen. He was a part of this family. A part of her.

No matter what happened after tonight, she'd always have that. But she couldn't stop herself from hoping for more.

CHAPTER SEVENTEEN

Simmer

Other than the fire's slow simmer and the faint background noise coming from the TV, the Madison house had fallen still.

Evan and Anna should be asleep like everyone else. Instead, they kept riding the coattails of the past, staying up late like they used to as teens. It wasn't fair to either of them to pretend things were the way they'd been then. But right now, Evan wasn't ready to let the moment go.

He could hardly look away from her. Propped up against the base of the couch, Anna stared into the flames. The soft glimmer trickling over her toned muscles tantalized him the same way everything about her had tonight.

Evan groaned inside. Her vulnerability with him these last forty-eight hours had made things hard enough. But being back here together topped it off. His willpower hung by a thread. Craning his head back, he closed his eyes.

She'd said herself she was overly emotional right now. He had to be careful.

"Don't tell me you're getting sleepy, Gramps." Anna nudged her shoulder into his and hiked up a brow.

He knew that look. Had seen it dozens of times. Another couple of minutes, and she'd get her second wind for the night. "Maybe you shouldn't have taken that long nap after dinner."

"C'mon, it's Thanksgiving." She squinted at the clock on the wall. "Okay, technically, it's already Black Friday, but still. We should be having fun."

It'd be a lot easier if fun didn't include torturing himself.

Anna crawled over to the brick fireplace, added two more logs, and yanked her hand back. "Ow."

"You burn yourself?"

"No." She lowered her finger from her mouth. "Splinter."

He reached into his pocket. "Let me get it."

"A Swiss Army knife?" A lopsided grin overrode her cheek. "Don't you think that's a little cliché, Sarge?"

Cupping a hand under hers, he dished her expression right back. "Thought I was supposed to be the one with all the jokes."

"Guess you must be rubbing off on me."

His brow slanted. "Can I have that in writing, ma'am?"

"Shut up."

He opened the knife, and she recoiled like he was about to drive the blade through her palm.

"You kidding me? I've seen your toes after some of your pointe classes. You push your body through levels of pain that'd make grown men cry. And you're freaking out over a tiny splinter? Give me that hand."

She held in a breath until she must've given up trying to think of a comeback. The air seeped out of her tight lips. "Not all of us are big, tough Rangers, you know."

"You're tougher than you think." He held her still to guide the tiny shard of wood out of her skin. A quick upward glance met an open appraisal fixed on his face. "What?"

Without releasing his eyes, Anna brought her thumb to his cheek and gently traced the indent left from a close combat fight. "New scar." A note of sadness tainted her words. "It's too bad life can't be like our make-believe games in the attic. Always the heroes. Never walking away with a mark from the enemy."

The pensive look on her face sawed through overlapping layers of yearning and honor. Evan lowered her hand from his cheek and dug inside for a teasing tone. "I thought battle scars were supposed to be sexy."

"Only if you know how to rock 'em." She rolled up her T-shirt sleeve and pointed to a chickenpox scar she'd earned in the fourth grade. "See this? It was a close call, but I made it out alive." She winked. "Sexy, right?"

As if her infectious laughter weren't enough on its own. "Very."

A flicker of doubt shadowed her expression.

Hunter trotted into the room before Evan could assure her. Beside the Christmas tree, he sniffed the air and scratched his ear with his hind leg, red fur floating all around.

Evan stifled a laugh, picturing Ms. Riza going crazy earlier making sure no dog hair ended up in any of the dishes. She should be thankful she didn't have a cat to keep off the table. That reminded him. "Is Mrs. Santos watching Bailey?"

Anna shook her head. "I saw her light on this morning, but I never got a hold of her. It's just one night, though. I left out extra food. Bailey will be fine."

Hunter lolled beside Anna with a heavy sigh.

Staring into the fire again, she ran the dog's wavy ears between her fingers while rubbing one socked foot over the other.

Evan couldn't help grinning. Right in front of the flames, those suckers were still probably freezing cold. At some point, the girl seriously needed to get her circulation checked.

His inward laugh tapered at the sight of her sobered expression.

"I hope Megan had a good time tonight."

That's what had her lost in thought? "It's on her top ten list."

"You think?"

"I know." Evan leaned an elbow against the brick ledge beside them. "She told me herself when I tucked her into bed earlier."

The contented glow beaming over Anna's face dissolved as fast as it came. "I hate thinking of her mom being alone on a holiday. She looked bad when we stopped by, didn't she?"

"Going through withdrawals can get pretty ugly. It's probably a good thing Megan's not there to see it."

"Withdrawals?" The pieces visibly fused together. Anna face-palmed herself. "I can't believe I didn't think of that." She scrambled over to the couch for her cell. "We shouldn't have left her. I mean, what if she needs to go to the hospital. Or—"

"Relax, I already called Harris." Evan scooted toward her on his knees. "He checked on Heather earlier and has someone scheduled to stop by in the morning."

Anna gawked at him.

"Why are you looking at me like you're shocked?"

"I thought I was supposed to be the one with all the sympathy." The corner of her mouth hiked to the left the way his had when he'd said he was supposed to be the one with all the jokes.

He pressed his tongue against his cheek. "Guess you must be rubbing off on me."

She shook her head. "You're something else, Evan O'Riley. You know that?"

"Just be sure to tell Reese I'm smoother than she thinks."

"Sure." Anna rolled her eyes. "Right after I tell Casanova you stole his nickname."

He chucked a throw pillow at her.

A moment of being caught off guard morphed into a trained reflex. She swiped the other pillow from the couch. "Oh, you don't want to start this, Sarge."

Not with *that* look on her face. He knew where this was going. He clambered to his feet and backed up, about to turn.

"Uh-huh. You better run."

A two-second head start didn't help.

In the kitchen, Anna cornered him beside the fridge and clobbered him with both pillows at once. He dodged a second swing, scooped her up at the waist, and reversed their positions. He pinned the pillows to the cabinets with his knees.

Relenting, she released them and squirmed to break free. Not happening. He gripped the counter on either side of her. "Where ya going?"

Laughter bubbled up. "Don't think you won." She braced her palms against his stomach, and her sassy grin turned to something else. Something that drilled into the center of his chest and latched on to the nerves spiraling in every direction of his body.

Hunter's nails clinked on the hardwood floor and kick-started Evan's breathing again. He let go of the counter, releasing the pillows and a situation he shouldn't have put them in.

Anna studied his face as though trying to interpret his reaction.

But the second he stepped back, she hustled toward the opposite end of the counter. "You know what we need?" she said way too quickly. "Life cereal."

What? Where'd that come from?

She withdrew two bowls from a top cabinet and stalled in front of the counter with her back toward him. "Like old times."

Back when he didn't try to cross any lines.

He warded off the effect she left on his voice. "We're not twelve anymore. I doubt Ms. Riza keeps kids' cereal on hand."

"She knew we were coming. She bought some. Trust me." Rifling through a bottom cabinet, Anna gave a satisfied grunt. "See?" She swiveled around with the white box in hand.

Evan nodded in concession while she fixed two bowls.

Crunching noises infiltrated the thick silence he'd inadvertently created between them. She ran her toe along the grout between the tiles, looking lost in thought.

He should say good night right now, walk away. Instead, he soaked in the sight of her under the warm light above the oven. Hair wound up in a mess on top of her head, cropped pajama pants exposing her dainty ankles, the tip of her upside-down spoon resting against her bottom lip.

Lying to everyone—including himself—didn't change the fact he was more in love with her now than ever.

With a slow exhale, he released the tension knotting his muscles. It didn't matter. Regardless of what happened after this week, he'd always share her past. That was enough.

Anna scrunched her brows together while munching on the cereal, probably disappointed it wasn't stale.

His chuckle elicited an upward glance. She lowered the spoon. "What's so funny?"

"This." He held out his bowl. "You. Us, standing in here like teenagers. All you're missing is that cherry Chap Stick you always carried with you."

She unburied a teal tube from the tiny pocket in her pants. "At least I've upgraded to Blistex." She set her bowl in the sink and rolled the balm over her lips. "Guess I haven't changed much."

"You say that like it's a bad thing." Evan placed his dish beside hers.

"You can't live in the past."

He swallowed the sting. "That doesn't mean you have to let it go."

She wiped strands of dog hair off her shirt. "What do you do when you have no choice?"

The ache in her eyes seized him as much as it had the day of her mom's funeral when she'd turned to him for affection.

"Then you build a future worthy of its memory." Evan pulled out the folded-up flyer he'd been carrying in his pocket.

"What's this?"

"Something I came across the other day."

The audition information for Hubbard Street Dance Chicago unfolded as Anna smoothed out the creases on the page.

"I know you're auditioning for Chicago Dance Crash, but Hubbard Street was your first choice once. I just want to make sure you're not settling now."

"Settling would mean I have an option." Shoulders crestfallen, she returned the flyer. "This is sweet, but I can't."

"Why not?"

"Because." She strode into the living room.

He caught up and turned her around. "Because why?"

"Because I'm not interested in reliving my mistakes."

"That audition was five years ago."

Anna sank onto the couch. "Not everything changes with time, Evan."

The dejection in her voice weighed him down beside her. He raised her chin in search of the right thing to say. But instead of words, the pulse he'd failed to keep under control all day took over again.

His gaze glided down the slender slope of her neck and back to her mouth. If he slipped his fingers into her hair, he wouldn't be able to turn back.

Her green eyes found his, wide and luring. The same transparency she'd shown last night and this morning invited him in. One breath closer, and there'd be no space left.

She traced her fingertips over his hand and brought his palm to her lips.

His muscles pulled taut against her softness, his skin reflecting the heat radiating off hers. "*Anna.*"

But instead of heeding his warning, she prodded him closer. Past the limits of his willpower. Cupping both her cheeks, Evan swallowed hard—wanting this to be real but even more afraid it was.

"*You think she cares for you? Wait till she finds out what you've cost her.*"

Dad's voice joined flashes of holding Anna in his arms while she came undone after her mom's burial. He searched her eyes. Same as then, the emotional havoc going on drew her to him for comfort, confused her into thinking she wanted more than friendship. But even if she truly did this time, it'd end the minute she knew what his failure had cost her.

He bolted up, raked his hands through his hair, and ordered his erratic breathing to slow. This was exactly why he didn't go through with being her full-time security detail from the beginning. His role in her life mandated boundaries, self-control. Her safety was too important to compromise. He couldn't keep messing things up.

A flicker of disappointment moved through her eyes and gutted him down the middle.

"Bells, I'm sorry."

Alone on the couch, she closed her arms across her torso and wouldn't look at him.

"It's not—"

"What you want." She clasped her elbows. "Yeah, I got that part. Please don't make it any worse."

His heart sank past the floor. She had no idea how much he hated letting her think he didn't want her. How much he wished the feelings she had right now were real. And that love was enough to right his mistakes. But he knew better.

He breathed out slowly. "There's no point wishing for something you can't have."

She bristled. "Thanks for clearing that up."

"That's not what I meant. I—" The rumble of tires brought a car outside into view. An Escalade. Evan swung a glance from the window to Anna. "Down. Now." Without pause, he leveled her on the couch and braced for gunfire.

Footsteps clamored outside, but no gunshots came. His body, still taut from the reaction Anna spurred, relaxed over hers until he met her gaze. Instead of open eyes inviting him in, shielded ones warned him away. Heartbeats pounded against him with frustration instead of passion.

The front door opened. One of her dad's men rounded the doorway, gun and flashlight drawn. Williams.

Evan rolled off Anna onto the floor and shot up to attention beside the couch.

Shifting his focus to Anna, Williams brought his wrist mic to his mouth. "Radiance secured."

The resentment of hearing her code name hollowed her eyes even more. Anna huddled her knees to her chest and drew herself deeper into the shell she'd erected because of Evan's lack of control.

He fisted his hands. If there weren't a possible threat outside right now, he'd clock himself in the face for hurting her again. But doing his job was the best way he knew to love her.

Evan hustled to follow Williams out front and scanned the area. No sign of anyone around. No stirring. Nothing but the steady lap of waves from the lake.

"How'd that car get past you?"

Williams didn't acknowledge the hint of accusation Evan had no business slinging. "Whoever it was knows our schedule. Must've slipped in while we were changing shifts. I never even saw them until they skidded around the corner."

"Did you get a visual?"

"Negative."

Evan faced the wind, shoved his hair off his forehead, and waited for the chill to rid him of anything but focus. Michelli's guys had been lurking as they'd been doing this whole week. But this time, they'd made it known they were here for a reason. Why? A warning? A message?

Whatever their intention, it was another confirmation Evan belonged out here instead of on the couch. As much as it killed him to know Anna wouldn't understand, it was the way things had to be. For both their sakes.

CHAPTER EIGHTEEN

Splinter

The *ding* of an incoming text jolted Anna awake. Rolling away from the crease in the couch, she blinked back the morning sunlight. Glimpses of Dad's living room filtered through the web of hair across her face and killed any possibility of yesterday being a bad dream.

She padded around the cushion for the phone, thinking it was hers. But when she swiped the screen, someone named Hernandez popped up. From the looks of it, he'd sent several unanswered texts pushing Evan for an answer about reenlisting.

"I haven't decided that yet."

Because he thought she needed him here?

Evan sat on the floor against the couch with his chin to his chest, still watching out for her even dead asleep. Anna couldn't resent him for that. He'd told her he knew where they stood. She was the one who put him in a position to confuse those feelings.

Of course he'd want to comfort her. He didn't know how to do anything else. If she didn't start proving she could handle being on her own, the compulsion to protect her could end up driving him to give up his career in the army.

Guilt poured in. His guys counted on him. How could he say no to them? And how could she ever begin to ask him to choose?

She couldn't. End of story.

Evan's happiness was too important to her. He'd return to Georgia, and she'd go back to pressing on as she had the last five years. Except this time, she'd find the courage to be strong and say good-bye.

She eased off the couch as soundlessly as possible.

From the doorway, Anna looked him over again and rubbed the knick on her finger. He'd removed the splinter but not his words. *"There's no point wishing for things you can't have."* That truth had impaled her the night she lost Mom, burrowed deeper the day Evan left, and would stay lodged inside her all her life. She simply had to accept it and move on.

She jogged upstairs to the bathroom and stood in the shower until thick steam fogged every thought and emotion. Her focus didn't need to be anywhere but on her audition. For Mom. She had to find a way to make this work.

A good hour later, Anna hustled downstairs—dressed, packed, and ready to leave.

Whisper-yells funneled through the doorway leading to Dad's study. She peeked around the corner to find him caught up in some kind of intense conversation with Evan. "You better find some boundaries, young man."

A sense of failure flickered down Evan's stiff pose. Empathy flared. She'd been on the receiving end of Dad's lectures enough times to know how it felt.

"Lay off, Dad." She entered the room. Whatever he was upset about, she could guarantee it wasn't Evan's fault.

They both startled at her intrusion, but neither met her eyes.

Anna zeroed in on Evan's tousled hair and the rumpled clothes he still had on from yesterday. Boundaries? Did Dad think they'd slept together? Perfect. What was one more awkward moment to add to the mix?

"We stayed up late, talking. That's it. Evan crashed on the floor."

The stinging sensation prickling her cheeks didn't come close to the deep blush climbing both the guys' necks as they fumbled for a response.

A sunbeam stretched across the carpet and onto Evan's back. Anna slowed toward him. "Is your shirt wet?" A bad feeling twisted in her stomach.

He peered behind him, followed her finger to the soaked fabric clinging to his skin, and dropped his gaze to the carpet. "It's nothing."

"Don't tell me it's nothing. Tell me what's going on?"

Evan looked from her to Dad and back to the floor. "I was checking the brakes on the cars out front."

"Brakes?" Comprehension gnawed at her gut. "*That's* why you wanted to take my car to the shop. Because you're worried someone's tampering with it."

Dad set a folder on his desk and strode around the corner. "You're staying here today, Annabelle."

"Excuse me?"

"The roads are too dangerous."

She wedged open the blinds. White sheets of glimmering snow blanketed the ground. No. Not today. "The storm was supposed to hit tomorrow."

"Looks like it got a jump start on the weekend. And it's only going to get worse."

Anna slung her bag over her arm. "Then we better leave now. I'm not missing my audition." Too much was at stake.

"Honey, this isn't the time to be thinking about dance."

He'd never told her he thought art was a waste of time. He'd never had to. Moments like these said it loud and clear. "I'm sorry you don't get it, Dad, but dance is my *life*."

"And you're mine." He pushed off the desk. "Please. The case goes to trial on Monday. Just stay here until then. That's all I'm asking."

"The trial has nothing to do with me."

Dad swiped a folder off the desk and caught her arm as she turned. "Michelli's made it about you. And he's made sure I know. Why do you think his men were here last night?"

She tugged her arm away. "No one was here. Michelli's in custody. You can't freak out just because an SUV passes the house." She darted a glare at Evan. "Both of you need to drop this."

The gray in Dad's eyes deepened. "Dang it, Annabelle. This isn't about being overprotective."

"That's exactly what it's about. What it's *always* about. If you didn't suffocate us with security, Mom wouldn't have skidded off the road, trying to get away from her detail." Her words shot out with harbored resentment she hadn't meant to reveal.

Dad clutched the folder, looking backhanded.

She willed away the tears mounting from a place inside she couldn't afford to open. "I'm sorry. I know it's not your fault. But you can't change what happened to Mom. None of us can. Spending your life trying to protect me isn't going to bring her back." Didn't he see that?

"And pretending it was an accident won't either."

"Dad—"

"They were here, Annabelle." He handed her a plastic-covered photo from the folder.

"What's this?"

"A message for me to lose the evidence I have on Michelli or lose my daughter."

Evan stood beside the window, face unreadable.

A picture of Mom's totaled car glared up at her. Every horrific feeling from that night clawed down her body as if she were reliving it all over again. "Where'd you get this?"

"They left it on my windshield last night." Dad cupped her shoulder. "One photo for another."

Michelli was behind bars. He couldn't have done this. "It's just someone thinking they can coerce you into throwing the case. Don't let them intimidate you. They want you to fold."

"And I want you alive." His brow creased. "But I can't ensure your safety unless you let me."

Burying her fear, Anna shook her head. "I won't cower to them."

"And I won't let them take another of my girls away from me."

She backed up. "I'm sorry, Dad."

Evan moved from the window. "Anna, please."

"Give me the keys."

He remained still, eyes beseeching.

She looked between the two of them, knowing she wouldn't win this fight. "Fine. I'll take the 'L'. Tell Megan I'll be back to pick her up after the audition." She hustled outside.

The door flew right back open, followed by Evan jogging after her. "Bells, wait." He caught her hand. "Stop being so stubborn, and think this through."

"You think I haven't?" The lake's bitter wind clenched her throat in a familiar grip of fear. "You think I haven't wondered every single day since my mom died?" Anna started to shake. "He can't be right, Evan."

Rather than argue, he caressed her fingers with such tenderness, she almost broke on the spot.

She withdrew and clutched her arms. "If they killed her, it means she was wrong. No matter how much you invest in the world, darkness still wins. It means everything I've dedicated my life to has been for nothing." He didn't understand what that would mean. What it'd do to her.

"You can't really believe that."

The same emptiness that had nearly destroyed her five years ago closed in with the snow. "You're right. I can't. It almost paralyzed me once. I won't live my life believing Mom's was a lie."

Evan edged forward, stopped himself, and then started again. "Anna, listen to me. Your mom's life wasn't for nothing. And neither is yours. There'll always be evil in the world."

"I know. Which is why I can't give up on dance, and why you can't give up on the army." Drawing herself together, she looked him head-on. "It's time to let go, Evan."

She needed to show she could do this without leaning on him. His men needed him more.

"To let go of what?" His usual bravado surrendered to a hoarse whisper.

"Of wishing things were different. You said it yourself."

His gaze strayed to the pavement. "I'm sorry for messing up last night."

Messing up. Because he thought anything other than friendship between them would be a mistake? She shoved down the traitorous tears coating her throat and turned. "Please stop apologizing for the way things will always be."

He caught her elbow again. "What do you want me to do?"

"I want you to say good-bye." The desperate plea belted out in a tangled mess of feelings she couldn't maneuver through anymore.

From the look on his face, it might as well have been a sucker punch. He released her arm.

Wincing at his expression, she reached for him and the words she wanted to take back. "Evan, I'm sorry. That's not what I meant. I ..." What could she say? All she was doing was making things worse.

Her flushed skin burned against the snowflakes collecting on her forehead. She backed up, needing the dance floor and the one place of escape. "I have to get to the studio."

Turning away from her, Evan yanked open the car door. "Get in."

She glanced up. "You don't have to take me."

His unyielding gaze said otherwise.

With time running out, Anna climbed in and gripped the fringes of hope that she still had a chance to salvage what she and Mom had started together. She couldn't lose Evan and dance in the same day. Not again.

A drive that should've taken thirty minutes multiplied into ninety. Between the slick roads, bumper-to-bumper traffic, and the nagging possibility that someone might've tampered with his car, Evan took caution to a new level.

He'd checked the brakes, the engine, and the lines. Everything looked clear. Anna might be right about Michelli's guys tossing around threats without any backing. Still, something didn't add up.

At least he'd already had Anna's car towed to the shop. Maybe he'd slip the mechanics a few more bills to get them to stall. Whether she liked it or not, she needed to lie low and stay off the roads until the trial was over. The audition was an exception.

Anna drew her feet into the seat and kept her eyes on the road. Same way she'd done the whole ride. An hour and a half of electric silence felt like an entire day of it. Knowing there wasn't a thing Evan could do to make it better was what ate at him the most. He couldn't take it much longer.

She chewed her pinky, probably going over her routine in her head. Either that or replaying last night over and over again like he was. Man, he hoped not. He hadn't done a single thing right.

Her feet slid to the floorboard as she pulled out her phone again. She huffed something indecipherable. "You're gonna have to take me straight there. I don't have time to stop at the studio to warm up." She dropped her fist to the dashboard.

He should've insisted she get to sleep early last night. She didn't need any more stress. Not today.

One regret bled into another until Visceral Dance Center finally came into view. Evan pulled into the plowed lot and lined up her door with the walkway leading to the entrance.

Anna hustled out of the car with her bag, stopped, and turned. Words she didn't have to say poured through her eyes. "Evan, I …"

He leaned across the seats. "You're going to be amazing."

A watery smile stood in for a response. She paused a moment longer and then raised her chin and pressed forward. She might not've been a soldier, but she was a fighter.

Evan snagged the closest parking spot. Brushing off the snow from his sleeves, he approached the door but stopped himself from entering.

"*I want you to say good-bye.*" Anna's words latched on to his raw nerve endings and sank all the way to his core. He never should've walked back into her life. He belonged out here, where he could protect her instead of hurting her again.

Staying outside, he traded one storm for another and waited for the crisp scent of wet asphalt to clear his head. He knew his place in Anna's life wouldn't amount to more than being her bodyguard. He hadn't left for the army in search of a way to change his role. He'd left, searching for a way to be worthy of it. And here he was, still letting her down.

The wind's icy prongs stabbed his ears. One blow. Another. It jabbed until numbness spread and allowed the bitter truth to settle. Anna was right. It was time to let go.

CHAPTER NINETEEN

Wreckage

Evan released his mom's hand and stretched. His stiff joints creaked with the rigid hospital chair, but the movement didn't wake her. He picked up the empty Styrofoam coffee cup he'd been refilling all night.

"She's in good hands, Mr. O'Riley." The nurse jotted something in her chart. "You should go home and get some sleep."

Sleep definitely wasn't happening. And going back to his hotel would mean returning to the same drawing board he'd been going over nonstop since he'd taken Anna back to her apartment yesterday. At least while staking out the front of her building, Evan felt like he was doing something halfway useful.

Between him, Harris, and Murphy, they'd kept Anna under surveillance around the clock, but there'd been no sign of Michelli's men. No hint of foul play. The lack of activity gnawed at him. What was their next move?

He massaged his neck. Five more days, and the trial would be over. Seven more, and Mom would be home recovering.

From the doc's updates, the prognosis seemed hopeful. Evan looked her over. She exuded strength even in her sleep. Maybe she didn't need him as much as he'd thought. Maybe Anna didn't either.

From inside the folds of his wallet, he withdrew the weathered paper that never left his person and smoothed out the wrinkles over his knee. The words on the page were branded inside him as much as his oath to be a Ranger. If not more. He'd tried to honor them the best he could, but maybe it was time to admit he couldn't.

He scrolled to the text from Hernandez waiting for his response about reenlisting. An incoming call cut him off in the middle of a reply.

Evan swiped the screen. "Murphy, you good? What happened?"

"Jeez, O'Riley. You need me to spike that hospital coffee? Take a load off, bro."

"Sorry." He reclined in the chair. "What's up?"

"I'm just calling to let you know your girl's on to you."

Evan sat right back up. "What do you mean?"

"I mean, she knows you've got Harris and me watching her. Some kid named Shaun just came knocking on my car window. Said Anna was hot about you not telling her."

Considering Anna hadn't spoken to him since the audition, "hot" probably didn't begin to cover it. "Did Kid President have anything else to say?"

"No, but someone else apparently does."

"What? Murph—"

"Evan?" A woman's voice came on the line. "It's Robyn, Anna's coworker. How you doing, sugar?"

He glanced from his mom to the note in his lap and returned it to the well-worn spot in his wallet. It didn't matter how he was doing. "I'll be better if you tell me what's going on."

"Straight to the point. My kind of guy." She chuckled. "Look, baby, I know Anna doesn't like anyone all up in her business. But sometimes that girl needs a good head slap to knock some common sense into her. I know *you* know what I'm talking about. Stubborn as—"

"I'm sorry. I don't mean to be rude." He stuffed the wallet into his back pocket. "But I thought we were getting straight to the point."

"Well, dang, honey. You're just as slow as Anna, aren't ya?"

Okay, he didn't have time for this. "How about you just let me talk to her?"

"That's what I been trying to tell you. She ain't here."

His stomach lurched. "Where is she?"

"At home. Packing."

Packing? Evan jetted from the chair and whirled around the doorway. "I'll be there in five."

With the storm picking up, hardly anyone was on the road. He probably shouldn't have been either, but Anna was more important.

He slid into a parking spot beside the curb and hopped out at the same time Murphy exited his Jeep. Sucker had gotten there first. "How'd she get by you?"

Murphy cocked his head. "Guess you're not the only one trying to be sly."

Playing him at his own game. Why did that not surprise him?

"You got a bulletproof vest on? From what that kid was saying about how ticked she is, you might need it going in there."

"I can handle Anna."

"Sure you can." Murphy opened his door.

Evan grabbed the side of the trim. "Hey, do me a favor before going home?"

"Shoot."

"Anna's dad sent a car to take Megan home yesterday. Would you mind swinging by Brookfield Apartments to make sure everything seems cool?"

Murphy clasped his hand. "I got ya, bro."

"Thanks, man." Evan leaned in for a half hug. "I appreciate it."

He flicked a glance at Anna's windows. "You got enough problems to deal with."

"Thanks for the vote of confidence."

Leaving the door halfway open, Murphy started the ignition. A classic Casanova grin climbed up his cheek. "Be sure to give her my number." He puffed out his shirt and rubbed his chin. "You know, after she throws your sorry butt to the curb."

Evan swung the door shut. "Get outta here, punk."

Murphy's throaty laugh filtered through the window as he pulled away.

A cloud of exhaust and snow spun around Evan. Blowing against his hands to warm them, he peered up at Anna's apartment again. Murphy might not be that off base about her reaction to seeing him. He jogged across the street to the front door. Only one way to find out.

Inside, Evan hustled up the steps, taking them two at a time. His footsteps echoed off the walls all the way to the top. He rapped a knuckle on Anna's door and cast a backward glance at her neighbor's apartment. No barking. No sound, period. The quiet unnerved him.

He banged the door harder. "Anna, it's me. Open up."

A scrambling noise stirred from inside. The deadbolt clicked, and she cracked the door open far enough to allow a sliver of a view into her place. "What do you want, Evan?"

"I want to know you're okay."

"Why don't you go ask the guys you have keeping tabs on me?"

"Bells, don't be like this." He nudged her to let him in.

She grabbed a throw pillow from the couch and clutched it to her stomach, face turning red. A glimpse of their high school logo peeked out from behind the pillow.

"Is that—?"

"No." Backing up farther, she swiped a second pillow and covered the bottom half of her shirt.

He pulled them away. "My old wrestling sweatshirt?"

"Technically, it's mine now since you left it here." Anna blew a strand of hair out of her face. "You know. Because of statute of limitations … or … whatever."

How did the girl pull off sexy, infuriating, and adorable all at the same time? And why did she make it so hard to focus?

He pushed his gaze from her to the cardboard boxes covering the couch. Bailey circled over one and curled into a ball on top of whatever was packed inside it.

"You wanna tell me what's going on?"

"I'm moving out." Anna strode to the bookshelf along the wall and went back to wrapping her knickknacks in newspaper. "Time's up."

"Your landlord gave you till Wednesday. There's still—"

"I didn't make the cut." She dropped the paper and clutched the box. "If you'd stayed and seen the audition, you'd understand why."

The tremble in her voice raked over him.

She shoved another item into the box closest to her. "I should've stayed home Thursday. Should've trained harder. I can't believe I messed this up."

"They're the ones who messed up by not taking you."

"No. It was me. I wasn't focused. I ..." She let out a long breath. "It doesn't matter. It's over."

"It's just one audition." Evan reached in his pocket for the flyer he'd shown her Thursday night. "There's still the one for Hubbard. It's only a little over a week away. We can talk to your landlord."

"There's no *we*, Evan." Her arms drifted to her sides as though weary of straining. A torn expression met his and softened her hard shell. "I'll always be grateful for knowing you want to take care of me. But this isn't an op. It's my life."

Her words speared him but not as much as watching her buy into something that wasn't true. "A life you're throwing away."

"What's that supposed to mean?"

"This." He flicked the box's flap. "You, giving up on your dreams."

"Me?" Her eyes turned a fierce green. "I'm not the one who walked out on my dreams and ran away."

The blow caught him below the belt. "I didn't run away."

"No? Then what do you call ditching everything we had planned and running off without even facing me first?" She hedged him backward. "Why'd you really leave, Evan? What were you afraid of?"

The fact she didn't already know was the very reason he hadn't told her.

She kept advancing. "All this time, you've blamed your dad—hiding behind the fear of failure, thinking you have some kind of inadequacies you have to make up for."

He stumbled backward over the truth he didn't want to admit.

A dangerous mix of emotions laced each step marching her closer. "You go off, thousands of miles away, willing to fight God-knows-who rather than risking what might happen if you stay and give yourself half a chance at what you don't think you deserve."

His back pressed into the kitchen counter behind him. Shock rooted him in place until agitation boiled to the surface and freed his voice.

"You want to talk about hiding?" He straightened away from the counter. "You ostracize yourself from your family out of fear, blame your dad for the very thing he's fighting against, and let guilt keep you from pursuing your own dreams."

Her expression darkened. "At least I try."

"No, you settle. You walk around, challenging everyone else to live with courage, but you keep none for yourself. If you did, you wouldn't be writing off your top choice company."

He jutted the flyer out at her. "You want to call me out on being afraid of failure? Fine. But at least admit you're afraid of success. 'Cause I think you're sabotaging your career on purpose. So, you tell me who's hiding."

Fist clenched, Anna opened her mouth, clamped it shut again, and lowered her arm.

The fight between them drained with a pent-up exhale. "I can't go there, Evan. A career with a company would consume me."

"Only if you let it."

"I'm not strong enough not to." Dejected eyes blinked away from him. "I let Mom down like that once. I can't lose myself again."

He lifted her chin. "You won't."

"How do you know?"

"Because I won't let you."

He enclosed her in his arms. He'd fight with her every day if he had to, would face his fears and sacrifice his heart like he should've done from day one no matter what it cost him. She deserved all her dreams.

Anna sank into him and let the silence drain the last of the tension away until her stubborn exterior crumbled under fears of her own. "Don't you ever wish you could give up on it all? To tell that thing inside you to walk away?"

He breathed against her hair. "We don't get to choose what steals our hearts." No self-mastery, training, or logic would change that truth he lived with every day.

Evan drew her tighter. But instead of allowing him to keep holding her, she slinked out of his embrace and returned to the boxes on the floor, shield back in place.

"What are you doing?"

"I'm finishing packing. Which is what you should be doing, too."

He crossed the living room. "What are you talking about?"

"I saw the text from your comrade about re-upping." She swiped the ceramic frogs off the shelf and encased them in an extra layer of newspaper. "They need you there, Evan."

He ran his fingers over the couch arm's wooden edge. "You want me to leave?"

Her hands stalled over the items in the box, her gaze locked inside it. "It doesn't matter what I want."

"It does to me." He turned her toward him. "What do you want, Bells?"

"The same thing I've wanted all my life." The words rushed out.

He searched her face for an explanation.

Craning her head to the ceiling, she pushed her hair off her forehead with the back of her wrist. "Never mind."

"Just talk to me. What is it? Dance?"

"*You*, Evan." She balled her sweatshirt's cuffs in her hands. "It's always been you."

His whole body froze. He'd taken an M4 rifle to the chest more times than he cared to count, yet her words just knocked the wind from him with ten times the force. "What did you just say?"

She shook her head and returned to the box. "Forget it. Like I said. It doesn't matter."

Breaking the paralysis, Evan curled his fingertips under hers and brought her to him.

She landed a palm over the dog tags under his shirt. Her brow furrowed. "You left for a reason." The storm outside had nothing on the battle behind her eyes. One he knew too well.

"That doesn't mean I wanted to." How could he make her understand?

"I thought we just said no more hiding." She tipped her head to the side, smiled sadly, and retracted her hand. "You skipped town the week after I almost kissed you. You can stop worrying about hurting my feelings. I get it."

That couldn't seriously be what she thought.

Pulse hammering, Evan inched toward her. And with all the courage he had, he lowered the guard shielding her from the truth. "I've never wanted anything more in my life than to have kissed you back that night. But you'd just lost your mom, Anna. You were hurt, confused. Of course you'd turn to me for comfort. And God knows I wanted to be there for you. But I was scared, too. Afraid you'd regret it when everything settled. Afraid I'd lose you when you found out I ..."

He swallowed. If he'd told her everything and given in to what he felt, how much would have changed? The risk had been too high. It still was, but he couldn't walk away this time.

With a hand to her cheek, he traced a thumb along the corner of her mouth. She drew in a breath at his touch. The torn expression she'd shown all week resurfaced, but now, he understood why.

"Evan, I—"

"Stop talking." They'd let enough words stand between them. If she truly wanted this, too, he'd give her all he had, would pray it was enough.

His fingers trailed over the soft skin behind her ear and into her hair. Each heartbeat brought him closer until his lips touched hers for the first time. Slow and unassuming, Anna kissed him with the same tenderness he'd fallen in love with from the very beginning.

Evan lifted back to search her face, wanting to savor every part of this, of her. The pulse beating through his wrist mingled with the one fluttering on her neck. His fingertips grazed her collar, and the flush claiming her skin begged his lips to cover every inch.

"Evan," she breathed against him, his name like a song washing over him.

She glided her hands up his chest and into the back of his hair with such earnestness, her response shot his heart rate past what he could control. Giving in, he traced his free palm down to the small of her back and pulled her torso tight with his until everything dissolved except her. Her distinct scent, her warm lips, her soft body pressed to his. Nothing existed outside the awareness of finally holding the woman he'd always loved in his arms.

Backed against the boxes, Anna balled his shirt in her fingers and tugged him into her as if she couldn't get close enough.

Instinct seized him. He claimed her mouth, her neck, wanting no space between them. No hindrance to separate them. A tiny noise escaped her throat and fed the all-consuming love taking over. Every locked-away emotion crushed into her with the passion he'd held for no one else.

Breathing hard, Anna leaned back but didn't let go.

His chest rose and fell, grappling for stability, for words. "Bells ..."

"All this time." A sheen of tears glittered her warm cheeks. "Why didn't you ever tell me?"

The same reason he shouldn't have now. The battle that never relented edged him backward.

Green eyes, deeper than he'd ever seen them, studied his for an answer she deserved. Transparent. Beseeching. They burrowed into him and dislodged the secret he'd kept buried. Willing it back down, he forked his fingers through his hair.

But she wouldn't let him pull away. Not anymore. "What is it?"

Heart pounding, he met her gaze and inhaled. "There's something I need to tell you."

Her body stiffened and sent dread raking over his. Would she forgive him?

Another breath. "Anna, I ..."

A clamor in the stairwell pulled their attention to footsteps behind the door. Bailey lifted her head from her paw and slanted her ears toward the noise.

Evan's eyes shot to Anna. "Back bedroom. Go."

"I'm not hiding."

He clenched his hands. "Anna, this isn't the time—"

"So, someone's in the hall. It's an apartment building. It could be anyone."

Men's voices approached. Evan dipped his head. "How many of your neighbors speak Italian?"

The doorknob jingled.

He strode to the window and peeked through the blinds. He had to get her out of here. His gaze bounded off each angle until it landed on the steel railing along the bricks. "Fire escape." He led her to the bedroom and opened the window.

"What about Bailey?"

Did she ever think of herself first? "I'll come back for her."

With Evan right behind, Anna shimmied through the window and down the ladders. Once they hit the pavement, he pressed a palm to her back and prodded her forward. "Keep moving." He scanned the area, checking cars, windows, rooftops. "Act casually."

She scoffed. "Someone just flung me into a Jason Bourne movie, and you want me to be casual about it? Right."

He kept forgetting she wasn't used to the adrenaline, wasn't trained to harness it. But at least the primal instinct to escape seemed to have finally kicked in.

At his Accord, he checked under the car for any sign of tampering and then cranked the ignition. "I want you to drive straight to Harris's precinct. Don't stop until you're in front of his desk. You hear me?"

"What are you gonna do?"

He looked behind her. "I'm gonna finish this."

"Evan." She grabbed hold of his shirt. "Let's just get out of here."

Releasing a breath, he raised a hand to her neck. "I'm right behind you. I promise." But he had to take these guys down first. No more slipping by him.

Anna lifted on her toes to kiss him and leveled her passionate eyes with his. "Be careful."

With a reassuring nod, he leaned into the car as she slid into the driver's seat. "Straight to the station. Don't slow down. Don't look back. I mean it."

As soon as he closed the door, the tires spun over the snow and squealed, but Evan didn't move until the taillights disappeared around the corner.

He breathed in, out. Honing the intensity she ignited, he steadied his heart rate and redirected all his senses to his surroundings. Every sound. Every movement. It filtered through and mobilized him back to the apartment building.

At the front door, he drew his Sig and eased inside. After clearing the stairwell, he crept up the steps toward Anna's door, gun still raised. He turned the knob. Locked. He pressed an ear to the door. No sound. Where were they?

A sinking sensation plowed into his stomach. He slung a glance back at the entrance. *Decoy.*

Pulse skyrocketing, he flew down the stairs and barreled outside again. He combed the area until he found a gray Beamer with tinted windows. Someone rolled the driver's side window down, letting a puff of smoke spew out. The guy behind the wheel flicked a cigarette butt to the ground and smirked right at him.

The car sped off the second Evan launched forward. He grabbed his cell. Each unanswered ring accentuated the beats striking his ribs. *Come on, Harris.*

"Relax, O'Riley. I still have ten minutes till my shift. I'll be there."

"Anna's en route to you. She's in my car. The minute you see her, you call me." He jogged up the street to where he could hail a cab. "I'm on my way."

"What's going on?"

"Michelli's guys played me. They flushed us out. Knew I'd send her alone." He swore away from the phone. Why didn't he see it coming? He ran a hand down his head and clenched the back of his hair.

"Slow down. Tell me what happened." A beep blared in the background, the garbled voice of dispatch following. "I gotta go, O'Riley. I'll call you back."

"What was the call?"

"An accident. On South Drexel Boulevard."

Evan hung up, tapped Anna's number, and hustled around the corner. Ice-cold air seared his lungs the harder he pushed. Muddied snow splashed over his sneakers hitting the pavement. The call went straight to voice mail. He redialed. "C'mon, Bells."

Backed-up traffic stretched down the road. His stomach tensed. Shoving his phone in his pocket, he slowed to a stop and froze until the shriek of police sirens kicked his body back into motion. He eased forward. One step. Another. An all-out sprint drove him through the throng of people crowding the sidewalk.

Glass and wreckage covered the street. He wedged between people's shoulders, straining for a clear view. A single car sat sideways in the middle of the intersection. An Accord. *His* Accord. The impact from another vehicle had caved in the passenger side. The driver's side door hung open. No one inside.

He sprang from the curb and scoured the scene. Blood on the trim. Anna's smashed cell on the asphalt. He rammed a palm into the doorjamb. This wasn't happening.

The last of the day's warmth faded with the sunset behind the skyscrapers.

Flashing white lights circled the car's panels as a cruiser skidded to a stop beside him. "O'Riley?" Harris jogged up.

Evan scanned the area in search of cameras, snipers, anything. Faces stared back from every direction. All but the ones he needed to see. They were gone. And they had Anna.

CHAPTER TWENTY

Trust

Evan's hotel desk chair whined as he wrenched backward away from stacks of photos and papers. Staring at page after page of notes all night was starting to turn him cross-eyed.

It'd been almost a full day since the wreck, and still nothing. No clues. No direction.

The helplessness that'd destroyed him as a kid mounted in his chest. Evan vowed he'd never be that defenseless again. He'd trained to avoid it. Now, here he was. Just as powerless to do anything. He pushed out of the chair and started to pace.

A knock at the door interrupted the silence.

Grabbing his Sig from the desk, Evan waited. Listened.

A second knock came hard. "Don't make me bust down your door, O'Riley."

Casanova. Evan strode over, checked the peephole, and unlocked the bolt.

Murphy strolled in with a brown paper bag and drink carrier. He gave Evan a once-over. "Dang, bro. Ever heard of sleeping?"

Evan holstered his gun. "Not until we find her."

"Well, you at least gotta eat." He set the items on the table, unfurled the bag, and pulled out two white cartons with foil tops. "Chicken parm or fettuccine?"

Italian aromas infused the stale air circulating in the closed-up suite. "Parm."

Murphy handed it to him with a plastic fork pinned against the lid.

Evan plopped into the closest kitchen chair and dug in. The first bite warmed his insides and stimulated the hunger he'd been suppressing. When had he last eaten? The hours were starting to run together. Hours he was losing.

A wave of unease rolled in his stomach.

Murphy flipped his chair around and straddled it. "This is what I'm talking about, right here, dawg. Food energy. You won't do Anna much good without it."

Like he was doing her much good holed up in this hotel right now.

Twirling pasta around his fork, Murphy glanced up at Evan's face. "I know I said girls dig the whole dark knight mystique, but you might be pushing it."

Evan touched a knuckle to the bruise on his temple. A few Advil had lessened the throbbing enough that he'd almost forgotten about it. "Yeah, I, uh, might've paid Adele's Little Italy a visit last night."

"You what?" Murphy lowered his fork. "Bro, you're lucky they didn't kill you."

He shook his head. "They have what they want. They're not interested in attracting any more heat."

"Still. Next time you wanna do something reckless, do me a favor and call me first."

Evan nodded in concession. He shouldn't have gone there alone. But after seeing Anna's blood on his car, he was past the point of rational thought.

A high-pitched meow sounded from under the table. Bailey rubbed her cheek against the chair leg and stretched her front paws up his calf. He scooted backward, and she jumped into the seat with him.

Murphy fished in the bag for a napkin. "So, what's the lowdown? Any word from Harris?"

Evan hoisted one of the coffee cups out of the carrier while Bailey pawed around his lap for a comfortable position. "He's got shields canvassing the area still. One witness saw a white van fleeing the scene. Said the front fender looked pretty smashed up."

"They got a BOLO out?"

Evan scoffed. "That van's long gone."

Murphy shrugged with his brows. "True. What about prints from Anna's place?"

"Nothing. Not even on the doorknob." Evan hunched against the chair back. "They were just toying with me, man."

"I bet her pops is freaking out."

He didn't know the half of it. "He's got the entire PD working the case."

"No doubt." Murphy swallowed a bite. "Pays to have a position of influence."

Not if it wasn't enough. The case went to court tomorrow. If they didn't find Anna in time, Mr. Madison would give in to Michelli's threats and let him skate. No way he'd risk his daughter's life. Which meant Evan had to secure her before the prosecution presented their case. There was no other choice.

Evan banged a hand against the table. Bailey jumped down at the same time Murphy jabbed his fork in the air at him. He opened his mouth, but Evan's cell cut him off.

He snagged the phone from the table and swiped the screen. "Harris, tell me you got something."

Harris's delayed response said enough. "Every unit in the city's on alert. We're gonna find her."

Evan needed Anna safe in his arms. Now.

"The second we get a ping from her ID or credit cards—"

"They don't want her money. They want leverage." Evan pushed back from the table, his jaw ticking with frustration. "You should be treating this as an abduction."

"We are, but we have to cover every angle." A heavy exhale filled the line. "Anna's like a sister to me, O'Riley. I won't rest till she's safe."

That made two of them.

"But you gotta trust me to do my job."

Bailey planted her paws on his shin and meowed again. Evan unhooked her claws from his jeans and patted her head, but her crying persisted. He tore off a piece of chicken from his dish and held it out for her. She gobbled it whole.

He sent a backward glance to the cat dish in the kitchen. Empty. She was probably starving. Man, he was a lousy pet sitter.

The thought smacked him in the face. *Anna's neighbor.*

He bolted from the chair. "Harris, meet me at Anna's apartment. I think I may have found a lead."

Evan and Murphy made it to Anna's in less than ten minutes. With it being Sunday and the snow still coming down, traffic was a fraction of its normal bustle. Harris was still en route, but Evan wasn't about to waste any more time.

On the first floor, he pounded the landlord's door.

Mr. Reyes cracked it open. "No solicitation. I have you arrested."

Something about his Asian accent and small-framed stature undermined the threat.

Murphy glanced at Evan with an is-this-cat-for-real expression.

Evan kept his voice even. "Apartment 2C. Open it."

"Come back with a warrant."

"I doubt you want to make this a public spectacle." Evan pressed his fingers to the door to keep it open. "The media will have a field day if there ends up being a dead body in one of your apartments."

The guy's face paled. "Dead body?"

"You seen Mrs. Santos lately?"

Mr. Reyes fumbled a set of keys off a hook beside the door. "I figured she was out of town."

So had Evan. No crossing her in the stairwell. No barking. Anna being unable to get a hold of her. It made sense. But something about it had left him unsettled.

He tugged the landlord out by his shirt. "Let's go." The clock was ticking.

Murphy brought up the rear to the second floor. In front of Mrs. Santos's apartment, Mr. Reyes twisted the key in the lock. A look of dread plummeted down his face, taking the color in his cheeks with it.

Evan moved him behind them. "Go downstairs and wait for the cops. They'll be here any sec."

Mr. Reyes scrambled down the steps without hesitation. Evan couldn't fault him for fleeing. No telling what they'd find on the other side of this door. Maybe nothing. Maybe the kind of scene no civilian needed to see. Either way, he had to find out.

Gun in hand, he jutted his chin at Murphy. "On my mark." He turned the knob. "Three, two, one." They swept inside and cleared the room. No odor of decomposition, but a lingering stillness hovered throughout the dark apartment.

Murphy entered the back bedroom while Evan checked the first.

"Clear," they both called.

Evan lowered his Sig, his chest caving. He was sure they'd find something. Anything. He slammed a palm into the doorframe and backed against the opposite side.

What was he missing? The bedroom showed no sign of the woman or her dog. Nothing looked disturbed or missing. The place looked ... perfect. If Michelli's men had been here, they'd obviously cleaned up after themselves.

"Yo, O'Riley. In here."

Evan pushed off the trim and followed Murphy's voice into the bathroom. Other than a faint hint of bleach hitting his nostrils, the room only offered more untouched, empty space.

Murphy held up a hand. "Wait for it ..." He swung the door shut with his foot. The light caught a smidge of blood along the bottom corner of the doorknob.

Maybe the thugs weren't as thorough as they thought.

"Don't touch anything in here." As much as Evan wanted to tear the place apart with his bare hands now, he knew Harris would ream him out if he tampered with evidence.

He whipped out his cell, but police chatter and heavy footfalls climbing the stairs eliminated the need to make the call. He holstered his Sig, rounded the bathroom doorway, and met Harris in the hall.

Harris stood down. "Got a vic?"

"No." Evan nodded to the bathroom. "But you might want to start sweeping nearby dumpsters." The thought turned his stomach. If they could kill an old lady, what did that say about Anna's chances of getting through this alive?

Harris peered around the frame and reached for his shoulder mic. "Twenty-two to dispatch."

"Dispatch. Go ahead, Twenty-two."

He strode into the bathroom, his conversation trailing in after him.

Murphy patted Evan's back. "Good call, bro."

Maybe on this part of the case but not on finding Anna. The gravity of not knowing where she was or if she was okay closed in on him.

He kicked off the hallway wall and reentered the bathroom. If Michelli's guys had overlooked the blood, they had to have tripped up on something else. He just had to find it.

Another officer came in with a camera and a yellow marker for documenting evidence.

Harris motioned to the bloodstain and withdrew a pad and pen while the guy shot a handful of takes. "Get Detective Michaels on the line and tape off the scene."

"Copy that." The officer strode out with the camera in hand.

Harris gave Evan a wary stare. "This doesn't mean Anna's dead."

"It doesn't mean she's not."

"She's their only bargaining chip."

Would keeping her alive make it worse? He blanched at what Michelli's men were capable of doing. He should've cut them off before now. Should've figured it out. He'd been scouring the city for their base, and they'd been right under his nose, banking on him expecting them to be somewhere less obvious.

He balled his hands. They'd been messing with him this whole time, flaunting how close they could get to Anna without his knowing. How easy it was to track her routine, to study her.

His thoughts darkened. They'd probably been in Anna's apartment, too. Planted bugs. Or worse, hidden cameras. If they'd swept her apartment as clean as they had this one, there likely wouldn't be any evidence to trace back to them. But just the idea of the creeps watching her on video made his blood boil almost as much as the possibility of what they were doing now that they had her in person.

Evan's knees buckled in anger. He squeezed his tension-knotted shoulder and blew out a hard breath.

From this angle, the bathroom light caught a scrap of paper behind the trash can. It looked like a torn-off piece of a menu.

He stretched around the base of the toilet to grab it with a piece of toilet paper, stood, and flipped it around.

Harris leaned over him. "Is that …?"

"Mario's Pizza." He met Harris's gaze. "The Port District," they said in unison.

Evan launched off the sink and into the hall.

"O'Riley, hold up." Harris jogged after him. "What do you think you're gonna do?"

"Whatever I have to." He reached for the doorknob. Every second mattered.

"Not alone, you're not."

"I wasn't asking for permission." Evan stopped in front of the door. Harris was just trying to help. Seething under his breath, he stole a minute to unclench his fingers before turning. "With all due respect, your boys aren't going to get within a mile of those docks without tipping them off. I'm trained to be invisible. I can't ruin the chance of locating which warehouse she's in before they're on to us and move her."

"I don't like it, O'Riley."

Evan clamped a hand on Harris's shoulder. "You want me to trust you to do your job. But right now, I need you to trust me to do mine."

Harris uncrossed his arms. "You need backup."

"Already got it." Evan met Murphy's gaze. "Time to suit up, soldier."

CHAPTER TWENTY-ONE

Shadows

Anna's eyelids fluttered open. Once. Twice. Fragments of a dark room came in and out of focus as she blinked over the dried-out contacts glued to her corneas. Labored breaths chafed against her chapped lips and something in her mouth. A gag?

Panic speared through the haze clouding her senses. She lurched up, but a cold metal edge strained against her wrists and tugged her right back down. Handcuffs.

Flashes from the car crash reignited a surge of pain throbbing from her temple down to her shoulder. She'd barely seen the van coming before it'd rammed into the side of Evan's car, hurling the left side of her body into the door and window.

Wherever she was, she had to get out of here. She struggled to sit up again, but the cuffs sawed deeper into her wrists. Each movement rocked acid farther up her throat. Head swimming, she squeezed her eyes shut and waited for her muscles to relax.

Four slow breaths caused the concrete ground to stop spinning. She had to concentrate. Feeling around with both hands, she gripped a pipe and followed it along with her fingers. Damp and corroded, it curved upward into the wall with no opening to slip the cuffs through.

It must be some type of bathroom. No shower, just a toilet and sink from what she could tell. Unmaintained. Freezing. Inside a basement or warehouse, maybe.

Somewhere behind her, tiny claws scurried across the floor. Anna drew her legs in tight to her stomach. The cold from the ground seeped through her jeans and joined a gust of briny air rippling in from a doorway with a pungent stench of fish. Was she by the lake? A dock?

Deep male voices with foreign accents filtered in from outside. Michelli's men.

A rush of heat eclipsed the chill claiming her body. Anna wrestled the cuffs harder. A burst of light stabbed at her eyes and speckled her vision with black dots until a broad-shouldered man with an out-of-control beard came into view above her.

"'Bout time you woke up." Without losing his smirk, he flipped up the toilet seat and unbuttoned his jeans.

Anna wrenched her head away, but the rancid odor of urine still singed her nostrils. Bile burned up her esophagus.

A rough grip clasped her arm as he unlocked the cuffs and yanked her to her feet. She rubbed a thumb over the raw flesh left from the metal. He dragged her forward and clenched her arm so tightly, she fought back a whimper of pain.

The industrial lighting lit up a massive, open-walled room cluttered with stacked pallets. Two more men paced along the front entrance point. She scanned the area in an effort to gain her bearings. A glimpse of a barge outside removed any uncertainty. They had her in the Port District.

The guy dragging her must've noticed her comprehension. He shoved her toward another man sitting on a crate. Her gaze shot from the tattoo peeking out of his collar to the automatic rifle in front of him right before she lost her balance.

Her chin collided with the crate's edge, the impact dropping her to the floor. Swallowing the metallic taste of blood filling her mouth, she raised a hand to her jaw, but Grizzly Adams heaved her up before she could assess the damage.

Tattoo Guy tapped his gun against the crate while scrutinizing her profile. Anna squirmed against the other guy's crude hold when a derisive laugh rasped into her ear. "Give it up, *ragazza*. You're not strong enough to fight."

Fury invigorated her weak muscles and leveled her shoulders. "I'm strong enough for this," she said through the gag. Thrusting her foot behind her, she slammed it into his kneecap.

A low-seething yelp freed her from his grasp. She sprinted for the exit. The sound of a chamber loading a bullet echoed behind her, but Anna kept her eyes on the lake outside. Almost in reach.

An oversized man with a gun across his torso edged into her path and blocked the doorway.

She stopped and backed away. A glance to her right and left offered nowhere to run. Sweat rolled into the gag clogging the shriek no one would hear. There had to be another way out. She made it only two steps before being yanked back by the hair.

From behind her, fingers clenched her arm with enough force to leave marks. Grizzly Adams wrenched her head backward. Something cold and round pressed into the nape beneath her ear.

Tattoo Guy lunged from the crate and cast his partner a warning glare. "Boss gave us orders. She stays alive."

"For now." Hot breath poured onto her skin. "Don't worry, *ragazza*. I'll be sure to tell Daddy you said good-bye."

Anna closed her eyes, fighting back fear, until every raging thought subsided. Except one.

Evan.

Low-hanging clouds obstructed the moonlight and darkened a night Evan spent five years dreading ever having to face.

Anna had been gone for twenty-four hours. He knew the statistics. Knew the rate at which the odds of survival in a case like this plummeted. It's why he hadn't stopped searching, not even to sleep.

Crouched behind a barrel, he craned his head toward the snowflakes hitting his overheated skin and thanked God Michelli's hired guns didn't have "low key" in their vocabulary. It'd taken Evan and Murphy less than two hours to narrow down which warehouse they had Anna in.

Evan's fingers clenched at the thought of her locked up in there. Slow, even breaths pressed his back deeper against the metal container until his heart's steady tempo aligned his focus.

Angry gusts of wind coming off the intersection of Lake Michigan and the Calumet River stormed across the docks. Merciless. Driven. The same way he needed to be right now.

If this turned south, Michelli would walk during tomorrow's trial, and Evan would lose the battle he'd trained for.

This wasn't the time to let doubts assail him. He'd made a promise. One he'd die keeping. Even if that moment ended up being tonight.

Evan checked the mag on his Sig, butted it back in, and radioed Murphy on the other side of the transit shed. "How many guys you count?"

"At least four on the inside. Armed with nine millimeters."

They'd easily taken down two other thugs patrolling the docks. But even with Harris's units holding the perimeter, Evan had a feeling it'd turn ugly fast once gunshots fired. He needed to get Anna out of there.

"All right," Evan said. "Let's smoke them out. Stand by to move."

"Copy that."

They each lit a fire in the barrels closest to the entry point.

On cue, two men came out to inspect the black smoke billowing in the wind. Evan gripped the man on his side in a sleeper hold. Three gunshots popped off before he went down. The echo shuddered across the terminal.

Evan signaled to Murphy. "Move in. Go, go, go."

They dove inside and took cover behind two steel beams. Shell casings from automatic rounds thundered against the pavement. Evan raised his brows at Murphy. "Only nine millimeters, huh?"

He shrugged. "What fun would a raid be without upping the stakes?"

Evan shook his head at him. "Cover me."

Murphy fanned out, gun firing. Evan sprinted up two rows and backed behind another pillar. The stench of blood, sweat, and gunpowder clouded the air. He needed to get into close combat range fast.

At the sound of the magazines emptying, Evan and Murphy both darted forward. One from the left, the other closing in from the right.

Seeing Anna on the ground with a blood-soaked gag in her mouth and terror in her eyes throttled him. Vehemence like he'd never known drove him straight for the tattoo-covered guy with the automatic weapon. Evan hooked a blow to the guy's rib cage and took one to the jaw with the butt of the rifle.

Vision blurring, Evan dropped his gun.

A muffled scream from the floor pulled him back to the scene in time to dodge another swing.

Evan rammed a shoulder into the guy's stomach, bulldozed him into a crate, and wrestled the rifle away from him. Clutching him by the shirt, Evan slammed him against the boxes.

A bloody smirk spread to the cold, dark eyes egging him on. "You gonna kill me?"

It took everything in Evan not to. "No, but you might not have as much luck in prison."

A haunting laugh shook down the guy's body as if recharging him. He broke Evan's hold and sprang for Anna. Murphy tossed Evan his gun. But the guy already had Anna in a choke hold, her body a shield. He pulled a handgun from his shin and aimed it from Evan to her. A wild expression dared Evan to make a move.

Instead of fear, remorse streamed from Anna's eyes. Tears didn't dilute the message they held. She wanted him to take the shot.

Keeping his gun trained on them, Evan shook his head.

Another dark laugh fed the guy's misguided sense of power. "Don't worry, Ranger. You can't win every mission." He ran the barrel down Anna's neck.

Evan kept his eyes on hers, praying she remembered their signals from when they played in the attic. She gave an almost-imperceptible nod, and he readied his finger on the trigger.

"Maybe not, but I only need to win one."

Anna thrust her foot behind her and dropped facedown. Evan took the shot, hitting middle mass. One look at the bullet hole in his chest, and the guy collapsed to the pavement. Evan kicked the gun away, glanced at the other gunman, already down, and nodded at Murphy.

Rumblings rang from outside. Harris and his men would be moving in, but so would Michelli's. Evan knelt to the floor beside Anna and untied her gag. Breaths came hard and fast as she grabbed hold of him.

He pulled her close, nothing getting to him more than the tremor shaking her body against his. He scooped her up from the ground and looked to Murphy. "How many rounds you got left?"

He checked his mag. "Enough to have your back."

Tires squealed out front, sirens not far behind. Murphy covered them as they exited the shed and sprinted for the town car waiting for Anna. Evan opened the back door, lowered her inside, and stepped back.

She caught his arm. "What are you doing? Let's go!"

Everything he wanted to say to make her understand amplified the sweat bleeding through his clothes. Doubts wrestled with promises until he didn't know which was right anymore.

"Evan?"

Please God, let her forgive him. Inhaling, he brought a radio from his belt to his mouth. "Radiance secured."

Her clasp on his arm faltered.

He'd executed the op without taking a single bullet. But nothing could've left him more paralyzed than the look of betrayal confiscating the trust in her eyes.

Blue and white lights cut into the darkness as two patrol cars skidded onto the scene. Evan ducked in the car and caught John's gaze from the driver's seat. "Move out." He swung the door behind Anna and backed up.

The car took off, leaving a hollow sting in its wake. Evan shoved it down. Anna was safe. That was all that mattered.

Two uniforms steered the men Murphy and Evan had smoked out into the back of a cruiser while Harris's partner carted the other thug from the transit shed. The scumbag smirked at Evan. "You think this is gonna keep Michelli from walking tomorrow?"

"Maybe not, but this will." Of all people, Marissa strolled up with Harris, carrying a manila folder in her hands. She stopped in front of them and flashed Evan a don't-look-so-surprised expression. "Told you I was working on a big story."

With a haughty glare pinned on the man in custody, she flicked the folder with her red-tipped nail. "Dates, transactions, clients. I'd say your boss is going away for a long time and taking quite a few people with him. Turns out Mr. Michelli's been in bed with the CEO of Carmichael Enterprises for a good decade."

"Carmichael Enterprises." Evan stared at her. "As in the city's largest shipping company?"

"You got it." Her glossed lips sprawled into a glowing smile as though prepping for the headshot that'd be beside her newly acquired column in tomorrow's paper.

"How did you ...?"

Her contented grin tugged to the left. "You're not the only one who's trained to follow a lead, Evan. I'm a journalist. It's what I do."

Comprehension registered. CEO ... The executive from the gala. Evan ran his tongue over the corner of his mouth. He couldn't fault the guy for falling victim to Marissa's charm. She was a pro. Had even fooled him for a time.

Brows together, Evan looked from her to Harris. "You knew about this?"

Harris shook his head. "Not until she came down to the station earlier."

"A heads-up would've been nice."

"You were in the zone." Holstering his gun, Harris grinned. "Didn't want to ruin your chance of being invisible."

He wasn't going to let that one go, was he?

Murphy moseyed up beside Marissa. "Props for the element of surprise. I'll give ya that."

She flicked her chin toward the transit shed. "Not too bad yourself."

He shrugged. "I might've played Call of Duty once or twice."

Evan rolled his eyes. Murphy could joke all he wanted. The guy was Ranger quality, all the way.

Marissa tipped her head at Casanova and prodded Evan off to the side.

He squared his shoulders, bracing for whatever she had to say.

But instead of lighting into him, she fiddled with the folder as though stalling for the right words. "Listen, I know you don't agree with my tactics, but I'm good at what I do. And believe it or not, I care about putting the bad guys away."

"Never said you didn't."

Marissa fixed her brown eyes on him, a sad smile on her lips. "You didn't have to." Looking away, she ran a finger over the top corner of the folder. "Truth is, I might've pushed the line. On reporting and on us." Her gaze drifted back to him. "But this is my life, Evan. I can't apologize for that."

He raised a shoulder. "Again, didn't say you had to."

"Your eyes say enough." She pinched her bottom lip between her fingers, let go, and clasped her arm. "I want to thank you for caring enough to look out for me all this time, despite how ... *challenging* I've been." She edged closer. "I don't regret us, you know."

"Marissa ..."

She waved it off with the folder and readjusted her suit jacket. "Now, take some advice from someone who knows when she's losing a good thing, and go after the girl you really want."

Except he'd just lost that girl for good.

CHAPTER TWENTY-TWO

Broken

Anna gripped the leather seat in front of her. "Turn this car around, John."

"I'm afraid I can't do that. Mr. Madison's orders are to take you straight home."

It wasn't her home anymore. It hadn't been for years. And this was exactly why.

The second the tires breeched the driveway, Anna gunned out, stormed inside, and wheeled into Dad's study.

He lowered his cell to the desk. "Annabelle, thank God."

She stopped him with an outstretched arm. "How could you?"

"How could I rescue my own daughter?" His brow creased.

"That's not what I meant. Evan, Dad. I'm talking about Evan. How could you ask him to be on your payroll?" She paced the carpet to keep from shaking. "Is this about his father? About their class? Evan was never good enough for you, was he? Is that why he left after high school? To earn enough status for you?"

She strode right up to him, fingers balled tight. "What'd you say to him to make him leave?"

He cupped her shoulders. "Annabelle, stop. I treated that boy like a son. You know that. I was just as shocked as you were when he left. Even more so when he approached me a month ago."

"What are you talking about?"

He let go and ran his fingers through both sides of his graying hair. "Evan *asked* to be your security detail during this case. I kept a car at your apartment at night, but he said he was the only one who could get close enough to protect you without you knowing. That it had to be that way."

Dad might as well have thrust a gavel through her chest. Anna backed up in search of the wall to steady her. She replayed the last week through her mind, screening for details to prove him wrong.

Her stomach churned. Blackbird. Running into Evan at the restaurant … Their paths hadn't randomly crossed. Evan planned it, setting her up not to suspect anything, to trust him.

Dad's eyes softened. "He said he had a promise to honor."

More like an obligation to fill. One he lied about.

"When I caught you scolding Evan in here the day after Thanksgiving, it was about overstepping job boundaries, wasn't it?" Each time a piece of the story fused together, another piece of her heart came undone. "This whole time he's been with me, I thought …"

Nausea seized her again. Pain throbbed. But this time, it pulsed from that place inside her she'd vowed would never own her again. "I'm such an idiot."

"Annabelle."

Gripping the door trim, she circled into the hall, her legs barely holding her.

Headlights streaked through the windows as tires crunched over the snow in the driveway. Evan hustled around a Jeep's bumper.

A mix of anger, hope, and desperation ushered Anna outside. She couldn't distinguish between the emotions. Just knew she needed answers, needed him to make it okay.

Evan slowed a few feet away. Dried blood covered a gash above his eye. His five o'clock shadow looked like it'd won the battle for his jawline two days ago. But the war in his eyes hung on.

The snow falling in front of the porch light cast broken shadows over his face. And she knew right then. He didn't have to say a word. It was true. All of it.

She clutched the railing. Wind moaned across the yard and cut through her as if she weren't even there.

Evan inched forward, overlapping footprints left in the powder-coated walkway. "Anna, I—"

"Lied to me."

He dropped his gaze to the steps, breathed in, and slowly raised his eyes to hers again. "I'm sorry. You can't know how hard that was for me."

Hot tears stung, but she refused to look away. "It wasn't hard for you to walk out of my life senior year without batting an eye. Spending a week pretending you wanted to be around me should've been be a piece of cake."

Visible urgency drove him toward her. "You think it didn't *kill* me to leave you that night without saying goodbye? It took everything in me to walk out of that auditorium."

She let go of the railing and hugged her arms to her waist.

"But seeing your Mom's empty seat at the audition, knowing it could've been you, that I was responsible ..." He craned his neck to the sky and released a hard breath.

"What are you talking about?"

"I wanted to stay, Bells. To make sure Michelli never came near you. But what was I supposed to do? How was I going to fight them? I had no skills. No experience. Nothing. And if I would've stayed long enough to hold you one more time, I never would've left to change that."

Snow landed on her skin, his words sinking deeper.

"Those first few months of being apart were the hardest I'd ever gone through." He climbed the next step. "I wouldn't have survived Basic if I didn't have Harris here watching over you for me."

Visions of Harris interacting with her the last five years threatened to knock her backward. His stopping by the rec center, checking in at her apartment, driving her home on one of his random patrols. It'd all been a job. None of it real. She thought he was being a good friend. Thought he'd genuinely cared. Had everyone been lying to her?

"I didn't join the army as an excuse to walk out of your life." Another step brought Evan closer. "I joined to train so I could come back to defend you."

Frustration drove her nails into her palms. "Stop using that cop-out. I didn't need another bodyguard, Evan. No one asked you to protect me. You left by choice."

"I left because I made a promise."

She advanced. "To who?"

His jaw flexed in and out as though fighting something else he couldn't tell her.

"Who, Evan?"

A slow blink lifted an anguished gaze to hers. "Your mom."

"What did you just say?"

Staring at the stoop, he released a long exhale. "She brought her car into my dad's shop before the accident." He pinched the bridge of his nose. "She stayed while I did the inspection, kept talking about your future and how I belonged by your side. That she trusted me to look out for you if anything were ever to happen."

Anna shrank back.

He took out a folded-up piece of paper from his wallet and toyed with the worn corner. "I thought she was just concerned about you graduating and the dangers of us moving downtown. None of your dad's cases had ever shaken her up before. But I should've realized this one was different. Should've realized she was charging me to protect you in case …" His voice caught.

Anna stared past him. Why hadn't he or Mom ever told her this?

Evan inched forward until she stopped him with her eyes. Deep-seated remorse bled through the tough exterior he used as a shield. "You don't know how much I want to rewind time. What I'd give to go back and double-check her brakes, to pick up on the things I missed."

Tears overran Anna's bottom lashes. "What are you saying?"

His jaw rippled. "It's my fault, Anna. I could've prevented the accident if I'd been more observant." Shoulders crestfallen, he closed his eyes but then stood tall and determined as the soldier he'd become. "And I know nothing I do can make up for failing you both that day, but I swore I'd never stop trying." He extended the paper to her.

Anna unfolded the creased, weathered page to the sight of Mom's handwriting along the top of the inspection invoice.

Promise me you'll always guard Anna's heart with your life, Evan. And never lose sight of who you are.

The words shook every part of her. Anna dropped the paper to the ground. Mom couldn't have known she was going to die. But why'd she go to Evan? And why didn't she tell her? Torrents of unanswered questions laced the snowy haze closing in.

"I didn't even see the note until my dad pointed it out later." Evan reached for her but stopped himself. "When I realized what she meant, I tried to honor her wishes. I thought once I had the training I needed, I could come back and be on your full-time detail like she wanted. That keeping the promise would somehow right the mistakes I made and enable me to stay a part of your life."

He shook his head like he was naïve. "But the realization of what that would mean didn't fully hit me until I came back and saw you with Jack Calloway. On your detail, I would've been watching your life move on with someone else while standing beside you every single day—keeping things between us strictly professional, pretending I wasn't in love with you and that the guilt wasn't eating me alive. I didn't know if I could do it, Anna. So, when I came home, I—"

"Home?" Confusion twisted the blade of betrayal even deeper. "You came back?"

"Every leave." Earnest eyes held hers. "I always made sure you and my mom were safe, taken care of."

"And never once told me? All this time, you let me think …" She backed up.

"I'm sorry. I know I messed up. I swear I was trying to do right by you the best way I knew how." He faced the starless sky. "As hard as it would've been to be your detail, I didn't want to let you or your mom down again. But then with my mom relying on my financial support, and my team counting on me for leadership, I didn't know what to do. Protecting you from a distance seemed like the only way. Until the Michelli case came up, and I had no choice but to step back in—"

"Stop." She couldn't listen to this anymore. She braced a hand to his chest, but he didn't back away.

His heart pounded under her palm. "Bells, please …"

"Don't." She recoiled, desperate for his embrace, yet too hurt to trust it anymore.

A storm of regret blazed in his hazel eyes. "I'm so sorry. For not being honest with you. For causing you any more pain. I wanted to tell you so many times. You have to under-stand—"

"Leave." Anna looked away. "Please, just go."

A passing car rumbled around the curve behind him. He didn't move. Stillness pressed in until nothing but the sound of breathing stood between them. "I know I lost the right to ask you to believe me, but I love you, Bells. I always have." A hoarse whisper tore at his voice.

The patter of snow landing onto the porch from the rail drew her gaze up from the ground as he strode down the stairs toward the driveway.

As soon as his taillights faded, Anna slid down the door, cradled her knees to her chest, and waited for the numbness spreading to her bones to reach her heart.

CHAPTER TWENTY-THREE

Choice

Cramped in his mom's Ford Focus, Evan reached into the empty cup holder for the twelfth time since they'd been driving. Of all things, he left his cell back at the hotel. Not like it made much difference. The only person he wanted to call him wouldn't. Ten days of not hearing from Anna made it clear she wasn't ready to forgive him. Would she ever be?

The question stung, but he wasn't running away this time. He'd been a coward for too long.

Anna had every right to resent the way Evan had gone about protecting her through all this. She could even shut him out of her life for good. He'd always known that'd be a risk, and maybe he deserved it. But if he had to do it all over again, he'd still sacrifice the right to be with her for the assurance of her safety.

Michelli'd been indicted and his business shut down, justice was served for Mrs. Santos's death, and Chicago's streets were one black market operation cleaner than they'd been in the last ten years. And more than anything, at least Anna knew the truth now.

A soft whimper came from the passenger seat as Mom adjusted her seat belt.

Evan glanced over. "You all right?"

"Better than you."

He cast her a sidelong glance.

"I lost a lung, honey. Not my heart."

Please tell me we're not back to this again. "We've been through this, Mom. I'm fine."

"Mm hmm." She pointed ahead. "Make a right at the light."

A truck on their left merged into their lane and sprinkled the windshield with muddied overspray. Evan snapped on the wipers. Though the snowstorm ended a week ago, its remnants continued to brand the streets with reminders of a night he'd probably relive forever.

They turned off the main road. He knew the area but still wasn't sure where they were headed. Somehow, Mom's vague, "*a needed stop*" didn't bode well.

"Are you sure you're up for being out today?"

She waved off his question with a flutter of her hand. "Take a left at the corner."

He peered past the cars parked along the street toward a glimpse of some kind of park. His foot slipped off the gas pedal. The dark wrought iron fence up ahead all but speared right through him. It wasn't a park. It was a cemetery. She couldn't be serious.

Mom's cold hand covered his arm. "It's time, sweetheart."

The heck it was. He tightened his grip around the wheel. "Dad didn't even deserve a proper burial. What makes you think he deserves our respect?"

"He's your father."

Evan grunted. "He gave up that right a long time ago." The anger festering inside him collided with the undeserved compassion coloring Mom's eyes. "How can you possibly want to come here?"

Her gaze returned to the entrance. "Being cooped up in the hospital has a way of interrupting your routine. After missing three Mondays, I was starting to miss it."

His hands slid down the wheel and dropped to his lap. He had to have misheard her.

A honk from behind them set him on edge. Still lost for a response, Evan inched the car off the road and into the cemetery.

"Up here on the right." Mom gestured ahead. "Just past that statue."

He parked and turned the keys in the ignition. His body moved on autopilot, but it felt like he was trudging through mud-coated trenches.

He blinked away from the glare on the snow-crusted ground. "I don't understand. You're saying you come here every week? Why?"

An aged smile stood in for her reply. She opened the door. "Can you give me a hand?"

Reluctantly, Evan unloaded a wheelchair from the back and helped her into it. Her overall recovery had been progressing faster than he'd expected. But her gentle wisdom seemed to know when not to push it.

She bunched the front of her scarf over her neck while he wheeled her to Dad's plot. The engravings on the headstone glistened in the sunlight and seared into him. He turned away.

Mom stretched behind her shoulder and patted his hand. "Your dad was a good man, Evan. A good man who lost himself."

The disdain heating his body mocked the bitter wind stabbing from both directions. "You think that's an excuse? You think half of America doesn't deal with disappointments in life every day? Drinking was a cop-out."

"Any more than pride?"

His jaw twitched. "Nothing justified the way he treated us."

"You're right."

And yet she'd endured it all those years. Guilt tore into him and shook his grasp around the wheelchair's handles. "I should've gotten you out of there a long time ago."

"Oh, honey." She brought him to the front of the chair. "I stayed because I had hope in the promise your dad and I made to each other. To our family."

"He forfeited that promise, Mom. You had every right to leave him."

"I know that, but I'll always love the man I married. I'm not saying his actions were excusable. Or even that he deserves forgiveness."

"Then what *are* you saying?"

"I'm saying I made a choice. Whether right or wrong." Tear-filled eyes looked up at him, and his knees nearly gave way at the silent plea they held.

"And you want me to change mine?"

"That's not for me to ask. Come here." She tugged him down so he knelt to her eye level. Lifting her hands to his cheeks, Mom studied his face. "You were always such a fierce-ly protective boy. Always took on more responsibility than was yours to carry. So much so, you ended up shielding this big heart of yours from any pain."

Her gaze roamed past him to Dad's grave at the same time her hands slid to her lap. "But also from love, from seeing how much you have to offer. It's there, Evan. What I'm ask-ing is for you to give yourself permission to see it."

A slow tremor built behind his ribs. Huffing, he rose. "Don't worry about me knowing my worth. Dad made sure I never forgot exactly what I amount to." He gripped the back of his hair to keep down the words she didn't need to hear him say.

"Evan David, look at me. Self-worth isn't something any-one can give or take away from you. It's something you choose to live. Same as self-doubt." She took his hand. "We all get a say in what rules our lives."

He'd essentially told Megan's mom the same thing not long ago. But now that the choice was in front of him, he re-alized the costs.

Anna was right. She and Mom both were. He'd run away, thinking he was valiant, when really it was fear. Shame. He'd let his dad's words choke out his self-esteem like the weeds winding around the headstone. But after so long, he didn't know anything else. Didn't know how to change it.

Mom squeezed his hand and inclined her head toward the car. "I'll give you a minute."

As she drifted in the opposite direction, Evan stood between one parent and the other—between two entirely different responses to pain and heartache.

A pricking sensation burned behind his eyes. He stood against the wind, a soldier of resolve coming apart, piece by piece. His greatest battle might begin with confronting his dad. But ultimately, it'd end in facing himself.

He wasn't sure how long it would take or if he even could. But as minutes passed in that quiet cemetery, he wrestled for a place in his heart willing to start.

In the distance, a Bulls coat caught his eye. Was that …? He cupped his hands around his mouth. "Shaun?"

The kid popped his head up, and Evan jogged over.

Shaun clasped his hand. "What are you doing here?"

Evan hooked a thumb behind him. "Just, uh, having a few words with my old man."

A level of empathy no kid his age should have flashed over his face. "At least you know where your pops is."

Unlike a majority of the kids who went to the rec center. Evan hadn't thought about that until right now. Was the pain of abuse worse than the pain of abandonment? His stomach knotted with a glance around the graveyard. "You visiting someone?"

Shaun pulled his book bag straps together across his chest. "My grams."

"I'm sorry to hear that."

He shrugged. "Around here, you get used to saying good-bye to peeps."

Maybe it was time they changed that. He'd probably assumed Evan had bailed on him, too. "Hey, listen, I've been brushing up on my three-pointers. You mind if I come by the rec center tomorrow?"

He raised a brow. "Thought Miss Madison was still mad at you."

"Yeah, well." Evan scratched his jaw. "I'm kinda hoping she won't stay mad forever."

"Good luck with that. My cousin says girls are like cats. Once the claws come out, it's over."

Evan laughed. "Thanks for the relationship advice."

"Free of charge." Shaun sported a lopsided grin way too telling for his young age.

Evan pulled him into a headlock and rubbed his knuckles over his head. "All right, Dr. Phil. How 'bout you just worry about bringing your A game to the courts tomorrow, 'kay?"

"Psh." He shoved away from Evan and resituated his backpack. "I always got game, old man. You're the one who needs to be worried."

If Anna was gonna be there tomorrow, he was probably right.

"We can ball right now, if you want?"

"Actually, I have a few errands to run." Out of habit, Evan patted his pockets for his cell. Empty-handed, he looked back to where Mom sat patiently in her wheelchair. "Tomorrow, though. Promise." Evan extended a hand, and Shaun leaned in to give him a half hug.

"A'ight. Later."

Evan hustled over to the car and helped Mom into the passenger side.

"Who was that?"

He looked across the field to the plot that must've belonged to Shaun's grandma. "A new friend." And with any hope, the possibility of new beginnings, too.

The smell of acrylics swirled around Anna as if Mom were flitting throughout her workroom with a paintbrush in hand.

Hunter wedged his snout through the tiny opening in the door and butted inside. With an assertive hiss, Bailey bounded off the windowsill and scurried under the daybed along the back wall. Unfazed, the dog trotted over, planted his chin on Anna's thigh, and raised his sappy brown eyes at her.

She laughed and rubbed him behind the ears. "I know, buddy. I miss Mom, too."

Sunshine filtered through the blinds and splashed warm colors onto the canvas in front of her. Canary yellows and burnt oranges blended into the forest greens and indigo blues. Vibrant. Vivid. The painting Mom started years ago came more to life with each brushstroke Anna added.

Seated on the stool, she took in the power of art. She didn't have Mom's knack for painting, but it didn't matter. That was part of its magic. As long as an artist created from her heart, her work carried soul, impact. The kind that colored over the world's gray with hope.

How could she have gone this long believing that for everyone but herself?

The floor creaked behind her. Anna turned to find Dad standing in the doorway in a suit without the jacket.

Hunter plodded over and sat by his side, panting.

Dad slanted a glance past her to the easel. "It's beautiful. Reminds me of the ones you two used to paint together."

She looked back at the abstract piece. "Except she's not here to turn all my blunders into real artwork."

Chuckling, Dad ruffled Hunter's ears. "She had a way of doing that on and off the canvas."

That she did.

The ache of missing her swelled throughout the entire room. Anna set the brush down, lifted the apron over her head, and cradled it to her lap. "Mom knew, didn't she? That she was going to die?"

"No, sweetheart." Face creased, Dad made his way toward the window. "But I think she knew the risks of the danger Michelli posed to our family."

Hunter lolled on the carpet between them.

"I don't get it. If she really believed she was in danger, why was she trying to ditch her security?" The moment she said it, Anna realized she'd been doing the same.

His chin sagged. "She wasn't running from her detail, Annabelle."

"Then what was she running from?"

Leaning against the windowsill, he stared outside as though looking back in time. "She thought she saw someone outside the house that night. John secured the area. But when he told her it was clear, she asked him to keep an eye on you girls." A distant smile touched his lips. "You know how stubborn she was. Once she got a hold of something …"

"She never let go." Must be where Anna picked it up from.

Hunter's ears rose as if contributing his agreement.

"She called me at the office. Said she'd snuck out and was on her way there."

"Why?"

A long breath redirected his eyes toward her. "To draw whoever was at the house away from you."

Anna dropped the apron to the carpet. "What?"

"I told her to go back, but she wouldn't listen. The second we hung up, I called John, called the cops, but …"

"It was too late." Another layer around Anna's secure world crumbled to the floor. Tears burned. "She died protecting me?"

The corners of Dad's eyes crinkled above a heartfelt smile. "She died loving you, honey." He pulled her into a hug. "Same as I would."

And Evan, too. The sacrifices the people she loved had made for her were more than she could comprehend.

"You're her greatest work of art, you know. You and Reese both."

Tears soaked into his dress shirt under her cheek. And in the safety of a father's embrace, Anna let go of the last of the pieces she'd fought so hard to hold together. "I love you, Daddy."

"I love you, too, sweetheart." He cleared a tremor in his throat, leaned back, and looked at her with his steel-gray eyes. "I'm sorry for holding you too tight. It was never because I didn't believe in you and your talent as a dancer. It's because I've wanted to keep you safe, close."

"I know." Evan was right about Dad, too. He wasn't the enemy. He brought light to darkness just like Mom did, only in different ways. But both had the same starting point—the one Anna had missed. Until now.

Her eyes closed with a slow exhale. After spending five years striving to guard her heart, it shouldn't have come completely undone in only two weeks. It made even less sense for the place she always thought had caged her to be the one to give her wings.

"I'm sorry for being so stubborn. For making it hard on everyone to protect me and for pushing you all away." Was it too late? Did she still have time to make it right?

Dad squeezed her arm, smiled, and let go. "You almost ready to head out?"

"Yeah. I just need a minute to make a call first."

He nodded his understanding. "I'll be downstairs."

Hunter wandered out after him, leaving a floating trail of dog hair behind.

Anna pulled her feet onto the stool and tucked them under her legs while grabbing the phone. Evan had been gracious enough to give her time and space. But the more that passed, the more certain she became that neither made sense without him.

With a shaky hand to her ear, she waited for him to answer. His voice mail clicked on instead. "Evan O'Riley. Talk to me."

She slid her legs out from under her in a scramble to find her voice. "Evan, it's me. I, um … clearly don't know where to start."

She laughed softly. "But I know it begins with I'm sorry. You were right. About so many things I had all wrong. To be honest, I'm still sorting through a lot of it, and I know it might be too late. But if you haven't left Chicago yet, would you meet me at 1147 West Jackson Boulevard today? I have something I need to tell you. In person."

CHAPTER TWENTY-FOUR

Promise

Evan pulled into his hotel after getting Mom settled at home and running his errands. While coming out of the elevator, he tossed the key to his new apartment in his hand, still reeling from the way everything had come together.

Around the corner, someone bounded straight for his legs. "Mr. Hulk!" Megan squeezed her bony arms around him. "I missed you."

He looked from her to her mom a little ways down the hall. "What are you guys doing here?"

"You mean aside from appeasing my daughter's nonstop request to see *Mr. Hulk?*" Smiling, Heather lifted off the wall. "Sorry to just drop by."

He unwound himself from Megan's precious hug. "It's no problem. Everything okay?"

"Yeah, it is, actually." Heather approached in an outfit hanging from her gaunt frame. At least her sallow cheeks had regained some color and her eyes held a clarity he hadn't seen from her before. "Everything's good now, thanks to you."

Evan deflected her misdirected praise. "You made the courageous choice, not me. And if there's anyone to thank, it should be Anna."

"I know. I will." She brought Megan in front of her. "But I needed to thank you, too. For helping to put Jamie away." A hint of shame tinted her blue eyes. "I'm not used to having people root for me and Megan like you and Anna have. I'm used to them looking at me and only seeing one thing. After so long, it's all I saw, too."

"I know the feeling," he said with more understanding than he wanted to admit. He'd accused Anna of settling, but he was the one who let his belief about himself limit his future. He scratched the back of his hair. "Guess that's why we need friends who see past what we see." Since being around Anna again, nothing had hit home harder.

Heather lifted her gaze from the carpet. "I'm starting to understand that." She gathered Megan's hair off her shoulders. "Corporal Harris got me connected with a support group. Things are still gonna be hard for a while, but … I think we're gonna be okay."

"I'm glad to hear that."

"Me too." She offered one more smile and took Megan's hand. "We should get going."

Megan let go and flung her arms around Evan's legs again. "Will you come to my dance recital next week?"

Man, this girl was trying to melt his heart. "Wouldn't miss it for anything."

Heather pried her away. "Okay, kiddo, let's go."

Evan waved good-bye while trying to disentangle his heart from his vocal cords. He needed to call Anna.

Letting the door swing behind him, he made a beeline toward his cell on the kitchen counter, where he'd left it. Halfway over, a knock stopped him short. Megan had a little stubbornness in her, didn't she?

He opened the door. "Okay, one more hug, but—" His hand slipped off the door's edge.

"Sorry, Pipsqueak. I didn't come for hugs." Reese shifted in front of him. "But you could at least invite a pregnant lady out of the cold hallway."

He blinked until his voice caught up to the movement. "Uh, yeah." He held the door open for her. "Sorry. I wasn't expecting to see you."

"The blank stare kind of gave you away."

Chuckling, Evan waved off any unease. This was Reese he was talking to. The queen of telling it like it was.

He swiped a jacket from the doorknob and nudged his open duffel bag underneath the coffee table. "Excuse the mess. I'm checking out tomorrow, so I'm in the middle of packing up."

"You heading back to Georgia?" She reclined against the side of the couch and folded her arms over her stomach.

"Actually, no. I just signed a lease on an apartment uptown, near my mom's place."

Now Reese was the one with the blank stare. "Wait, so, does that mean …?"

He tugged on his ear. "It means I didn't reenlist."

Her hands slid down her coat. "I'm sorry, what?"

"I served my country for five years. It's time to serve my family and pursue the things I gave up on when I shouldn't have."

"Things like ...?"

"I'm renting studio space in a gallery off North Lincoln." He picked up his camera and sat on the desk. "Your sister did a pretty good job calling me out on being afraid of failure."

Reese smiled as if having a proud mentor moment. "Then why have you failed to go see her?"

"That's different." He scrolled through the frames from their day in the park. "I'm not hiding anymore. I'm just trying to give her what she needs right now. She asked me to leave. Until that changes, I'm not gonna push."

"Men are so slow." Reese arched backward and tottered off the couch. "Let me give you the easiest lesson you'll ever get on what women want. It's three P's, so you can remember it." She held out one finger. "Women want to be pursued." She extended another finger. "Provided for." A third finger. "And protected."

He almost bumped a stack of photos off the desk. "You sure you know your sister? 'Cause I'm fairly positive those are the last things she wants."

Reese rolled her eyes. "Trust me."

He shook his head.

"Okay, look." Crossing her arms, she countered his obstinate gaze. "I'm not gonna pretend I like the way you went about everything, but ..." She swayed her head. "I understand now. And so does Anna."

"Doubt that. And I'm not sure it's fair to expect her to anytime soon." He retrieved the key to the studio from his pocket and added it to the ring with the apartment key.

Reese crossed the carpet, sobering. "Evan, listen to me. You didn't have anything to do with our mom's death. Dad took her car to the Priority shop two days before the accident. And even if you'd been the last one to check her brakes, Michelli could've tampered with them any time after that. You can't blame yourself."

Another shop? He stared at her. "I don't understand. Why'd she take it to me if she already had an inspection lined up?"

"My guess? She was probably looking for a way to talk to you alone. I think Mom was making sure she said everything she wanted to in case she lost the chance."

He shouldn't have missed the cues. "I should've known something was wrong. Should've told someone. Been more thorough."

"You were just a kid, Evan. And trust me. All of us feel we should've been more vigilant. But there's no point going down that road." Her expression softened to a smile of concession. "What matters is she obviously knew you and Anna belong together and wanted to make sure you did, too. She believed in you and what you have to offer." Reese squeezed his arm. "If you want to carry the weight of anything, carry the truth of that."

He exhaled. "I'm trying." But he'd already waded through too many mistakes. He wouldn't risk making any more. As much as he wanted to make it right, he had consequences to deal with. "I lied to her, Reese. I ran away when I should've stayed. I walked out of two of her auditions."

"So, don't miss the next one."

"What next one?"

"She's at Hubbard right now."

His jaw locked, right along with every muscle in his body. He darted a glance at his cell on the counter. Had she called to tell him? Would she want him there after everything?

Reese angled in front of him. "Why are you still standing here?"

He jogged to his phone and then on to the door.

"Aren't you missing something?"

He stopped over the threshold, peered back at Reese standing there with her hands on her hips, and hustled over to give her a kiss on the cheek. "Thanks."

"You're welcome. But that's not what I meant." She wriggled her keys from her coat pocket and waddled toward the door. "I'm driving."

She had to be joking. He shuffled behind her at a snail's pace. "I might have to carry you."

"Don't even think about it." She swung a finger at him. "I know you're all Mr. Buff now, or whatever, but I'm telling ya. This water weight is one match you don't want to take on."

His laughter echoed into the hallway as the door swung shut. The weight he could handle. Reese's wrath? Maybe not.

Fortunately, all the swelling must've gone straight to her feet. And the gas pedal.

Only ten minutes later, she lined up her Audi with the curb in front of Hubbard Street Dance Center. Massive images of dancers decorated the top half of the building, and Evan could almost feel the creative energy flowing from inside.

He looked from the entrance to Reese.

"Go on," she said. "I'll be there in a sec."

With a quick nod, he climbed out into the cold. But once inside, his internal thermostat spiked. Voices and footsteps clamored in the crowded entryway. Dancers, families, instructors. Years of training and anticipation charged the atmosphere with a palpable current. He sifted through the throng of people, the need to find Anna driving him to the front.

From the right, a side door opened and released the soft tenor of a song he recognized. He bolted to the door before it closed and slipped into the darkness cloaking the side of the stage. A spotlight flickered beyond the curtains. *Bells.*

The anxiousness that'd been ratcheting his pulse since he left the hotel faded at the sight of Anna coming to life on the floor. The music, her movements, the lyrics—it extended inside him to a place where fear finally yielded to truth.

When Mrs. Madison asked him to take care of Anna, she didn't mean to protect her as a bodyguard. She meant to love her as a soul mate. And now, he might've ruined his chance of keeping the only promise that mattered.

The overhead lights warmed Anna's skin and blinded her view to the panel of judges seated in the auditorium. Attuning herself to nothing but the music, she completed four chaîné turns with her arms rising from lower second to a high V.

Her heart breathed with each extension she made, each glide across the floor. She held a sous-sus in fifth position, faced stage left, and stepped into an inside single pirouette.

She'd let go of the pressure to make callbacks, left her nerves at Dad's house. Right now, none of that meant anything. The scene from her first audition played through her mind. But this time, as she faced Mom's empty seat, Anna realized her responsibility wasn't to change the world. It was to give all her heart to whatever she did and trust it to leave its mark, even if she never saw how. The beauty of art wasn't in the outcome. It was in surrender.

Freedom whisked through her as she pliéd in a final close.

The judges might as well not have been here. Regardless of her scores, she'd danced with every part of herself. Nothing withheld. No walls. No fears. As she lowered her heels to the hardwood floor, Anna breathed a breath of release.

Offstage, she jogged into Mr. Jamison's arms stretched open for her.

"You nailed it, Anna. I'm so proud of you."

"Thanks."

Behind him, Evan's face came into view, Dad's and Reese's not far behind.

A backstage worker hurried over to Evan and twisted her head mic away from her mouth. "You can't be back here."

"He's with me." Relief and nerves rushed Anna toward him. "You got my message."

He patted his pockets. "No, actually, Reese stopped by. Long story."

Mr. Jamison cleared his throat.

"Oh, uh, Mr. Jamison, this is Evan." She waved between them. "Evan, this is my dance instructor."

"Your dance instructor." Evan shook his head, an unreadable smile on his face.

"Yeah, why?"

"Nothing." His grin turned into an almost self-conscious laugh. "I'm just a real idiot sometimes. That's all." In the silence, he rubbed his clean-shaven jawline. "Bells, listen—"

"You said enough the other night. It's my turn to talk." She tugged him off to the corner. The curtain brushed against her back and neck as she prayed for the right words.

"You shouldn't have lied to me, Evan. And you never should've blamed yourself for what happened to my mom. But you're not the only one who messed up."

Anna bent her toes back and forth against the floor. "I've been so set on trying to carry out Mom's legacy, I ended up missing the entire point of it. That's why she went to you. Because she knew I'd need help figuring this out."

The next dancer's music cued up, and Anna pulled Evan farther offstage. "She made me promise to pursue my dreams, but she didn't just mean dance. She meant you." Anna looked behind him toward Dad and Reese. "She meant family. The people who anchor me. Because the truth is, I'd lose myself if I didn't have you in my life."

Evan held her gaze, deep breaths moving in and out with the same intensity as hers.

She rested a hand to his chest. The heart that'd always held hers thundered under her palm. "I'm not saying I have all the answers. I don't know what life will look like with you in Georgia or overseas while I'm here. And I know there'll always be another Michelli, another case. The dangers don't stop. But I'm in love with you, Evan O'Riley. And I want to risk sharing that love with you every day."

When Anna finally took a breath, Evan hung his head for so long, her muscles tensed.

She started to lower her hand, but he covered it with his and brought her closer.

He raised his fingers to her cheek. "There'd be no greater honor than devoting my life to loving you. To stand by you no matter what you pursue." He swallowed. "But I won't ever stop protecting you, either."

Anna met the same fierce hazel eyes that'd looked after her since they were five. His protection wasn't a cage. Or an obligation. It was love. The kind she finally understood.

She leaned in. "And I'll never stop letting you."

His gaze gravitated to her mouth, already kissing her before their lips ever touched. And in the arms of a promise that'd kept them together all this time, she laid down her fear of the future to be with the one who shared her past.

Moments

One Year Later

Fresh pine, baked gingerbread, and mint hot chocolate filled Evan and Anna's living room to the brim with the fragrance of Christmas and new traditions.

Evan admired the sight of his friends and family surrounded by the simple elegance Anna brought with her wherever she went.

Seated beside Mark on the love seat, Reese bounced their son on her lap, looking even more exhausted now than when she was pregnant. "We could've had Christmas at Dad's, you know?"

Anna looked up from the tree skirt, where she and Megan were wiggling a new cat toy in front of an unimpressed Bailey. "I know." She rose, strolled over to Evan's side of the couch, and lounged an arm across his back. "But we wanted to host on our first Christmas as a married couple."

Married. Evan rolled around the word. Their new reality still hadn't fully set in.

Mr. Madison returned a picture of Anna and her mom to the fireplace mantel and leaned an elbow over the bricks. "Well, you know Ms. Riza's expecting everyone over for a big dinner tomorrow night."

Anna chuckled. "Of course she is. The woman wouldn't know what to do if she didn't have people to entertain."

"Says the girl who's been running around all night, playing host." Evan pulled her into his lap and handed her a present. "Your turn to open."

She dropped the tissue paper from the bag onto the floor and withdrew a double feature DVD of *The Breakfast Club* and *Pretty In Pink*. "You didn't."

"I did." He reached in for the bonus treat. "And don't worry. I bought the popcorn from Garrett's three days ago, so it'll be perfect."

She twisted toward him with a goofy grin on her face and pressed her lips to his. "You're the best."

"Stale popcorn?" Reese scrunched her nose. "You guys are so weird."

"I think they're adorable." Evan's mom scooped up baby Jonathan from Reese and cuddled him. "And they're going to give me cute little grandbabies just like you. Isn't that right?" she said in a high-pitched baby voice.

Anna's neck flushed. "Um, not for at least a few more years. I doubt Hubbard Street would be too keen on choreographing a routine around a prego lead dancer."

"What's prego?" Megan peeked out from behind the tree while Bailey frantically clawed to get away from her.

The room lit up in laughter.

"Never mind, kiddo." Biting back a smile, Heather ruffled her hair.

Beside them, Murphy flaunted a mischievous grin at Evan and raised his glass toward Anna. "I think we should toast to Hubbard Street for enabling you to float this starving artist."

"Real funny, tough guy." Evan rolled his eyes.

Anna leaned backward to hook an arm around Evan. "Sorry, but if you want to talk about the success in this family, talk to the guy who's sold enough prints to buy out the entire first floor of the gallery."

Heat climbed Evan's neck and spread to his ears.

With an impressed look, Murphy raised his glass higher. "Not too shabby, bro. You know, I could pose as a model, if you're looking."

Heather gave him a shove. "The only person who'd ever hang a print with your face on it in their house would be you."

"Ohh ... girl's got jokes. Okay, I see how it is."

Ignoring their banter, Evan placed another gift in Anna's lap, eager to take the limelight off himself. "One more," he whispered.

She peeked inside the bag, squeezed it shut, and spun toward him. "Electric slippers?"

"To warm those ice picks you poke me with every night." His lips pulled to the left, barely suppressing a laugh.

Her eyes tightened as she slid her fingers up his shirt. "You really want to start this?"

He scrambled her hands away from his now-goose-bump-covered skin and held her at the waist. "We just need to get you electric gloves, and we'll be all set."

She brandished that sassy grin of hers and walked her cold fingertips up to the back of his neck. "I'm pretty sure I already have a lifetime hand warmer right here."

Evan held her hungry gaze.

"Gag." Reese rose from the love seat. "I think that's our cue to leave the lovebirds' new nest."

Mark helped her with her coat while Mr. Madison did the same for Mom. Heather and Megan joined them in the entryway, followed up by Murphy.

He clasped hands with Evan. "There you go, showing me up in the romance department again." Murphy cut a glance toward Heather. "Now I'm gonna have to go work the Bruce Wayne persona I picked up from you."

A year later, and he still hadn't let that one go. Evan fake-punched him through the doorway.

After saying all their good-byes, he and Anna crashed on the couch in the glow of the Christmas tree lights. Bailey came out of hiding and curled up at the opposite end of the cushions.

"Hot chocolate?" Anna asked.

"Later." Evan pulled her to him and nuzzled her neck. The same flush from earlier inched up her skin, but this time his lips got to follow it. She sighed against him, pressing in. Her natural fragrance overrode all the competing ones until the entire room faded to just her. He might not be a Ranger anymore, but she'd kept his laser focus skills sharper than ever.

She leaned back with the look on her face that never failed to undo him. "Can we make a new promise?"

"Name it."

Her compassionate, headstrong green eyes steadied his. "Let's promise to live moment by moment, one at a time. Savoring each one to the fullest."

Evan's fingertips skimmed her soft cheek and slipped into her hair. With his thumb brushing her ear, he brought his lips to hers and sealed a promise he'd live every day of his life. Starting right now.

A WORD FROM THE AUTHOR

Thanks so much for reading *Arms of Promise*. One of the best parts about art is the way it connects with each of us differently. I'd love to hear your thoughts on the story. Email me anytime.

Make no mistake about it. Your voice matters. I'd be incredibly grateful if you'd take a moment to leave a review on retailer sites to help new readers discover Evan and Anna's story. Reviews are a tremendous help to authors, which in turn allows us to keep writing more stories for you. Thank you so much for your support. I can't do it without you!

For a behind-the-scenes look into *Arms of Promise*, visit: http://crystal-walton.com/behind-scenes-arms-promise/

Love audiobooks? *Arms of Promise* is now available on Audible and iTunes. Grab your copy and experience this romantic suspense come to life through narration.

ACKNOWLEDGEMENTS

Dave, after fourteen years, your arms of promise continue to anchor me during the "for better or worse" seasons along this lifetime journey. Thanks for standing by my side.

Erynn—the editor with the world's most expansive vocabulary—thanks for sowing your humor and tough love into another manuscript, for letting me ramble endlessly until I finally found that little thing called clarity, and for refraining from coming to my house to clobber me when I kept interrupting Anna and Evan's first kiss. It's a privilege to work with such a gifted editor and supportive friend.

Melanie, thank you for walking with me through the countless pull-my-hair-out moments, the what-in-the-world-am-I-doing doubts, and the squeal-I'm-so-excited hopes during every stage of this book. Even more than an encouraging critique partner, you are a treasured friend.

Victorine, thanks, once again, for all your help creating a cover to fit the characters and story beautifully, and for giving me hard critiques when I need them.

Sara—girl, Anna would be one naïve dancer without the intervention of your expertise. Thank you for enduring my endless questions and emails. Your gift as an artist has touched me many times, and I'm so blessed to partner with you in sharing a story that celebrates the beauty of dance.

Rachel, thanks for standing in as my resident pet expert, name choice suggester, and suspense protocol checker. What would we do without crime shows? Especially ones with blue-eyed beauties?

Franky and Rachel, thanks for fitting this story into the nonstop schedules that come along with being a mom and author. Your critiques and suggestions have once again helped me polish and tighten another manuscript.

Julie, thank you for offering your super sharp proofing skills. I'm so glad we've connected and get to share in our love of New York and in books. You're a joy to work with.

Mom, Beth, Nora, and Katie, thanks for encouraging me to hold on to hope during the many moments I've been ready to let go.

Kevin, thank you for speaking into my life on our trip to Malawi. Your charge to be God's paintbrush to cheer this dark world continues to be my mantra as an author and is part of what inspired this book.

To all my readers who've taken the time to leave a review and help spread the word about Evan and Anna's story, your support and enthusiasm are an immense blessing. I can't make it as an author without you.